Advance Praise for
Queen of Spades

"A magical debut—literally. This tale is both spare and sprawling, gritty and otherworldly, both an homage to the complex psychology of gambling and a cautionary tale for those watching from the rail. A ridiculously satisfying read."
   —Jamie Ford, *New York Times*-bestselling author of *Hotel on the Corner of Bitter and Sweet* and *Songs of Willow Frost*

"Michael Shou-Yung Shum's *Queen of Spades* is a remarkable debut by an enormously talented young writer who has produced a literary delight that circles the dead center of a very dangerous pleasure—casino gambling. The novel is a perfectly rendered view of gambling from the inside, the dealers and their overseers in the casinos. People work but with vastly different objectives. Some are company men and women, others—and some here in *Queen of Spades*—not so much. The novel is a lovely and complex gambling fairy tale that twists and turns in intriguing ways on its way to a most satisfying conclusion."
   —Frederick Barthelme, author of *Bob the Gambler*

"Good God, this book is fantastic. I was hooked from the very first page and found myself fully invested in all the characters set in and around this out-of-the-way casino in the Pacific Northwest. It's so hard to believe this is a debut novel, because the author's sense of pacing and balance and heightening of suspense and anxiety is so expertly developed. I found myself thinking about this book whenever I stepped away from it, and had to keep it with me at all times, in case I had an extra minute or two to read. A perfect blend of humor and pathos, singular characters, and a peek behind the curtains at the inner functioning of a casino all make this a fascinating read. I can't wait to sell this to folks."
   —Mary Cotton, bookseller, Newtonville Books

"This book is a highly satisfying read with a wonderful ending. Magic runs throughout the story, but is it magic, or is it the math of odds and gambling? I spent a lovely weekend reading this novel. I'm left feeling like I might just get lucky, too. And I'll never forget, to the discerning hand some playing cards are heavier than others."

—Doug Chase, bookseller, Powell's Books Staff Pick

"*Queen of Spades* shimmers with suspense and a magical sense of forces just beyond our ken. Debut novelist Michael Shou-Yung Shum deftly deals hand after narrative hand, initiating the reader into the mysteries of the gambler's universe, its language, laws and gorgeous arcana. I felt I wasn't so much reading as leaning over a high-stakes gambling table as this quartet of vulnerable characters played for their lives. How will the cards fall? How will their lives transform? And who is the elegant and mysterious Countess who watches it all from her high-backed chair? An addictive and wholly satisfying reading experience."

—Marjorie Sandor, editor of
The Uncanny Reader: Stories from the Shadows

"In *Queen of Spades*, many unlikely and uncanny events transpire, all against a brooding and moody Pacific Northwest somehow reminiscent of both *Twin Peaks* and *Crime and Punishment*. How has an American writer created a brand-new nineteenth-century Russian classic in 2017? His name is Michael Shou-Yung Shum, and he has."

—Margaret Lazarus Dean, author of *Leaving Orbit*

"*Queen of Spades* raises gambling to a metaphysics that reminds us being in the world is an amalgam of gratuitous rules, chance, danger, and faintly Borgesian sleights-of-hand. Many may read Shum's smart, fast, impressive debut as a how-to fiction about betting, but at the end of the day it's really all about the epistemologically and ontologically incomprehensible all the way down."

—Lance Olsen, author of *Dreamlives of Debris*

"In a spellbinding structure that spirals around the mysterious Royal Casino, *Queen of Spades* weaves a cast of high-stakes dealers and gamblers closer and closer together as if within a spider's web. Though their games are staked on chance, these characters' lives intersect by fate, destiny and magic. Michael Shou-Yung Shum has written a luminous and mesmerizing debut, a novel I couldn't put down."
　　—Anne Valente, author of *Our Hearts Will Burn Us Down*

"Gambling—is it luck or applied theory? Dealer Arturo Chan, newly arrived in Snoqualmie, Washington, and beguiled by a wealthy bettor known only as the Countess, thinks he's getting close to the answer. Chasing after a clue to the Countess's inscrutable playing system, Chan finds himself at the crossroads of chance and manipulation, surrounded by colleagues and bettors with aspirations of their own."
　　—Ruby Meyers, bookseller, Annie Bloom's Books

"*Queen of Spades* is a paean to the deeply human thrill of gambling—part fond portrait of casino life, part poker-faced mysticism, part exploration of the risks we're willing to take in search of meaning. Michael Shum has imagined a world in which cosmic forces are at play, populated it with odd and charming seekers, and turned them loose among the games of chance to seek their destinies. Like drawing just the right card to a longshot inside straight, what they find—and what we read—seems at once astonishing and dazzlingly preordained. A remarkable and original debut, rendered in impossibly lucid prose."
　　—Michael Knight, author of *Eveningland*

"In *Queen of Spades*, Michael Shou-Yung Shum has crafted a deceptively simple meditation on obsession, human frailty, and the possibility of magic that all of us, gamblers and otherwise, hold in our innermost hearts. An elegantly structured, deeply fulfilling tall tale that left me wanting more."
　　—Matthew Flaming,
author of *The Kingdom of Ohio*

Queen of Spades

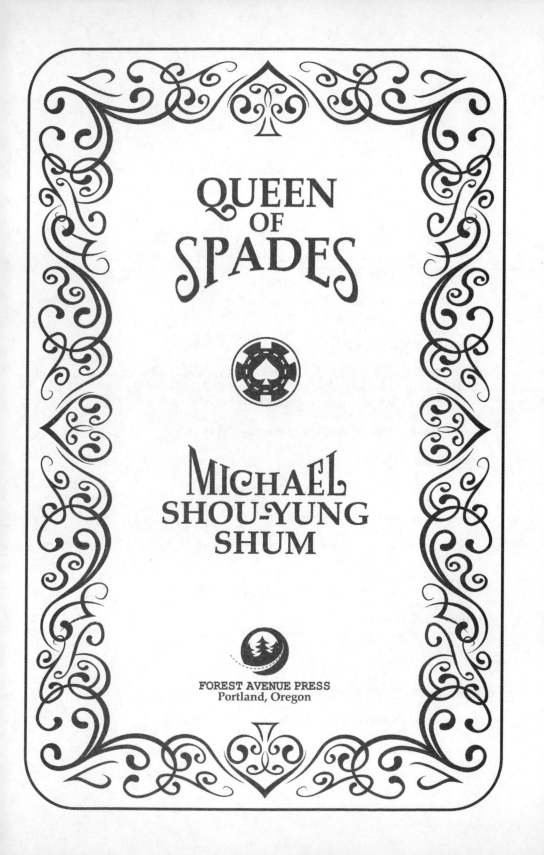

QUEEN
OF
SPADES

MICHAEL
SHOU-YUNG
SHUM

FOREST AVENUE PRESS
Portland, Oregon

Figure 1 and Figure 3 illustrations by Ciaran Parr
Figure 2 and Queen of Spades illustrations by Gigi Little
Cover design: Gigi Little
Interior design: Laura Stanfill

Vectorized Playing Cards 2.0 - http://sourceforge.net/projects/vector-cards/
Copyright 2015 - Chris Aguilar - conjurenation@gmail.com
Licensed under LGPL 3 - www.gnu.org/copyleft/lesser.html

An early draft of the first chapters appeared in *Spolia* in 2014.

ISBN: 978-1-942436-31-7

Library of Congress Cataloging-in-Publication Data

Names: Shum, Michael Shou-Yung 1971- author.
Title: Queen of spades / Michael Shou-Yung Shum.
Description: Portland, Oregon : Forest Avenue Press, 2017.
Identifiers: LCCN 2017007822 (print) | LCCN 2017026001 (ebook) | ISBN
  9781942436331 (ePub) | ISBN 9781942436317 (pbk.)
Subjects: LCSH: Casinos--Fiction. | Gambling--Fiction.
Classification: LCC PS3619.H857 (ebook) | LCC PS3619.H857 Q44 2017
(print) | DDC 813/.6--dc23
LC record available at https://lccn.loc.gov/2017007822

1 2 3 4 5 6 7 8 9

Distributed by Legato Publishers Group

Printed in the United States of America by United Graphics

Forest Avenue Press LLC
P.O. Box 80134
Portland, OR 97280
forestavenuepress.com

To my dearest Jaclyn,
in this fourth year of our blessed union

Contents

Dramatis Personae

The Countess

Arturo Chan, Dealer

Barbara, Streaky Gambler

Stephen Mannheim, Pit Boss

Chimsky, High-Limit Dealer

Gabriela, Casino Manager

Dr. Sarmiento, Neurologist

Dr. Eccleston, Spiritual Advisor

Theo Sommerville, Dr. Eccleston's Apprentice

Dimsberg, Recovering Gambler

Faye Handoko, Reporter

Jean-Paul Dumonde, Former Pit Boss

Simon and Quincy, Club Owners

Henry Fong, Bookmaker

Frances Murphy, Bookmaker's Mother

Shirley and James Harris, the Cursed Couple

The Spiky-Haired Boy

Thomas, Dr. Eccleston's Son

Dayna, Leanne, Bao, Rumi, Lederhaus, and Derek, Casino Staff

and all the Regulars

A Transformative Hand

I FIRST MET THE INDIVIDUAL described herein as Arturo Chan when we worked together at Highway 9 Casino in Lake Stevens, Washington. He was a pit dealer and I a part-time poker dealer, working nights to supplement a meager graduate student stipend. During breaks, we would discuss in the employee lounge the books we read—we both greatly admired Kawabata's *House of the Sleeping Beauties*, I remember—and this mutual interest in *belles lettres* not uncommon among the dealing class gradually grew into a private confidence. I learned Chan had dealt one of the most astonishing hands of the twentieth century, in 1984, during a hand of Faro—a game similar to Roulette but played with a deck of cards. This particular Faro table, Chan explained, was the last of its kind in North America. The table had, in fact, shut down immediately after the hand in question.

Utterly fascinated by this card story, I offered to piece together his recollection of the events leading up to its deal, rendering them into the narrative you now hold in your hands. As part of this arrangement, Chan provided me with a file cabinet's worth of carefully ordered, handwritten personal reflections and unusual "dealing exercises" from the time period in question. A sample of the latter follows:

1. Close eyes and breathe deeply through nose into pit of stomach. Count to three. Exhale.
2. Focus on shape of breath—expanding and contracting.
3. Repeat for ten breaths.
4. Eyes shut, hold deck of cards in preferred hand.
5. Deal slowly, sensing weight of each card, into two decks: Light and Heavy.
6. Open eyes and decks. Determine whether paints [Jacks, Queens, and Kings—ed.] are in one deck, cardinals in the other. Errors most likely with Nines and Tens.
7. When mastered, switch hands.

Despite my proddings, Chan never demonstrated, at the tables or otherwise, the kinds of showy technical expertise that other dealers were prone to advertise in public. I believe this was due to the fact that Chan never considered these exercises mere tricks, but rather an important part of a personal practice toward the discernment of small differences, a sort of aesthetic and political stance of refinement that lay in quiet opposition to the gross, broad strokes applied by culture in our fast-moving society. For Chan, taking care and paying attention were foundational to establishing congruence with the forces of the universe, which I imagine as an enormous, rolling wheel we move either with or against.

As author, I took the liberty of organizing and naming each chapter in *Queen of Spades*, but the scenes rendered remain the province of Chan's memories, distilled through fictional conventions of timing and characterization. Chan's notions of risk, fortune, and luck appear as a faint, ghostly presence in these pages, one that I hope readers find quite powerful and calming. Chan had that effect on the people around him—his tables were always the liveliest and best-natured—and my only hope is that some of his mystical influence touches you now, dear Reader, wherever you happen to be at this moment.

MSS
Atlanta, July 17, 2017

BOOK ONE:
ROYAL CASINO

Part of human life escapes from work and reaches freedom. This is the part of play that is controlled by reason, but, within reason's limits, determines the brief possibilities of a leap beyond those limits. Play, which is as fascinating as catastrophe, allows you to positively glimpse the giddy seductiveness of chance.

—Georges Bataille, "Chance"

Located a stone's throw off the interstate leading west out of Seattle, about fifty miles before it turns into a treacherous passage through the Cascades, there appears around a bend the magnificent sight of the Royal Casino. The wearied traveler is filled with the hope of good fortune, and there is nothing about the spacious parking lot, immaculate grounds, or sumptuous High-Limit Salon—one of the only rooms in the world in which hands of Faro are still being dealt today—that serves to dissuade these impressions.

—*The Complete Guide to*
American Gambling Houses 1984

The Audition

AUDITIONING NEW DEALERS WAS ONE aspect of his job as pit manager that still interested Stephen Mannheim after nearly forty years in the trade. Off the beaten path of the Vegas, California, and Atlantic City casinos, the Royal attracted to its doors the oddest sorts of characters seeking gainful employment, drawn to the Pacific Northwest by the quiet beauty inherent to the region. There was something in the trees, it was oft repeated, and Mannheim, who had lived within these pines and shadows all his life, had never considered there was anywhere else he should be.

That May night, he had clocked in at eleven p.m. as usual, and received word from the swing shift supervisor that a man named Arturo Chan had arrived to interview for the newly open dealing position on the graveyard shift. Three days ago, Mannheim had lost one of his best dealers, a woman named Crystal, to a rival casino in Snoqualmie, and the existing dealers had had to work five downs out of six rather than their usual three out of four to cover her absence. Mannheim had taken his time filling the opening, but he knew if he delayed any longer, word would reach Gabriela, and she was the last person Mannheim wanted to disappoint. Although the rumors circulating among his loyal crew—that their boss was distracted, that something was wrong—were not entirely unfounded, Mannheim realized they could be dispelled with a single decisive act, and when he sat down with Chan in the employee lounge to discuss Chan's credentials, he was already looking at this new character with an eye toward hiring him.

Chan was clad in the traditional white tuxedo shirt and black pants of the auditioning dealer, and as they shook hands, Mannheim noticed Chan's fingernails were cut short and were exceptionally clean. Mannheim liked his solemn manner immediately, as he'd had problems in the past with more effusive dealers, ones who might berate a customer, or quit without any provocation whatsoever. In his starched, pointy collar, Chan looked positively severe. As he sat silently, Mannheim scrutinized a long list of Chan's previous dealing appointments—they ranged from coast to coast for a period of twelve years, requiring two full pages to delineate.

"You have quite a bit of experience," Mannheim said. He chose at random a casino in West Virginia. "Oh, I see you worked at the Blackridge. Was Farnsworth your manager?"

Chan regarded him and shook his head. "Sorry, sir. I knew of no Farnsworth."

"I see. He must've left before you got there." Farnsworth had been the name of Mannheim's cat. It was a little trick, Mannheim knew, but he'd caught enough prospective dealers in a lie that it was a useful little trick.

Chan continued: "My manager was Mr. Dumonde. His number is available under the references section."

Mannheim flipped the page and scanned it without reading. Then he looked at Chan. "The one thing that concerns me about your background is that you've moved around so much."

Chan nodded. "I have. But I've worked a minimum of

six months at every location, with the sole exception of Four Queens in Tunica, which closed due to a hurricane. In each instance, I've given at least three weeks' notice, and never missed a shift."

"So how long are you planning on staying this time?" Mannheim asked.

Chan paused and carefully placed his palms on the table. "My previous appointments were temporary—but I believe the Royal is different, sir."

"We think so," Mannheim said, smiling. "What can you deal?"

"Blackjack, Pai Gow, Caribbean Stud, Two- and Three-Card Poker—the usual. The only games I cannot deal," Chan said, "are Craps and Roulette."

"What about Faro? We offer that in the high-limit room here."

"Nor Faro," Chan added apologetically. "I've never had the opportunity."

"That's fine," Mannheim said. "In the pit, we only spread Blackjack, Pai Gow, and Three-Card." He stood up from the table. "Well, shall we?"

The two men exited the lounge and Mannheim led Chan across the dark patterned carpet—ingeniously designed to camouflage any chip that fell upon it—to the pit, which in that nether hour between swing and graveyard shifts was calm and subdued. They walked behind the velvet ropes into the center of the pit, where the assistant graveyard manager, Dayna, stood with her arms crossed. One of the high-limit dealers, Chimsky, was also there, chatting to Dayna about an upcoming boxing match he considered an extraordinary betting opportunity, a "mortal lock." Mannheim knew Chimsky and disliked him—technically, Mannheim was his superior, but Chimsky lorded over everyone in the pit the fact that he worked in the High-Limit Salon.

Mannheim tapped one of his dealers on the shoulder and indicated to her that she should step aside for a few hands. Chan positioned himself in the spot, and the two customers at the table, old Royal regulars, regarded the new dealer suspiciously.

"Hello," Chan said. "I hope you are well."

"We will be if you deal us some winners," one of the customers said. "Leanne's killing us tonight."

With the flick of an agile wrist, Chan was off. Mannheim and Chimsky stood and watched the audition, which consisted of three hands. The first thing Mannheim looked for was confidence in knowledge of the game, the rules and the payouts in particular. The second was speed and efficiency—the more hands dealt per down, the better for the house. And finally, there was that aspect of dealing that cannot be defined—style, for lack of a better word. Chan was unremarkable in the first two departments, but his idiosyncratic flair in sliding a card from the shoe, flipping it over using just the edge of the card, the overall effect created by his spider-like fingers as they traveled across the felt, mesmerized Mannheim. He understood why Chan had had so many previous dealing appointments: the man was an exceptional dealer.

"So what do you think?" Mannheim whispered. He knew Chimsky, who prided himself on being the best at the Royal, could always be counted on for a brutal but fair assessment.

"He's not very fast, is he?" Chimsky said. "He's solid enough for the pit, though. He's better than half the people here already." Chimsky said the last softly enough that exactly none of the dealers of whom he spoke could hear.

Mannheim nodded. There was something in Chan's serious manner, in his subtle dealing style, that bespoke some secret intensity. He reminded Mannheim of himself at a younger age, a slow-burning fuse ready to be lit—but by what? Mannheim had never discovered his own spark, and now it was too late for him. But afterward, in the lounge, after he informed Chan he was hired—news the man received with utter equanimity—Mannheim told Chan that he hoped he would discover what he was looking for at the Royal.

"Find yourself a nice place to live," Mannheim said. He recommended a building with furnished rooms several miles away, in downtown Snoqualmie. "Get acclimated to our little corner of the world. Come in tomorrow night and we'll get you started. Oh, and let me know the size for your vest."

After Chan departed, Mannheim—pleasantly diverted by the audition—returned to the pit to begin his nightly ritual, kibitzing with his dealers and regular customers. His mood was light as he listened to their tales of woe: bad beats in Blackjack, an unlucky DUI, a tooth that had mysteriously gone missing. Mannheim was laughing at this last story when he began to feel a wetness in his right ear—from the inside. He put a hand to the spot and when he examined his fingers, there was blood on them. Mortified, Mannheim excused himself and rushed to the employee bathroom, all the while applying pressure to his ear, but to little effect—he could feel blood dripping down the front of his hand, staining the sleeve of his jacket.

In the bathroom, he leaned his head against the wall of the stall and stuffed the afflicted canal with tissue. As he waited on gravity to stem the flow, Mannheim could not help but recall Dr. Sarmiento's warning that disturbing symptoms would arise as his condition worsened: internal bleeding, amnesia, fainting spells. Even unusual odors and halluci-nations. For a moment, Mannheim wished that the trickle wouldn't stop, that it would in fact surge, and he would bleed to death right then and there on the floor of the Royal, and be done with it all. But of course, after ten minutes, it did stop.

Mannheim carefully cleaned his ear, both the lobe and inside, washed his sleeve, and then made his way back to the pit, feeling slightly disoriented, his equilibrium off. There, he watched as the rest of the evening at the Royal unspooled around him, hardly taking any notice now of what Dayna, Leanne, and the others were saying. There was a note of doom in his voice whenever he confirmed the buy-in amounts shouted by his staff, or explained to a customer why they were no longer allowed any alcohol. In the back of his mind was the knowledge that there was a very good chance that Chan would be the last dealer he would ever audition, that he would ever hire at the Royal, for Mannheim was dying, and only he and Dr. Sarmiento knew this.

Chan's First Night

AT THE APPOINTED TIME, CHAN returned to the Royal, freshly groomed. From the cage, he received his name tag—*Arturo Chan, Pit Dealer*—and a red vest, size small. It shaped his torso nicely, and he could tell Mannheim was pleased by his neat appearance. He tapped in at a Blackjack table, replacing a rotund, curly-haired dealer named Bao who dashed off to smoke. There were two players at the table, a mother and daughter who each had fifteen dollars out, but seeing the dealer change, reduced their bet sizes to five dollars, the minimum.

"Good luck," Chan said, passing his right hand over the table with a flourish. He dealt them both pat hands—the mother a 20 and the daughter a 19—and then promptly dealt himself a Blackjack, with the Jack and then the Ace of Spades. "Story of my life," the mother muttered as Chan swept their bets. They each pushed out five more dollars. This time, Chan dealt the mother a 6-4 for 10 and the daughter a 5-6 for 11—and himself a 7. They doubled down and Chan stonewalled their hands with a Trey and a 4, respectively. "It never fails!" the mother exclaimed, glaring at him. When

Chan revealed that his second card was another 7, giving him 14, their spirits rose for a moment—only to be dashed when Chan dealt himself a third 7 to make 21. Disgusted, the pair left for greener pastures.

Mannheim, who had been watching, chuckled. "I think this casino is going to like the way you deal."

It took twenty minutes before Chan received another customer. A young couple sat down, holding hands. He offered them the deck to cut and the woman took the yellow cut card and plunged it in the middle. Chan deftly made the cut and inserted the entire thing into the shoe. Out of the first three hands, they won twice when Chan busted, and pushed when they all drew 18. The table gradually filled, seat by seat, so by the time Chan got to the cut card, there was only one empty chair. Chan was finding a good, steady groove, and occasionally he won a toke or two for himself from the young couple, who had taken a liking to him and were occasionally placing one-dollar wagers on his behalf.

It was in this kind of dealer's trance, during his third down of the evening, that Chan looked up from the hand he was dealing—a new player was taking an inordinately long time deciding to hit or stand—and noticed a small procession was negotiating its way through the pit, toward the exit. It was a group of valets escorting an extremely old woman. Chan was struck by her appearance—she wore a long, dark gown, and her fine white hair was pulled back high from her forehead by a gold circlet. In several spots, the skin on her face was nearly translucent, revealing a patchwork of veinery underneath, like the delicate marbling in a block of cheese.

"Sir, my card please," the new player at the table was saying. Chan realized he'd been distracted from the play of the hand. He quickly dealt the player an 8 to make 20, and busted himself with a King. But moments later, while he was making the payouts, his attention was again drawn from the table, this time by the sound of someone shrieking in delight.

"Yes!" a woman near the entrance was shouting. "Yes! Yes!" It sounded like the mother that Chan had dealt to earlier that evening. Her slot machine was going off, relinquishing its jackpot in an orgy of bells and sirens. And a most curious sight—Chan could see that just beyond the machine and its happy winner was the old woman, leading the procession of valets up the ramp that led out of the casino, taking no notice of the commotion at all.

"Hey dealer! Are you going to pay us or what?"

Flustered, Chan apologized. He finished the payouts and swept the hands, and as he slid the cards into the discard tray, he was glad to see that Mannheim hadn't seemed to notice his dawdling. For the rest of the down, Chan resolved to focus.

At the end of his fifth consecutive down, Mannheim tapped him on the shoulder and told Chan to go on break. "Keep up the good work," he said.

Chan wandered to the employee lounge, where two fellow pit dealers pulled a chair for him to join them. Leanne and Bao were friendly and gregarious, and after fifteen minutes of chatting about their respective dealing pasts, Chan asked them about the old woman he had seen leaving the casino. They were only too happy to respond. He learned that no one knew her real name, and that she was referred to by all the regulars and the staff as the Countess.

Every evening, Leanne said, she could be found playing Faro in the High-Limit Salon. She arrived at ten p.m. in a long, silver Rolls Royce limousine, and would gamble for three hours—no, it was four, said Bao. Until two a.m. precisely. All the while, her chauffeur, a young man who never spoke a word, stood stiffly by her side.

"She's sort of the queen of the Royal," Bao explained.

As they continued chatting about the old woman, a

shadow fell across their table and a loud voice interjected: "I couldn't help overhearing your conversation." Chan turned and recognized the heavyset bearded dealer who had been present during his audition—Chimsky. He was standing before them in his purple vest, drinking a cup of coffee. "You three may be interested in hearing how she fared in her gambling this evening."

Leanne sighed. "Go ahead, Chimsky. You're going to tell us anyway."

Chimsky smiled and sat down in the seat next to Chan's. "Tonight, she watched eight decks pass without placing a bet," he began. "Three whole hours. Then, with no warning, I see her quietly push out one green plaque onto the Deuce." Chan knew the green plaques at the Royal were worth $25,000 apiece. He leaned closer.

"Three Deuces had already come out during the deal," Chimsky said. "The only one left was her Deuce—the Deuce of Spades. I waited for the table to quiet. Then I threw down her card and there it was!"

For the only time that evening, Chimsky told them, a slight curl of a smile had escaped the Countess's lips. She waited calmly while Chimsky slid her winnings across the table—another green plaque to match the one she had wagered. She had not played another hand, although she watched until two a.m., as she always did. Then she had risen, ordered her car, and departed.

"Are you saying," Chan asked—it was the first time he

had spoken to Chimsky—"that she places only one bet over the course of an entire evening?"

"Not quite." Chimsky turned toward him. "Many nights she watches and doesn't ever place a single bet. But very rarely, she'll place two in a row. The last time was three years ago, and she won over a hundred grand."

"I remember that night," said Bao. "It was all the talk for about a week."

"So she plays a system," Chan said.

Chimsky laughed. "Of course. But I haven't been able to figure hers out. Once, I recorded every hand she played on my deal for a month, about a dozen total. I couldn't detect the slightest pattern."

"But who is she? How can she can afford to bet such large amounts?"

Chimsky shook his head. "No one even knows where she lives!" He looked like he was about to say more. "Ah, but look at the clock. The Faro table calls."

AT THE CONCLUSION OF HIS shift—the last four hours of which were unremarkable—Chan returned to the cheap, furnished room he had rented based on Mannheim's recommendation and tried to sleep. However, even with the windows papered over, there remained slits through which light penetrated and vexed his eyes, no matter which way he turned. Eventually, he arose and took a long shower instead, then made a pot of coffee and returned with a mug to the living room. Where a television normally would have sat stood an old trunk paneled in dark wood—Chan gazed upon this with some satisfaction and ran his hand over its leading edge.

When he lifted the lid of the trunk, the hinge activated a mechanism that elevated an inner shelf to the level of his waist. Upon the shelf were the books Chan had been collecting since early adulthood, antiquarian tomes on the history and art of gambling: the first edition of Yardley's *The Education of a Poker Player*, Rocheford's *Les Caprices du Hasard*, the classic *Gambling Systems of the World* by Martingale. Chan withdrew the Martingale and perused it for half an hour, seeking some mention of the system the old woman employed, but he found none that fit Chimsky's description. This reinforced for Chan what he already suspected—that the Countess's system was singularly hers.

He returned the Martingale to its place, passed a finger over the Rocheford, and selected instead a particularly slim volume in a mustard-green dust jacket, upon which was depicted in an art deco style gamblers in formal dress surrounding a vast table imprinted with cards. Chan carried the book, which was entitled *A Player's Guide to Faro*, to the couch where his coffee awaited. That morning, he'd asked Mannheim about the steps required to eventually be promoted to the High-Limit Salon, and Mannheim had said that there were no shortcuts—Chan would have to work his way up the seniority list, which could take years, and that in the meantime, the first thing he should do was familiarize himself with the rules of Faro.

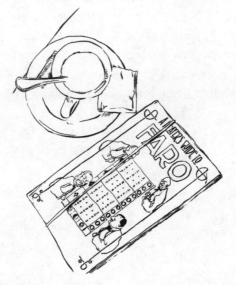

Figure 1. "Chan selected a particularly slim volume in a mustard-green dust jacket, upon which was depicted in an art deco style gamblers in formal dress surrounding a vast table imprinted with cards."

THE 13 RULES OF FARO

Players: Any number, although six is the comfortable maximum.
House Officials: A dealer and a manager who supervises betting
and serves as the case-keeper, keeping track on a board visible to
players which cards have been dealt and which are still available.

1. The house acts as the banker, and the stakes involved
   may be limited at the house's discretion.

2. Players purchase chips from the dealer to facilitate
   making bets. Their value is denoted by different colors,
   or numerals stamped on them.

3. The dealer sits before a table covered with a green or a
   blue felt cloth, on which are painted the thirteen cards
   of one suit, usually Spades.

4. The dealer shuffles and cuts the pack, then places the
   cards face down inside a metal box called a *shoe*. At one
   end of the box, near the top, is a horizontal slit, wide
   enough to permit the passage of a single card. The top
   card is always kept opposite the slit by four springs in
   the bottom of the box forcing the pack upward.

5. Having decided which cards on the Faro board they
   wish to bet on, the players bet by placing their chips on
   the cards selected.

6. The first card in a deck is known as the *soda*, and is not
   used, but discarded. The second card is the *winner*,
   and is placed to the left of the shoe in front of the dealer.
   The third card is the *loser* for that turn, and is placed

to the right of the shoe. There is a winner and a loser
for every turn.

7. Loser cards win for the house, and all stakes resting on
the corresponding card on the board are taken by the house.

8. Winner cards win for the players the amount of any bet
placed on the corresponding card on the board.

9. Whenever the winning and losing cards in a turn are
the same rank (e.g., two Kings, two Sixes, etc.), this is
known as a split, and the house takes half the chips
staked on them. This is the house's percentage, and can
be expected to occur about three times every two decks.

10. Each pair of cards is known as a *turn*. There are 25
turns in one deck of Faro. Including the soda and the
hock (the last card in the deck), there are 52 cards
total. At the end of each turn bets are settled, and new
ones made for the next turn.

11. When there is only one turn left in the pack (two cards
plus the hock), players may *call the last turn*, that is,
guess the order in which the last three cards will appear.
If the three cards are different, and the player
guesses correctly, the bet returns four times the stake.
If there are two cards the same, the bet returns twice
the stake.

12. When the pack is exhausted, a fresh deal is made and
the playing continues as before.

13. In case of a misdeal, all active bets are returned.

Two Temptations

FOR MANY YEARS, EVER SINCE he was a small child, Chimsky had followed the sport of boxing. In that time he'd witnessed the rise and fall of many champions—Bob Foster, Roberto Duran, and of course Ali—but this new fighter, Anton "Glove of Stone" Golovkin, was truly striking. No middleweight that Chimsky had ever seen, not even Hagler, carried as much power in his fists as the frightening Golovkin. During his recent ascension to the middleweight championship, the Glove of Stone had strewn in his wake a string of challengers, all stiffened by his concussive right to the temple or thudding left to the liver. Golovkin was 43 and 0 with 41 knockouts, and the two who'd survived the distance had done so at a heavy price to their own careers, neither having ever fought again.

Therefore, Chimsky considered it an absolute certainty that any bout that involved Golovkin would not go to a decision. In fact, Golovkin had knocked out his last fifteen opponents, and Chimsky had made money wagering on each of these contests. If only he could have restricted his betting to Golovkin! But of course, there were many other bets during this span of time—in many other sports—that were not nearly as reliable for his gambling bankroll.

But on August 18, in just three weeks' time, Golovkin was entering the ring again. His opponent was alleged to be his most challenging yet, although Chimsky did not think so: the stylish former champion Juan "El Matador" Coronado, who was returning after a two-year retirement in order to reclaim the laurels he still believed rightfully his. The rumor on the street was that Coronado was broke and needed the money. Despite the crafty southpaw's skill, Chimsky could not imagine any scenario where El Matador, now thirty-seven years of age, could defend himself against the marauding Glove of Stone.

The opening line was generous, with Golovkin only a 3-to-2 favorite. Normally, Chimsky would've bet five, even ten thousand on such an attractive number, but his recent losses had escalated in a frightening way, and his bookmaker, Henry Fong, was no longer accepting his bets until some of the debt was paid off. The last time they had spoken, Fong informed Chimsky that he was on the hook for $47,000.

It was a horrible feeling, knowing the fight could extricate him from this hole, but having no means to bet on it. Chimsky went so far as to ask some of the other dealers at the Royal if they were interested in staking him, but having been dissatisfied with previous tips, they all declined. The days passed and the Thursday before the fight, the line closed to 5 to 4, almost even odds. Chimsky grew desperate. He decided he would risk phoning Barbara and see if she would be willing to extend a hand. They'd spoken sparingly, ever since she'd joined the Snoqualmie chapter of Gambling Help, more than a year and a half ago now.

One of their rules, she'd told him early on, was that she should refrain from associating with anyone who worked in a casino.

Their main connection, however—before, during, and even after their marriage—had always been an interest in gambling, and Chimsky hoped the passage of time had brought Barbara to her senses. Before work on Thursday evening, Chimsky composed himself and dialed her number, listening to it ring six times before she answered.

"What is it, Chim?" She sounded tired.

"Hi, Barbara," he said. "It's good to hear your voice. How are you?"

"I'm fine. Everything's fine. Why are you calling?"

"I just wanted to see how you were doing, Barbara—I miss you. Are you still going to that—that thing you were going to?"

"It's called Gambling Help, Chim. And yes, I am. In fact, you're making me late for a meeting right now."

"Can't you skip it? Let's catch up."

"I have to go every day—that's how this works. You have to be constantly vigilant. And I'm late."

"Wait," Chimsky said. "I'll make it quick."

Barbara sighed. "Okay. What?"

"I need ten grand," Chimsky said. "Or even five would help."

"Ha! You're out of your mind, Chim. Even if I had that money, the last person I would lend it to is you."

"What if my life is in danger?"

"Not that I should care, but is it?"

"I'm on the hook, Barbara. For forty-seven large."

A long period of silence ensued, during which Chimsky grew hopeful Barbara was changing her mind. Then she spoke again, very slowly and evenly. "Chimsky, I'm about to walk out this door right now to go to a meeting. I'm trying to get my shit together, and you call out of the blue with all your bullshit, just like before, and I get caught up in it. But not this time. I'm getting better, Chimsky, and I hope someday you realize that you have an illness. Good-bye."

"Wait!" Chimsky said. "Don't you even want to know what the bet is?"

He heard her phone slamming against its cradle, and then the dial tone.

THE NEXT AFTERNOON, CHIMSKY LEFT his rooms at the Orleans Hotel and drove to the Royal, where he picked up his biweekly check from the cashier's cage. He was paid a minimal wage, the amount a mere pittance against his debt, but he had to placate Fong somehow. Afterward, he drove to another hotel across the street from the Orleans, its sister property known as the Oliver. He took an elevator up to the top floor, the seventeenth, walked to the end of the hall, and knocked on the door of 1717, one of the corner suites.

An enormous man with long blond hair, in a tank top and shorts, answered the door. "Yeah?" he asked.

"Hey, Quincy," Chimsky said. "Can you tell Mr. Fong I'm here to see him?"

"Wait here."

After several moments, Quincy returned and ushered him in; Chimsky followed him down a short corridor that opened out into a large living area. There was an entire bank of televisions—a half dozen—stacked on top of one another against a wall. Facing them was a long, circular white couch that surrounded a low coffee table, on which were two different-colored telephones. One was ringing, and the other was in the hand of a very tall, very thin man in a tracksuit, who was sitting on the couch and writing something down in a ledger.

"Seahawks plus three and the hook," Mr. Fong was saying into the phone. "Ten on the side and ten on the total, right? Okay. See you next week." He hung up and ignored the other telephone. "Personal line," he explained to Chimsky. "You're looking spry today."

Chimsky handed over his paycheck. He watched while

Fong looked it over, flipped to a page in his ledger, and made a notation. Quincy was in the kitchen, using a blender.

"He's making smoothies," Fong said to Chimsky. "Do you want one?"

"Sure," Chimsky said.

"Hey, Quincy!" Fong shouted. "Chimsky wants one too!"

"You got it," came the voice from the kitchen.

Fong showed Chimsky his calculations, the new total Chimsky owed minus his paycheck, plus the interest of another week: $46,375.

"That looks right," Chimsky said. "Mr. Fong, I actually have something I'd like to discuss with you."

"What is it?"

"The big fight tomorrow night."

"It's a good one. Who do you like? I say Coronado but Quincy says Golovkin by K.O."

"That's what I want to talk about," Chimsky said. "Can you extend me credit for the fight? I want to bet on Golovkin."

Fong laughed. "I thought we discussed this, Chimsky. No more bets for you until you pay down the number." He pointed at the ledger. "Get it down to less than twenty and we can talk."

Chimsky pulled from his pocket a scrap of paper that contained an itemized list he'd made that morning. He passed it over to Fong. "These are my assets," Chimsky said. "You can see I've got a car, a Saab, which is only a few years old, worth twelve grand easy. Then household effects: a new Zenith television, worth two. A nice stereo. A sushi maker. A pasta maker."

Quincy returned with three smoothies in tall glasses on a tray. Chimsky took his and drank half of it in short order. It was pineapple flavored and delicious.

"Quincy," Fong was saying. "Do you think we need Chimsky's sushi maker?"

"It's hard to say," Quincy said. "But it can't hurt."

"Those items I've listed add up to over twenty grand," Chimsky said. "It's all yours if I don't win this bet."

"It's already all mine," Fong said. "You owe me forty-seven grand."

"Plus my paychecks for the rest of the year," Chimsky said. "All I need is credit for one more bet, so I can start getting myself out of this hole."

"By paying me back with my own money," Fong said.

"Yes," Chimsky said. "By doubling it and then paying you back with it."

"And what if Golovkin loses? What then?"

"You can have everything."

"I told you I already own everything you have," Fong said.

"You can own part of me then," Chimsky said. "I can run errands for you, make you dinner, that sort of thing. Until you feel the debt is paid off."

"We may have to break your arms," Fong said, nodding at Quincy. Then he laughed. "I'm just kidding, Chimsky." He finished his smoothie and wiped his lips. "How much are you talking about exactly?"

"Fifty grand," Chimsky said. "If I win the bet, I'll win forty grand. That'll leave me six, seven grand in debt, and I can just work that off."

"And if you lose, you'll owe me almost a hundred," Fong said.

"Yes. But Golovkin's not losing."

Fong laughed. "What do you think, Quincy? Should we lend Chimsky another fifty grand?"

Quincy shrugged. "I think Golovkin's gonna win too," he said.

"You're going to have to excuse us for a moment."

"Sure," said Chimsky. When he realized Fong meant him, he went back out into the hotel hallway, and closed the door to the suite behind him. He stood there for several minutes, and then he sat down on the carpet to await Fong's decision. Finally, Quincy opened the door. Chimsky went back inside and stood beside the couch in exactly the same place.

Fong was regarding him carefully. "Are you sure you want this, Chimsky? You understand the consequences."

"Yes," said Chimsky.

"It's done then." Fong made a notation in the ledger. "Fifty grand on Golovkin it is."

"Thank you, Mr. Fong," Chimsky said. "I knew I could count on you."

He offered his hand to be shaken, but Fong did not move.

"Remember, Chimsky—if Golovkin loses, you won't have a place to rest your ass. In fact, you won't even have an ass."

As Fong returned to his phones, Quincy silently showed Chimsky to the door.

THAT EVENING, AS SHE HAD for a year and a half now, Barbara went to her seven p.m. meeting and sat in her usual metal folding chair, the one across from Dimsberg, her hands quietly placed in her lap. Typically, she tried to participate, to at least offer a kind word of encouragement to her compatriots, but this meeting, she found herself listening with only half an ear to their litany, and when it was her opportunity to testify, she averted her eyes and declined with a cautious smile. Instead, she found herself spending the hour discreetly examining the other members—their bony countenances, their pale, spectral features, their arms and hands mottled with discolored spots—noticing how none of them seemed to be getting any better, physically speaking at least, as if the effort of staying clean were draining the life out of their bodies. Was the same thing happening to hers?

Barbara had to suppress a sudden desire to feel the furrows on her own face.

After the meeting ended—finally!—she rose from her chair, preparing to depart as quickly as was polite, but Dimsberg was already there, obtruding upon her field of vision.

"Are you feeling all right, Barbara?" he asked. "You seemed kind of quiet, even distant, tonight."

She hated hearing her voice responding—obligingly, automatically. "Thanks for asking, Dimsberg. I've been swamped at work. I have to hire a bunch of temps this week, and I've barely started."

"I'd be happy to make some calls on your behalf," Dimsberg offered. He brushed her shoulder with his hand. Barbara recoiled inwardly, but maintained her smile.

"Thanks, Dimsberg—but you know, this is something only I can take care of."

"Say, Barbara. Maybe we can chat sometime—about your progress, outside of the group . . ."

Fortunately, at that moment, their social chair stepped in and began asking Dimsberg about the arrangements for their next potluck at the Community Center. Dimsberg appeared annoyed, but fielded the question nonetheless, which afforded Barbara another opportunity to leave.

"See you tomorrow," he said hopefully, with his gruesome smile.

"Good-bye," she said.

As she drove home from the meeting, the radio off, Barbara ran her fingers over her forehead, feeling the tension slowly ease from her temples. After several moments, she sighed and lit a cigarette using the car lighter: it was the same mournful atmosphere at the Community Center every night, and it had been wearing a little thin for months now. Wasn't all the suffering a bit *too much*?

But it wasn't just the other members. Not exactly.

It wasn't even Dimsberg—their "chapter leader"—though she disliked him most, with his obsequious manner, always apologizing for interrupting and then interrupting. Always touching her, when that was the last thing she wanted.

No, what was beginning to gnaw at Barbara—what she could only repress for so long—was the urge for action.

At this realization, she shuddered and had to light a second cigarette. She did not want to go through all *that* again, what made her join Dimsberg and his doleful crew in the first place. Two winters ago, she'd lost her television, and then her car, and then nearly her job after a manic two-week spree. At her high point, she'd been up over $10,000, but after all was said and done, she'd ended $12,500 in the hole. Worst of all, one awful morning, she was called in at work and told she was being demoted due to her strange, disordered behavior. "Are you on drugs?" one of her supervisors had pointedly asked.

Barbara had gone to her first meeting of Gambling Help because it seemed the sensible thing to do. There, everyone had spoken so kindly to her, assuring her they knew exactly what she was going through. Especially Dimsberg. Painstakingly, she had reestablished her position in life based on their support: she bought a used car from one member, and another had given her an old television, one that still required her to get up from the couch to switch on. And then, on another awful morning, behind the same closed doors, she had prostrated herself before her supervisors, volunteering for the thorny and thankless election project no one else would touch. She was given her old job back, albeit on a probationary basis.

Now, with the project looming and her sobriety still intact, Barbara resolved to be stronger. Her life was better without gambling—wasn't it? But the urge continued to unsettle her, and when she arrived home, she had to play several rounds of Solitaire on the coffee table—winning the last one—before she felt relaxed enough for bed.

The Referral

At the end of a long series of scans and tests, his neurologist told Mannheim his brain was riddled with lesions—"think of them as little, expanding holes," Dr. Sarmiento had said. "They've been growing for some time." Mannheim had been in a state of utter shock and had hardly comprehended the specific medical details she'd explained to him, other than her guess that he was only even odds to survive until the end of the year.

"What should I do?" he asked. "I'm scared."

"Don't you have family? Anyone close?"

"No."

Dr. Sarmiento, a quick-witted, plain-speaking woman who occasionally gambled at the Royal, placed a heavy hand on Mannheim's shoulder. "In that case, you should perhaps consider doing more of whatever you like. Damn the costs— don't leave anything on the table."

When she saw his look, she quickly added, "That's what *I* would do, in any case." She handed him a business card for a friend of hers, Dr. Eccleston, a "spiritual counselor," and said other patients in similar situations had found this sort of guidance helpful.

Then Mannheim had been allowed the room to himself for as long as he needed.

Afterward, he had stayed away from the Royal for two days, ignoring the messages accumulating on his machine from his staff. Mannheim was determined to take all at once the entire bottle of sleeping pills Dr. Sarmiento had agreed to prescribe him. But the longer the bottle lay sealed in his medicine cabinet, the less likely that outcome became.

Finally, the general manager herself, Gabriela, had called. She said that whatever was going on in Mannheim's life, she didn't care as long as he came back to work that evening. No questions asked. Moved, Mannheim had reported for his shift that night, and every night in the weeks since. It was the most natural thing to do, passing his remaining evenings among his dealers, in whose light company Mannheim found himself easily adopting a philosophical attitude toward his fate: he was doomed, but wasn't everyone?

Still, when he was by himself, it was impossible to forget.

Dr. Sarmiento said she believed it would feel for Mannheim like he was passing out. But of course, how could she know?

One morning in August, Mannheim had clocked out near dawn and driven to a twenty-four-hour hardware store. He bought a long, heavy length of rope. The cashier asked him if he was feeling all right, and Mannheim pretended not to hear. After returning home, he climbed up the ladder to his attic and tied the rope—which he had fashioned into a noose—around the rafter beam looking out over the trapdoor that led down into the house. Mannheim placed the noose around his neck, cinched it so he could hardly breathe, and sat on the edge of the open trapdoor, his legs swinging in the open space between floors. All Mannheim had to do was allow his body to fall into that space. He wanted to be thinking a wondrous thought when he did so, in that final snap of consciousness. But in that moment, he could draw only the faintest outlines of events from his memory. Mannheim became frightened—why couldn't he think of anything—any experience at all—worthy of this final moment?

Hadn't he ever been a child, laughing for the sake of it? Hadn't he ever fallen in love?

Sitting on his attic floor, regarding beneath him a house that suddenly baffled him, Mannheim lost his nerve.

LATER THAT DAY, WHEN MANNHEIM pulled up to the address on the business card Dr. Sarmiento had given him, he discovered a district of Snoqualmie he hardly ventured into, lined with tattoo parlors, art studios, and coffee shops. After having a falafel sandwich at a corner diner—Mannheim ate out as often as possible now—he walked the unfamiliar streets for the next twenty minutes, marveling at the array of services offered on the storefront signs: tarot card and palm readings, crystal ball, the rolling of bones, etc.

The street on which Dr. Eccleston's office lay, Mannheim discovered, was in fact an alley off the main boulevard of the district. Mannheim peered in the windows as he passed, until he reached the last shop in the alley—"Dr. Eccleston, PhD, Spiritual Counselor," the sign read, under a detailed rendering of a human brain, "Walk-ins Welcome." A bell jangled as he entered, and Mannheim found himself in a small, dark waiting room, the lights off and the curtains drawn. At first, he thought the place closed, but then he saw there was light coming from underneath the inner door to the office.

Mannheim sank into a woolly armchair to wait. In the darkness, he'd begun to doze when a voice from the corner— he had not even noticed there was anyone else in the room— startled him into full wakefulness.

"I can tell why you're here, sir," the voice said. A young boy was sitting in the far corner, behind a plant, swinging his legs. Mannheim could see he was wearing some sort of school outfit. "Dr. Eccleston says I'm gifted."

"Ahem, hello. And who might you be?" Mannheim asked.

"My real name is Theodore. But the kids at school call me Theo because that's twenty times cooler. Which do you like?"

"I think Theo is a perfectly fine name. My name is Stephen."

The boy slid off his chair and approached Mannheim. "My stepdad wants me out of the house in the afternoons when he's trying to sleep. He works nights, you see." He narrowed his eyes at Mannheim. "You work nights too."

"How do you know?"

"Everyone who comes here in the afternoon says they work nights. Unless they're wearing a suit. Then they're on lunch break."

"I see."

"Dr. Eccleston is teaching me how to read palms right now. She said I have to start with the basics. What I want to learn is how to channel dead people through a Ouija board. That's what empaths do, you know. Dr. Eccleston says I can learn to vacate my body and let a spirit in for ten minutes, before I swoop back in." The child demonstrated with his hand the dive of a hawk seizing fish out of a lake.

"Interesting," Mannheim said. "I'm not exactly sure that's what I'm looking for—"

"Give me your left hand," Theo commanded. "I'll show you." Mannheim did as he was told, and soon the boy was investigating his palm, pressing his nails into the soft areas. "That's what I thought. You have an abbreviated life line, sir."

Mannheim nodded grimly as Theo continued to probe his hand.

"Oooh!" he exclaimed. "I'm not a hundred percent sure— but you have a rare pattern in your palm! Dr. Eccleston calls it a simian crease."

"What does that mean?"

"Look," the child said. He held up Mannheim's hand to show him. "Your heart and your life line converge right here." Mannheim was directed to an area between his thumb and forefinger, right where he would've held the handle of a carving knife. "It means you're a lucky person."

"That's news to me," Mannheim said. He recalled sitting on the floor of his attic, the weight of the rope around his neck. "I don't feel like I'm lucky."

"Well, you are. Your palm says so. Something amazing is going to happen to you before you die."

"And how do you know that?"

"Because," Theo said, with the slightest hint of exasperation. "A medium can tell things, and then you read the palm to confirm you're right."

"I see. So how much are you charging me for this reading, Theo?"

He expected the child to say five, ten, or even twenty dollars, but the boy said he was gifted, and that a reading from him should cost a hundred dollars. Chastened, Mannheim withdrew the bill from his wallet and handed it over, which Theo accepted without hesitation and slipped into a pocket inside his school outfit.

Having paid the child so handsomely, Mannheim now discovered that he wanted more from the child. "So do you have any advice for me?" he asked when it seemed like none was about to be offered.

The boy thought for a moment. "Maybe you should stay awake as much as possible. Watch for this amazing thing to happen. Then you can die."

"What makes you think I have control over when I die?" Mannheim asked.

"You don't?"

It was at this moment that the inner door opened. Both Mannheim and the child looked up and saw the imposing silhouette of Dr. Eccleston darkening the doorway. She was attired in tinted glasses and a long white lab coat.

"Theo!" she boomed. "I told you that you must never turn off the lights when clients are here!"

The boy hurried and flipped a switch behind one of the drapes, instantly bathing the room in a harsh, fluorescent light. Mannheim was surprised to see that Theo seemed smaller—not younger, but undersized for his age, which could not have been more than ten. The room appeared now as just another waiting room, the shadows having hidden its more prosaic elements: the dropped ceiling, the drab carpet, the bell attached to the front door to indicate the presence of visitors.

Once the child had retired to his corner, Dr. Eccleston inclined her head politely toward Mannheim, held her office door open with one arm, and with the other beckoned him to enter.

Spur of a Moment

THE PHONE RANG SATURDAY EVENING in Chimsky's rooms at the Orleans—he had taken the night off in order to sweat his bet—and its loud tolling unsettled him and made him tighten the robe around his gray belly. He stared at the phone until the rings died out. Then, very carefully, he placed the receiver onto its side on the end table, and tried to refocus on the events that were unfolding on the immense television that encompassed an entire corner of his living room.

Things were not going so well out in Las Vegas for Chimsky. When he'd placed his bet, Chimsky had been absolutely sure of the outcome of the big fight. But now, with one round to go and the fight clearly headed toward a decision, his judgment was so clouded by his fear of losing that he had no idea what the scorecards would eventually reveal: whether Golovkin—and therefore Chimsky—had won, or whether Golovkin had lost, in which case Chimsky was fucked.

In the twelfth round, Chimsky could swear that Golovkin had gained the ascendancy, closing along the ropes with a battery of thudding blows against Coronado's horribly disfigured left eye. But Chimsky could see that Golovkin himself sported a face colored with bruises and a swollen cheek. The decision could go either way, Chimsky thought, a sentiment that was confirmed when the ring announcer proclaimed that the first judge scored Golovkin slightly ahead, 115–113, while the second preferred Coronado by the same margin. Chimsky held his breath.

"Say Golovkin," he pleaded.

An hour later, there was a sharp knock on the door. Chimsky found himself still sitting on the couch, although at some point he'd turned off the television. As the knock transformed into pounding, Chimsky rose and padded heavily down the hallway. When he opened the door, Mr. Fong stood there, holding a clipboard, ready for the accounting. He was accompanied by Quincy and another enormous man, red-haired, both dressed in movers' smocks. "I told you, Chimsky," Fong said. "You don't know shit about boxing."

Chimsky silently ushered them in.

Fong looked around the rooms while in the kitchen, Chimsky made Quincy and the other man—his name was Simon—cups of tea, hoping it would serve to soothe Fong's henchmen before whatever was about to transpire. They chatted quietly and were polite enough, Chimsky noticed, to not mention the fight at all. Fong came back into the kitchen after twenty minutes and began directing his men on what to remove from the apartment. They started with the enormous television and the couch on which Chimsky had so recently sat. Next went his king-size waterbed and the framed lithograph by Kandinsky that had hung over it. Eventually, sitting on a folding chair, Chimsky looked around and saw that everything of value had been taken from the premises. With the removal of the final item—the late Rajah's three-tiered cat tower—Fong calculated the grand total and showed his arithmetic to Chimsky:

"Your loan was for the amount of fifty thousand dollars, which I have added to your previous debt of forty-six thousand three hundred seventy-five. I have taken the liberty of withdrawing the balance in your checking account, five hundred thirty-seven dollars, as well as taking possession of your car, furniture, and household effects for twenty thousand, which I think we can all agree is an extremely generous valuation. The remaining balance of seventy-five thousand eight hundred thirty-eight dollars is what you owe us. Now, we need to speak about your plan for payment of this amount and its associated interest."

As if on cue, Quincy and Simon reentered the kitchen and took up a position behind Chimsky. He could feel their presence on the back of his neck.

"Start talking, Chimsky," Fong said.

"Well," Chimsky said. "I work in the High-Limit Salon at the Royal—but you know that already. I get toked an average of two dollars per hand, and I can deal fifteen hands per down, so that's thirty dollars per down. In a normal eight-hour shift, I deal twelve or thirteen downs. So that adds up to about four hundred per day, cash, not even counting my paycheck."

Fong did some quick figuring in his ledger. "That means it would take you over forty weeks to repay the loan. That isn't acceptable."

Quincy and Simon closed on Chimsky, who was still sitting on the folding chair, and dragged him off it, upsetting it. They stretched his right arm over the marble island in the kitchen as if it were a chopping block.

"I could work six days a week," Chimsky offered. "Or seven. I could work doubles."

"That's not good enough," Fong said.

Simon began twisting Chimsky's arm counterclockwise while Quincy held him down, and his arm felt like it was going to come out of the socket. The pain was excruciating, and Chimsky burst into tears at its intensity. "For God's sake, stop!" he cried. "You didn't let me finish!"

Simon stopped twisting his arm, but held it in position so the agony, still severe, had at the very least leveled off.

"Well?" Fong said.

Through the fog of pain, Chimsky seized on the hand he had dealt the Countess several weeks previous, the one she'd won with the Deuce of Spades. "I can deal you a huge winner!" he blurted suddenly.

"What?"

"I can deal you a huge hand—hands, even! As many as you want."

"How?"

"I've been practicing."

"You've been practicing," Fong repeated.

"I can manipulate the shuffle," Chimsky said. "Set the deck for you."

Fong paused, allowing Chimsky to plunge on.

"Come to the Royal a week from tonight. Sit at my table. Buy in for twenty-five, thirty grand. Watch a few hands and then start playing, maybe five hundred or a thousand a hand. I'll deal these hands straight from the shoe. Then after playing for a while, you can say you're about to leave. On the next shuffle, I'll set the deck. Bet normally until it gets to the last three cards. Then say that you want to call the last turn, and that you want to bet everything you have in front of you. I'll deal you a winner. You'll win four times your bet!"

Fong looked dubiously at Chimsky prostrate before him. "I don't believe you."

"I told you," Chimsky said. "I've been practicing for years— for twenty years! In front of a mirror so I can't tell what I'm doing with my own eyes! Please!"

Fong signaled Simon and Quincy to release him, and

Chimsky collapsed to the floor. His shoulder was on fire and Chimsky rubbed it vigorously, groaning in pain.

"Show me," Fong said. "Get your shoe."

"My arm," Chimsky said. "I can't even move it right now."

Fong laughed. "Don't be shy, Chimsky. We all want to see."

"It's my dealing arm!" Chimsky cried. "I think your apes dislocated it!"

"Hey now," said Quincy.

"He may be right, Mr. Fong—we did do a number on it," said Simon.

Fong laughed again and shook his head. "All right, Chimsky, you've made your case." He dismissed his men, telling them to finish packing the van. Then, when they were alone, Fong leaned down, close enough for Chimsky to smell aftershave and the faint scent of pineapple. "I admit your little idea intrigues me. One week from today, we'll return exactly two hours before your shift is scheduled to begin, and you can demonstrate for us what you're describing." Fong smiled and squeezed Chimsky's afflicted shoulder, causing him to cry out. "See you next week."

After their departure, Chimsky lay on the floor moaning, catching his breath. Slowly, he raised himself up on the counter and stared at the bare surroundings. They'd left nothing at all, except for Rajah, stuffed and mounted on a stand in the corner, regarding him with cold, emerald eyes. Chimsky knew he was as doomed as the cat. The fact was he'd been dealing for twenty-three years, and he knew no one who could set a deck the way he'd described, undetected, including himself.

There was no choice but to run. Chimsky waited a half hour, working up his nerve, and then took the service elevator down to the parking garage, to see if they'd taken his car yet. When the doors opened, Chimsky was relieved to see his Saab coupe was where he'd left it that morning. Only when he walked up to the car did he notice that somebody was already occupying its front seat.

It was Simon, the enormous red-haired man who had twisted his arm. Also, the one who had carried out his coffee table, which weighed two hundred pounds.

After exchanging a silent wave with him, Chimsky returned to the elevator and reevaluated the situation. So— all he had was one week to master the impossible. Or at least, Chimsky suddenly thought, at least well enough so that it would escape the notice of anyone at the Royal. As the elevator rose, Chimsky felt a bit of his resolve return. He knew that surveillance still used cameras from the 1970s— the black-and-white footage was grainy, with no sound, and was recorded on tapes that had been used hundreds, even thousands of times, erased every Sunday. There was a chance it would be impossible to tell from such poor resolution the minute acts of legerdemain required when the critical hands occurred.

Chimsky re-entered his apartment, which now contained just poor Rajah and the old wall-to-wall carpet from the Orleans. The air was noisy and cold without furniture to block its passage, and, shivering, Chimsky shut it off. After drinking two glasses of water to rehydrate his frayed nerves, Chimsky went to the hall closet and removed from the top shelf a roll of deep blue felt, his practice shoe, and a cardboard box full of voided sets of Royal playing cards. Carefully, he unrolled the felt on the countertop and flattened it with his elbow. The counter was about the same height as the Faro table when he sat on two phone books and the folding chair.

Chimsky took out a deck and fanned it over the felt face up, then face down. As he scrambled the deck and squared it for shuffling, he tried to focus his mind on the location of the Ace, the Deuce, and the Trey of Spades. Painstakingly, on each of the three riffle shuffles, he manipulated one of these cards onto the bottom of the deck so that eventually, all three lay next to one another. Then, very carefully so as to maintain the integrity of their sequence, Chimsky strip cut the deck. It was clumsy, but he finally managed to move the three cards to the precise middle, twenty-six cards deep, although his actions were so obvious even a child would have noticed. He then placed the deck next to his yellow plastic cut card and performed a one-hand cut directly to the location of the three-card sequence, so the Ace, the Deuce, and the Trey were now the top three cards in the deck. Then he turned the deck over and slid it face down into the shoe. He dealt the entire shoe out: the first time, it came out Deuce, Ace, Trey. Then they came out in reverse order: Trey, Deuce, Ace. The third and fourth times, there was another card shuffled into the sequence accidentally. But by the time Chimsky had done this a dozen times, the sequence was coming out right, although his actions were only slightly smoother. After several hours, when the deck he was using became too worn, he tossed it back into the box, took out another deck, fanned it out on the felt, reshuffled it, recut it, slid it back into the shoe, and started again.

Homework

CHAN CLOCKED IN AT MIDNIGHT, so for many weeks, he only ever set eyes upon the Countess as she was being escorted from the casino and returned to her car. It wasn't a procession he could possibly have missed. With a growing sense of anticipation, Chan awaited the approach of two a.m. every night, and when he saw her, a desire to watch the Countess gamble came over Chan—he especially wanted to deal hands to her.

One night in August when the start of his break coincided with her leaving, Chan followed her entourage outside to where her long, silver car sat gleaming underneath the casino awning. Before she stepped in, the Countess handed each of the valets a black $100 chip, and they bowed their heads in turn. Then, for a moment it seemed she had noticed Chan's scrutiny—her sharp eye had settled upon him, burning with an eerie vigor.

Chan had blushed, turned quickly, and reentered the casino. The look possessed a meaning that eluded him at the time, but later, lying restless in bed, he felt he knew what she asked of him: *Can you?*

• • •

ON HIS NEXT DAY OFF, Chan drove to the Snoqualmie Library, a modern, three-story edifice with a glassed-in atrium that occupied an entire block of downtown. Chan had heard that libraries in the Pacific Northwest were revered institutions, yet he was still impressed by the building's immense size, and the number and diversity of patrons he found inside, each deep in their own study. In a low whisper, the librarian at the information desk directed Chan to the second floor, where the archives of the local newspaper, the *Snoqualmie Intelligencer*, could be found. Chan carried with him up the wide marble steps a satchel that contained a spiral-bound ledger, a pencil sharpener, and two sharpened pencils. His plan was to discover for himself an account of the night from three years ago, the one Chimsky had mentioned, when the Countess had placed two consecutive bets at Faro and won over a hundred thousand dollars. There was something about Chimsky's story that Chan did not entirely trust, borne of the general suspicion under which he held everyone who worked in his field. There were many other tales he'd heard in the past that had proven fictitious under examination, and as Chan pulled from the shelf three large, leather-bound volumes of archives from the time period of the alleged incident, he was prepared for any outcome from his research.

The individual carrels were full in that midday hour, so Chan set his books down at a table with only one other user, a young man in his teens, pale faced, with dark liner around the eyes and spiky rigid hair dyed a jet black. A gold ring dangled from a pair of flared nostrils, and he glared at Chan, then moved his body so as to shield whatever he was reading. The boy's black leather jacket reeked of cigarettes and mildew, and as Chan looked him over, he surmised that each and any of these aforementioned qualities could have contributed to the fact that no one else sat at their table, despite the others being three- and four-full.

Chan, however, was used to dealing with (and to) unde-
sirables, and he paid little heed to his neighbor's paranoia.
Instead, he opened on the table before him the first volume of
archives and began to scan it page by page for some mention of
the Countess's big night. It was a slow, arduous task. As Chan
looked over each news story—about the school board, the city
planning commission meetings, a rise in petty crime—the
sparse, bare picture he'd held in his mind about Snoqualmie,
the town in which he now lived, slowly grew inflected with
texture, more colorful impressions. The mayor was some sort
of crackpot, apparently, having designated a particular day
of the month when all municipal workers could bring their
cats to work. Another story described a high school charity
fundraiser gone awry—in the midst of performing a difficult
dance move, a troupe of students had fallen from the stage
and injured themselves, one critically. Later on, the injured
student, now in a wheelchair, had made a triumphant return
to the high school gym at the halftime of an important district basketball game and received a standing ovation. At the
close of the volume, Chan read in its entirety a story about
a group of scientists who were claiming that the age of the
tallest evergreens in Snoqualmie had been previously mis-
judged, and that they were actually much older, by tens of
thousands of years. But his ledger remained empty—there
was still no mention of the Royal Casino, nor the Countess.

As he set aside the first volume and replaced it with the
second, Chan looked up and saw that the young man at his
table was casting furtive glances while scribbling something
down on a sheet of paper. Their eyes met for a brief moment,
and Chan, caught in the act of staring, managed a feeble
greeting: "Hello there." The young man snorted, slammed
shut the book in front of him—a medieval history book, it
appeared from the cover. Chan watched as his neighbor rose
from the table, carrying off with him the book and the notes

he'd been taking. At a wastebasket next to the stairs, the young man stopped, tore off the top sheet from his notes, crumpled it, and fired it into the bin with theatrical force. He then disappeared down the stairs, the sound of his heavy boots receding until it was quiet once more.

Amused, Chan returned to the volume in front of him. As before, he skimmed each page, bypassing an entire series of investigative reports on zoning decisions that had aroused the ire of the citizenry. Instead, he read about a retired local man who won a statewide lottery and remodeled the basement of his home to resemble a 1950s diner; a few pages further, a pair of newlyweds had vanished on their honeymoon near Snoqualmie Falls—several days later, their ransacked backpacks and a dismembered foot with a hiking boot still on it was discovered. Forensic experts attributed the unfortunate couple's demise to one or more grizzlies, and the *Intelligencer* ran a weekend edition that contained a pullout with numbered instructions on how to behave when confronted with the wild animals in the region. (You were never supposed to run, Chan learned—either fight back or play dead.) Chan was about to close the second volume when a small Local News item near the end, on December 24, caught his eye:

DISTRICT RECEIVES ANONYMOUS GIFT

Confirming previous reports, Public School Superintendent Cassandra Giles officially announced on Tuesday that the Snoqualmie Valley School District was recently the recipient of what she described as an "extraordinarily generous" donation from a private party.

The amount remains undisclosed, as does the identity of the benefactor. "It was a condition of the gift," Giles said, "that the donating party remain anonymous."

Giles further stated that it was the wish of the benefactor that the funds be spent on the district's math programs as a way to commemorate Winter Solstice. "We need new textbooks, a computer, everything," Giles said. "This gift will allow us to do that." She also announced that one third of the funds would be set aside to award scholarships to three local students, aged seventeen and below, who could prove Fermat's Last Theorem in the least number of lines.

Chan thought the Countess could be capable of such an award—so precise yet lavish was the prize. One third of how much? he wondered. On his ledger, he wrote down the name of the *Intelligencer* reporter, Murry Handoko. Then he moved on to the third and last volume.

By its end, an hour later, the name of the reporter was still the only mark Chan had made in the ledger. The bright afternoon had turned into chilly dusk, and he hardly had a lead. Chan stood and collected his belongings, replaced the three volumes on the shelf, and then approached the stairs. At their head, he paused at the wastebasket and, after glancing around, he reached into the bin and extracted the crumpled sheet lying on top. Flattening it on the cover of his ledger, Chan was surprised to see that instead of inscribing notes as he'd thought, the young spiky-haired man had been drawing: in a delicate hand, finely shaded in pencil, was a portrait of a grotesque face in an ancient, regal collar—it was a royal portrait, there could be no doubt about that, for underneath, the boy had written in a jagged block script: *Charles II of Spain—Cursed.*

THE NEXT MORNING, AFTER ANOTHER fitful night, Chan phoned the *Intelligencer*. "I'd like to speak with a reporter named Murry Handoko," he said to the switchboard operator.

"The only Handoko here works in Archives," he was told. "Please hold." Chan was transferred and after several moments, a female voice answered. "Archives. Can I help you?"

"I'm trying to reach Mr. Murry Handoko."

"Who is this?"

"My name is Arturo Chan. I have a question regarding a story he wrote about four years ago."

"Mr. Chan," the voice said, hesitating. "I regret I must disappoint you, but the person you are trying to reach is dead. He passed away last March. I'm his daughter, Faye."

"Oh! I'm sorry—"

"It took us all by surprise. Is there anything I can help you with?"

"I apologize for asking. But is it possible he left behind a notebook? The story ran on December 24, 1980. I wonder if there's more information than was published."

"Why do you ask? Is this a personal matter?"

"Not for your father, Ms. Handoko—but for me."

The voice paused. "What is this about?"

"It concerns someone extraordinary," Chan said, speaking slowly. "Your father may have crossed paths with her that day."

"Who?"

"I don't know much about her. She's difficult to explain—over the phone."

"This isn't some sort of joke, is it?"

"No, Ms. Handoko—I assure you it's not."

After a moment of silence, the voice finally informed him

of a cafe called Scribes, located in Old Snoqualmie, only a mile from Chan's apartment. A reporter's hangout. "I'll be there, Mr. Chan," the voice said, "during happy hour, at half past five today. Don't look for me. I'll come find you." Chan wrote the information on the ledger.

"Thank you," he said.

That afternoon was the first rainfall Chan had experienced in the Pacific Northwest—a persistent warm drizzle. Out on the streets of Old Snoqualmie, he saw he was the only one with an umbrella—everyone seemed perfectly comfortable walking in the rain, even stopping to hold conversations on the sidewalk as they got wet. The umbrella marked him, and Chan was thankful when he reached the awning of Scribes and was able to place it inside the door under a coat rack.

The cafe was crowded and loud at that hour, and Chan caught snatches of reporter jargon he didn't understand. He ordered a glass of hot water, which drew dubious looks from everyone within earshot—the clerk returned with a cup on a saucer and said there was no charge. Chan left two dollars on the counter and inched his way through the crowd to a high-top table in the corner, where he settled down to await Handoko's daughter.

Presently, a small, dapper woman broke off from the line at the counter and approached him, carrying a drink. "Mr. Chan, I presume?" She held out her left hand. "I'm Faye Handoko. Let me guess—you're a dealer."

"Yes," Chan said, smiling, as they shook hands. "How did you know?"

"The way you're dressed." Faye settled onto the stool opposite his. She eyed him carefully. "Where do you work? I don't believe you told me."

"The Royal," Chan said. "It's just off the highway."

"I know the place. Nice spot. How long have you been there?"

"Less than a month. I'm new in town."

"Welcome to Snoqualmie." Faye raised her glass and drank something dark out of it. Chan sipped his water. "So," she said after a moment, "I pulled my dad's story from the day you mentioned. It piqued my curiosity. What do you want to know about it?"

"I'd like to learn more about the mysterious benefactor," Chan said. "I believe she may gamble where I work."

Faye's eyes narrowed. "Mr. Chan, please don't tell me you're stalking one of your customers."

"No," Chan said. "It's not that. I'm interested in learning the way she gambles. I've never seen or heard of anyone who plays the way she does." Chan paused. "Do you gamble, Ms. Handoko?"

"Yes," Faye said. "Of course. But I usually play in Auburn—I know too many people around here." She lowered her voice. "When I gamble, I don't want any distractions."

Chan smiled. "Then you'll understand how unusual her play is: She either places no bets or one bet over the course of a whole evening. I was told by another dealer that one night three years ago, she placed two consecutive bets and won over a hundred grand. That was the story I was looking for at the library, when I came across your father's."

"And why do you think they're connected?" Faye said.

"The donation feels like hers. The parameters of the award especially. The way she plays is highly mathematical—a system."

"Does she win?"

"She must. Over the long term," Chan said. "Otherwise, why not play more hands?"

"Maybe she's cheap."

"She hands out at least a thousand in tips every night she comes. There's always eight or nine valets falling over themselves to escort her around the casino."

Faye laughed. "Okay. So you need to know more about her system, but first you need to know more about *her*."

"Do you think I'm misguided?"

Faye inspected his face closely. "No," she said, "you seem all right. You've done your homework, at least." She removed a small, black, leather-bound notebook from her satchel and placed it on the table next to her glass. "This is my father's notebook from 1980," she said. "Before we open it, you must tell me what you plan to do if you learn this system."

"I'll play it," Chan said after a moment. "If I can. Wouldn't you?"

"Yes. If you found out and told me."

Chan said he understood. "Thanks again for doing this," he said.

Faye flipped through the book to the month of December and showed Chan her father's shorthand, a jagged, near illegible script. "December 23, 1980," she said. "Cassandra Giles—that's the name of the superintendent. He spoke with her that day. There was a private donation—anonymous— you already know that. Amount undisclosed, but was told off the record it exceeded a hundred thousand dollars."

"Interesting," Chan said. "That's the right number."

"Here's something else," Faye said. She pointed to two numbers circled underneath the notes: a three and a seven. "My dad believed in seven basic rules of investigative reporting," she explained. "These must be rules that directly pertain to this story."

She flipped back to the front of the book. Chan watched her scan the pages, quickly and without fuss. "Here they are." She turned the notebook so Chan could see.

1. Avoid political affiliation.
2. Be equally aggressive with friend and foe.
3. Know your subject (do your homework!).

4. Do not use tricks or pretense unless absolutely necessary.

5. Do not exaggerate or distort the facts unless absolutely necessary.

6. Do not violate the law unless you are willing to suffer the consequences.

7. Never take someone's word for their identity.

Chan read rules three and seven again. Finally, he said, "I understand rule three—but what about seven?"

"This woman you're interested in," Faye said. "There must be information connecting her somewhere. Does she have a home? A car?"

"No one knows where she lives—I've asked around. But her car is unique: it's a silver Rolls Royce Phantom limousine, 1960s era. There can't be many of those on the road."

Faye nodded. "Not around here. But if it's registered, it can be traced." She recorded the information in the margin of the notebook, then closed it and returned it to her satchel. She looked at Chan. "If I have time, I'll look into it."

"I really appreciate your help, Ms. Handoko."

"Perhaps I'll see you at the Royal sometime." She slid her business card across the table—*Faye Handoko, Archivist*. "Good luck, Mr. Chan," she said, rising from her seat. "Remember to call me when you discover the secret to gambling."

"I promise," said Chan. They shook hands again, longer this time, and Chan wondered whether he shouldn't say more.

After Faye rejoined the crowd around the counter, Chan left Scribes and walked home to his apartment, his mind swimming with the image of the Countess's limousine. He imagined the long, silver car parked in its spot near the valet stand at the Royal—it would be there that night. Her car was the key—that's what Handoko had been reminding himself, and whoever happened to decipher his cryptic notes. In this excitable frame of mind, it wasn't until several hours later, when Chan was preparing to leave for the Royal in a downpour, that the thought finally struck him that in leaving Scribes, he'd completely forgotten his umbrella beside the door.

The Oblong Box

DURING MANNHEIM'S FIRST SESSION WITH Dr. Eccleston, she had brought out a small, gray tin-metal box with two dials on its face. She called the machine her "intaker," and before any further word was exchanged, she carefully connected a series of five diodes to Mannheim's temples, wrists, and chest. When this was done, he was made to lie back on a generously upholstered armchair, his feet on an ottoman and the back of his neck coming to rest against the pillow.

Dr. Eccleston sat next to him, beside an impressive desk that appeared to have been carved from a single tree. When she spoke, her pencil poised over clipboard, her voice was prim and measured.

"Please state your full name."

"Stephen Mannheim."

"Age?"

"Sixty-two."

"Occupation?"

"I'm a pit boss at the Royal Casino." Mannheim watched as Dr. Eccleston noted this on her clipboard. "I run the graveyard shift."

"So what brings you here today, Mr. Mannheim?"

"I was—ah, referred by Dr. Sarmiento."

Dr. Eccleston nodded. "And why did she refer you?"

Mannheim cleared his throat. "During our last visit, she informed me that I was dying. Not tomorrow, but soon."

"I'm sorry to hear that," Dr. Eccleston said. "She often asks me to consult in these kinds of terminal cases. What is your prognosis, if I may ask?"

"Six months—or less." *Your protégé knew this already*, he felt the urge to add, but resisted.

"Good," said Dr. Eccleston. "There's time."

Mannheim chuckled nervously. "To be honest, I'm not sure. The symptoms Dr. Sarmiento describes are highly distressing—amnesia, blackouts, hallucinations of all kinds. Suicidal thoughts." Unbidden, the noose returned to his mind, and Mannheim shoved it down. "I don't—can't—face this alone, at least not right now. I want to become all right with it—everyone dies, you know?" Again he laughed mirthlessly. "But I guess I'm not okay at this moment."

"Is there anyone else who knows?"

"No. There's not really anybody I can tell. Just my dealers, and I don't want them knowing. I don't think I could stand that. You see," he said with sudden emotion, "I am a quiet, unobtrusive man. I don't want to be made a spectacle of."

"I understand, Mr. Mannheim." She seemed to write for a long time. In the intervening silence, the machine emitted a low, steady hum. Then she said, "These symptoms you're speaking of—have you experienced any of them yet?"

"Yes," said Mannheim. "One morning, before I knew I was sick—it was *why* I went to see Dr. Sarmiento in the first place—I woke up in bed still dressed in my clothes from the night before, and in my pockets were receipts for random things, drinks, food that I don't remember ordering or eating." Mannheim's fingers trembled at the recollection. "Have you heard of such a thing?"

Dr. Eccleston nodded. "When the brain suffers trauma, it begins to compartmentalize, closing off the affected sections from unaffected ones. Your consciousness is becoming divided, like a portmanteau suitcase."

"I think I understand. But I'm not sure what I'm supposed to do about it. Dr. Sarmiento said it was likely to get worse. . . ."

"You can keep coming here," Dr. Eccleston said. She set down the pencil and leaned back in her chair, steepling her fingertips. "On a weekly basis. We'll work toward self-actualization—merging all your parts, ordered and otherwise, into as congruent a whole as we can make it. It will be messy at times, but determining. Does this sound all right for you?"

Mannheim found he was reluctant to accept such a recurring arrangement without thinking on it further. But then he remembered Theo—he would like to speak to the child again, he thought. "Yes," he said. "If I can meet with Theo as well."

"I see," Dr. Eccleston said, smiling. "You already appear to know how special he is, although he has hardly any training."

"Is he your son?"

"Nephew," Dr. Eccleston replied. She took off her glasses and placed them on the desk in front of her. Her eyes were wide-set and dark and penetrating. "I do have a son—at least I did once," she explained. "I'm hoping we find our way back to each other someday. But Theo is my charge now."

Mannheim found he could not stare into her eyes for very long. "Perhaps your nephew can benefit," he said, looking around the room, "from my, ah, situation."

"That's very kind of you to offer." Dr. Eccleston wiped the lenses with a tissue and neatly replaced her glasses. "Come back at three next Wednesday. That will leave twenty minutes for you and Theo to chat beforehand. Does that sound satisfactory?"

"Yes," Mannheim said. "It does. And thank you."

"I trust you will find our relationship gratifying, Mr. Mannheim." She reached for his hand and patted it reassuringly. "We're honored you would allow us to guide you in this manner."

Then she began unhooking the machine.

The rest of the week passed fairly uneventfully for Mannheim, who left Dr. Eccleston's office still not entirely convinced he should return. But the following Tuesday, the day before his next appointment, an odd series of events conspired to resolve his thinking on the matter. He left his house around half past twelve in the afternoon, intending to go to the bank to withdraw $200 prior to lunching at a new place he'd heard his dealers mentioning the night before, a Vietnamese restaurant called Forte, on the west side of town.

At the bank, he stood in line for a teller window, and when it appeared to be his turn, Mannheim approached, withdrawal slip in hand. However, the teller, a young man in his early twenties, instead waved forward the woman who had been standing behind him. Stupidly, Mannheim watched as they conducted their transaction, neither seeming to care he was standing right next to them. When they were finished, Mannheim thrust his withdrawal slip under the gap in the window, before he could be stymied again.

"Oh!" remarked the teller, startled, seemingly seeing him for the first time.

Mannheim withdrew $500—more money than he'd originally intended due to his peevishness at being ignored. In this aroused state, he entered the tasteful interior of Forte twenty minutes later, and was seated at a small table by himself near the bar. The server arrived and took his order, and although he usually did not drink before work, Mannheim decided he needed one to cool down. After his server left to place the order with the bar, however, Mannheim heard a loud voice saying behind him: "Hey Steve! Glad to see you made it home in one piece."

He turned and saw that the bartender, bespectacled with slick black hair, in a white striped shirt and bow tie, was addressing him. "Vodka tonic, lemon. I know already," he said, smiling at Mannheim and winking.

Mannheim was dumbfounded. He had never been to this restaurant before—he was certain of it. Nor had he ever seen this man who knew his drink, and, even stranger, his name, although no one had called him "Steve" for a long time, ever since he'd been in grade school.

Disturbed, he ate his bowl of vermicelli quickly, his back turned to the bar, feeling vaguely threatened, like an animal under scrutiny. When the server returned to check on his meal, Mannheim quietly asked for the bill. Then he wiped his mouth carefully, folded his napkin on the plate, and placed a twenty on the black plastic tray the server returned with. Out of the corner of his eye, Mannheim saw the bartender conversing softly with the other customers, two seniors in shabby, old-fashioned suits. He thought he could easily slip out underneath their notice, and quickly rose.

But as he neared the door, he heard the voice of the bartender again: "See you around, Steve. Like I said, glad to see you made it home in one piece!"

Mannheim turned and saw the bartender grinning at him, raising the pint glass he'd been polishing in a salute. The two elderly customers at the bar were laughing—at him? Mortified, Mannheim shoved the door aside.

Out of the restaurant, he walked haphazardly, his hands fairly shaking, hardly seeing where his steps were leading. How bizarre, how much of a stranger he felt to himself! What if these unsettling, disconnected moments came more frequently—became, in fact, the norm of his remaining days? Frightened and unmoored, it was only with the thought of tomorrow's appointment with Dr. Eccleston and Theo that Mannheim began to feel less disoriented. They would listen, he thought. They wouldn't brand him a lunatic, something to be pushed and tugged at, or worse, pitied and doddered over. They would see how mysterious he was becoming to himself.

Mannheim's stride grew slower, more measured, and before long, he found himself on a block he'd rarely ventured into, a street that ended in a quiet park. In the distance, children were playing on the swings; their laughter carried to him on a moist summer breeze, and he sat down on a wooden bench overlooking a small pond, staring around himself in wonder.

How curious this all was, after all!

Off the Hook

AS THE REST OF THE week passed and the hour of Fong's return neared, Chimsky settled into a routine he considered a kind of personal hell. During the afternoons, he practiced over and over the setting of the Faro deck at his kitchen counter, until his knuckles seized and would not straighten, his fingers throbbing and pulsing, their tips bleeding. In the evenings, Chimsky continued to appear for his shifts at the Royal—every hand he could practice seemed important now—conducted to and fro in his own car by Quincy and Simon. Even when he found time to nap, the Faro deck continued to confound Chimsky; he would dream he was setting the last three cards perfectly, but they would come out all wrong, sometimes not even playing cards but photographs of himself and Mr. Fong cut the same size.

Then on Friday, close to five in the morning, with only a single hundred-dollar bettor at the table, Chimsky attempted for the first time to set the deck in live play. After the initial scramble, he botched the riffle cut and the cards burst out of his hands everywhere. The result was a misdeal, an embarrassing moment when he had to call over his boss,

Lederhaus, to explain that the deck had been exposed prematurely. Lederhaus, who was aware of Chimsky's excellent reputation, was surprised but had ordered that all bets be pulled back, and for the shoe to be reshuffled. His boss hadn't been suspicious, Chimsky didn't think. But it was a demoralizing moment nonetheless.

Afterward, while they were waiting at a drive-through for Chimsky's order—Quincy and Simon were initially horrified but had grown accustomed to the dealer's dawn ritual of fast food after his shift—Chimsky overheard them chatting quietly in the front seat about a business venture they were entering. They were both aerobics instructors by day, and from what Chimsky could gather, they were preparing to embark upon a rather unusual enterprise: a private club that was combination hair salon, aerobics studio, and cafe. Fong was bankrolling the whole project.

"Exactly who is your clientele?" Chimsky asked from the back seat.

"We're aiming for the young and the young at heart. People who want to mingle," explained Quincy, turning halfway in the passenger seat.

"What are you calling it?"

"Well, I want to call it Hair & Now. But Simon doesn't know whether he likes that name or not."

"I didn't say I didn't," Simon said from the driver's seat.

"You said it might restrict our customer base. Why, because of the pun or the ampersand?"

Chimsky smiled faintly. It sounded like an odd venture, but he wasn't an entrepreneur. His food entered by way of the window and Simon paid for it, passing the steamy bag over to Chimsky. It was a pleasant little thought, opening a business of one's own. As Simon turned the car back onto the road and toward the Orleans, Chimsky ate his hamburger in silence. His nerves were completely shot from the events of the evening, and the food tasted oily and rich on his tongue.

"You know," Chimsky said after a long period of silence, "what Fong expects me to do is nearly impossible."

Quincy turned to face him. "We all believe you can do it, Chimsky. Mr. Fong doesn't extend a deadline for just anyone."

After they dropped him off, Chimsky tried to fall asleep, but was unable to. He missed his old life, his old bed—and yes, Barbara—terribly. Sighing, he arose and resumed practicing at the kitchen counter. By this point, Chimsky knew his movements were quite precise, but his accuracy was still only about fifty-fifty. Moreover, this was in his home, with no one watching. He could not guarantee to Mr. Fong that he would win; Fong just as easily could lose, and in a straight deal, he was likely to lose five out of six times. And then—well, there was no telling what Quincy and Simon would have to do to him.

But when Fong showed up at his door at precisely nine p.m., Chimsky found himself guaranteeing nonetheless that all was ready. Prior to their appearance, Chimsky had preset one of the decks. Then, under their naïve eyes, he simulated on his countertop a riffle shuffle and strip cut that was so fast that he could tell they were falling for it. He slid the deck into the shoe face down and dealt out the entire deck, including the last three cards in ascending sequence: the Deuce, the Four, and the Six of Hearts. Fong told him to do it again, and Chimsky did so, this time reversing the final sequence so that they came in descending order: the 6, the 4, and then the Deuce.

"I'm impressed," Fong said. Simon and Quincy whistled their approval and applauded.

"This is how I imagine it," Chimsky said. "My first down at Faro starts at eleven thirty. I'll deal straight for as long as you want to sit there. Then when you're ready, you'll say,

'Look at the time—I'll stick around for one more shoe.' That will be the signal. I'll set the next deck so that the last three cards appear in ascending sequence. Bet however you like based off that information."

Fong nodded. "And you're positive surveillance won't notice anything."

Chimsky was much less concerned about surveillance than he was about the more pressing concern raised by setting a deck that he hadn't prepared beforehand, doing it live, on-the-fly, on the blue felt at the Royal, with Lederhaus and all the other players watching.

"Everything will be fine," he assured Fong.

THE FARO TABLE WAS ALREADY close to full when Chimsky tapped in that evening. The Countess sat in her special, elevated chair, her driver at her side, hardly breathing in his gray chauffeur's outfit. He recognized some of the other players, regulars who were chatting with Lederhaus about the new lamps in the room, a set of three marble braziers. Chimsky said hello and began to deal. Ten minutes later, he looked up from a hand he was paying out and saw a bearded man in shorts and a purple Hawaiian shirt approaching, accompanied by Mannheim. It was Fong.

"Lederhaus, this is Mr. Murphy," Mannheim said. "He's come all the way from Florida to try his hand at our Faro table."

There was a discussion about lines of credit, and within moments, Chimsky was pushing Fong, now seated directly in front of him, two full racks of black chips—$10,000 per rack. "Good luck, sir," he said.

Fong played patiently. Chimsky dealt the first deck completely straight, with Fong betting between one and five black chips per hand. The other players at the table were wagering similar amounts. Only the Countess remained watching, marking down the appearance of each card with her eyes. When Chimsky got to the last three cards, Fong failed in his attempt to call them in order, and was down $300 after the first deck. Chimsky reshuffled and dealt the second deck, again straight from the box, and as before, bets were placed, pulled back, doubled, and lost. Once more, Fong attempted to call the last three cards and failed, and Chimsky eyed the man's chips and estimated that Fong had now lost approximately $700 in the session.

Fong made a show of it. "Perhaps Faro's not my game after all," he said loudly. "I'll play another shoe. If my luck doesn't change, I'm switching to Baccarat."

Lederhaus indicated to Chimsky he was changing the setup. Chimsky handed the old deck over to Lederhaus, unwrapped the new one, and fanned it face up across the felt in an arc, confirming that all fifty-two cards were there. Then he collected the deck and fanned it face down. In his mind, he isolated three cards: the Deuce of Hearts, the 7 of Diamonds, and the Jack of Spades. He had to make sure these three cards—the Deuce, the 7, the Jack—appeared in ascending order at the bottom of the deck. He scrambled the deck face down, and then it was time to perform the three riffle shuffles, strip cut, and one-handed cut onto a cut card that would move those three cards where they absolutely *had* to be.

Usually, Chimsky's movements were so practiced that he would kibitz with players while he shuffled, hardly even looking at what his hands were doing. Now, he hoped no one would notice that he was staring intently at the backs of the cards, so intently he could feel the collar of his shirt chafing against the back of his neck. Lederhaus was talking to Fong and the other players about property values in West Palm Beach compared to Seattle. But when Chimsky glanced over to the Countess in her chair, his blood froze. The eyebrow over her left eye was raised a shrewd quarter-inch, and the orb beneath looked straight into him—she knew!

Chimsky tried to swallow and nearly choked. It was too late to turn back now. The deck of cards lay face down next to the yellow plastic cut card, and Chimsky's fingers trembled as he faced the most delicate of the steps necessary to complete the setting of the deck. He had to cut directly twenty-six cards deep, and in his agitated state, he had no faith he could do it. He grabbed at the deck and cut it. He then slid the entire deck face down into the black metal shoe. The soda was the Ace of Clubs, which he discarded. While the players made their bets, Chimsky continued to wilt under the direct scrutiny of the Countess, who, in a departure from her usual practice of hardly deigning to acknowledge him, was examining his every move.

There are twenty-five turns in a deck of Faro, and the first twenty-three transpired in unremarkable fashion. As before, Fong played each hand, betting lightly. But then, on the twenty-fourth turn, Chimsky's heart sank when he saw one of his three cards—the 7 of Diamonds—appear in the window two cards too soon. So he *had* miscut it! In addition to the Deuce of Hearts and the Jack of Spades, there was now an interloper—the King of Spades, according to Lederhaus's case-keep.

"Call the last turn anyone?" Lederhaus asked. Chimsky wanted to signal to Fong to abort mission, but he was powerless, stuck behind the table. He watched Fong push his remaining chips in—about $19,000—calling out Deuce, Jack, and King, in ascending order, as they'd discussed.

"Anyone else?" Lederhaus said.

"I would like to call the last turn as well," the Countess said. She pushed across a single green plaque off the stack in front of her—$25,000. "In the same order as the gentleman here—the Deuce, the Jack, and then the King."

For the first time in the hand, Chimsky felt Lederhaus pausing, sensing that something was not quite right. The Countess almost never called the last turn, usually preferring to bet on a single card rather than three. But then Lederhaus recorded the bet and told Chimsky to go ahead and deal.

Fong looked confident, smiling even underneath his false beard. If only he knew that Chimsky had lost control of the deck, that the last three cards could come in any order—

"Chimsky, please proceed," Lederhaus said again.

It was down to luck now—pure chance. Chimsky took a deep breath, seized the top card and yanked it off. The crowd gasped—so did Chimsky—for the card revealed was the Deuce of Hearts.

"Yes!" Fong exclaimed.

The other players oohed and aahed, but the Countess continued to regard Chimsky boldly, hardly glancing at the Faro box at all. Chimsky looked down at his hands—they did not feel like his own. He flexed his fingers and allowed them to hover over the opening in the metal box. The next card had to be the Jack of Spades or he was finished. Chimsky closed his eyes and said a little prayer. Then, with a sudden flourish, he snatched the next card off the top of the deck.

Even before he opened his eyes, Chimsky could tell from Fong's cry of exultation that he'd done it. There on the felt for everyone to behold lay the Jack of Spades:

It was the most glorious card Chimsky had ever seen. In the midst of celebration, Fong high-fiving everyone at the table, the Countess's lips pursed as she received her congratulations. Chimsky was sure she was not going to say anything now—she had just won a hundred grand. And Fong had won almost eighty. As the commotion settled, Chimsky revealed for the sake of formality the final card in the deck— the King of Spades. Then Lederhaus told Chimsky to remove the deck and count it down, which was customary on hands of this size. While Chimsky did so, Lederhaus called upstairs to surveillance, who replayed the hand back and forth to confirm its legitimacy. Because the outcome of the hand had been as much the result of chance as of manipulation, Chimsky was not surprised when they reported back after several minutes that everything seemed fine. The winning bets were paid out, and Fong toked Chimsky with a messy stack of black chips, smiling all the while.

"You're too kind, sir," Chimsky said as he collected his tip.

Then the Countess took one of the green plaques off the four she had just won. Slowly, she pushed it toward Chimsky.

"Please break this for me," she said. "And keep five for yourself."

"Madam, are you serious?" Chimsky said. "I can't possibly—"

"You've earned it," she said, eyeing him narrowly. "Haven't you?"

Chimsky laughed nervously. "Your generosity is extraordinary—and greatly appreciated, madam."

She said nothing, watching him as he made change. When he was done, he realized Lederhaus had been tapping him on the shoulder for some time. "I think that's enough excitement for one night, Chimsky."

The crowd groaned at his removal, and he acted as if he were being pulled against his will, but Chimsky was glad for the involuntary EO—he could not go through *that* again. He basked in the glow of the table's admiration for just a moment longer. Then, once he was clear of the Salon, he hurried to the locker room and changed quickly, his fingers still shaking.

He wondered if he would encounter Fong or his buddies again that evening. But as he walked out to the employee lot toward his car, he saw—for the first time all week—its driver's seat empty. The door was unlocked, and the keys were in the ignition. A note stuck underneath the wiper blade read: "Nice job, Chimsky. Consider yourself off the hook. For now."

Chimsky's face widened into a grin. He folded the note and put it in his pocket. Then he took a running start, leaped into the air and whooped. He felt ten years younger, as light as a feather, and even looked it for a moment. His pockets flush with the six grand Fong and the Countess had tossed him, there was no question how he would celebrate, having restrained himself for so long. He wanted to call Barbara and tell her the good news, ask her to join him—but would she even care? He'd phone her later. Instead, he pulled out of the parking lot, merged on the expressway, and headed west toward the nearest casino.

A Painted Man

CHAN'S MOTHER AND FATHER BOTH died when he was a small child—his mother of breast cancer when he was seven, his father in a single-car accident just months later—and he had been raised by his maternal grandmother at her home in Scarsdale, New York. It was his grandmother who'd instilled in Chan an interest in gambling, although she went to great lengths to prevent her young charge from being exposed to such activity. She loved playing mahjong with her guests, who were numerous and frequent, and after dinner, Chan would watch them retire to the study, where through a closed door, he could hear their exclamations and the unceasing clatter of tiles long into the night.

When Chan asked his grandmother what was happening inside, she told him he was too young.

Out of her regular visitors, there was one who especially intrigued and frightened Chan, a man with long, dark hair and a painted face who appeared only once every several months, and always alone. When he came, dressed invariably in shirt and tie, there was no dinner. His grandmother would be agitated on these occasions, and she would send

Chan to bed with a bag of potato chips. Then she and the stranger would sequester themselves in the study, where Chan could hear them arguing—the man's voice high pitched and loud, his grandmother's subdued and contrite. The man never stayed long—only a half hour at most—but his grandmother would remain in the room, not emerging until the next morning, exhausted and shaken.

Chan had learned never to ask his grandmother about these visits. One time he had persisted, and she had struck him on his left arm with a long-handled ladle, leaving a welt. Later, she had come into his room, where he lay on the bed crying softly, and apologized, stroking his shoulder. "That man is not a good man, Arturo," she said. "Please don't ask me again about him."

Tuesday night was especially slow at the Royal—after the big hand on Saturday night, the casino still seemed to be in a state of recovery—and when Mannheim asked if anyone wanted an EO, Chan had volunteered and was granted one. He went home, showered, changed, and at five minutes to two, he was sitting in civilian clothes behind the wheel of his hatchback, a full tank at the ready, watching the long, silver Phantom parked near the valet stand at the Royal. As he waited, Chan imagined where the Countess lived, a hidden estate in the mountains, perhaps, far from the casino, lying in ruin.

Within moments, the Countess and her entourage emerged, and she was delivered into the rear compartment of the Phantom. The driver got in with one last look around, and the taillights came on. Chan felt the low thrum of the powerful engine resonating through the floorboards and into his feet, which began tingling. He started his hatchback and fell in line behind the Phantom, leaving the span of a city block between them. A light rain was falling. The young man ahead drove confidently—never braking unnecessarily, always taking turns at the optimal speed. Chan imagined the Countess inside, the smoothness of the ride lulling her into a post-Faro stupor—was she drinking? As Chan kept pace, he thought to himself that he liked the idea of some rejuvenating fluid passing across the threshold of her ancient lips.

They drove quietly through the city, and then the Phantom turned onto the freeway heading north, which at this late hour was given over to their two vehicles, and the occasional tractor trailer they passed easily. The young man was pushing the Phantom, going eighty, then ninety miles an hour, the trucks disappearing in the rearview as quickly as they came upon them. Chan's hatchback strained under the pressure, the stress of the chase causing the loose joints of the front axle to rattle and jar Chan. In this trembling cabin, the miles began ticking by, one after the other. Chan kept the radio off so as not to alter the spell that bound him to the streaking taillights of the Phantom—he was drawn into a kind of reverie by them, swimming in front of him.

It was more than ten years ago, the previous time he had followed someone. A man with long, gray hair, in a disheveled shirt and tie, had boarded a gambling boat Chan was working on. The man hadn't recognized Chan, because the last time they had seen each other, Chan had been twelve. But Chan knew him immediately: it was the man who had visited his grandmother in Scarsdale—he could not mistake the man's painted eyes, nor the distinct high-pitched voice as he berated the cards to do his bidding. "Trey!" he would yell, startling the other players. The man won every bet he made at Blackjack for an hour, doubling on hard 12s and 13s, splitting 10s, hitting on a 17, even—the man not only seemed to know what cards Chan held, but also what was coming next from the shoe. He seemed to be able to stare *into* the deck.

Chan had never seen anything like it. Perhaps this was

the secret shared between the stranger and his grandmother behind the closed study door. After the man was finished gambling, up well over $10,000, Chan watched him get into a taxi, and Chan followed it to a cheap motor lodge on the outskirts of town. He crept in the muck alongside the man's room—the window was half-raised and the smell from inside, of burning oil and incense, was overpowering. Through the filmy glass, Chan had seen the small man, now shirtless, sitting on the floor before the mirror: in one hand the man held a syringe. His other arm was restrained by rubber tubing the man pulled taut with his teeth. The man injected a clear fluid into the tattooed bicep of his left arm—the tattoo, Chan remembered, was of a bull's eye. All the while, the man muttered numbers, repeating them in a trance as his hold on the syringe slackened. "Deuce . . . Trey . . . 7 . . ."

Chan had discovered in this moment that there was a kind of secret he was not interested in uncovering after all; he had staggered away, revolted.

He had never seen the painted man again.

The Countess was different, though—she wasn't like any of the other peculiar gamblers Chan had come across in his travels, going on occasional hot streaks among many cold ones, relying on vague mysticism and narcotic substances to harness their luck. Her methods were far more deliberate, scientific even. Chan didn't know *how* he knew, but he was certain she was not gambling to win money—she played as a test, as an investigation, the same way Chan was investigating her—as a reason to live. But for all her singularity, he could not understand why there was so little known about her—where she lived, for example.

It wasn't until Chan looked at the clock on the dash, and saw that it was half past five in the morning, that it began to dawn on him why this particular piece of information was so difficult to come by. It was for the most practical sort of reason: the arrow on his fuel gauge was pointing toward just a quarter tank left.

Yet Chan felt unwilling to give up after he had pursued the Countess so far. He drove another eighty futile miles in the pre-dawn darkness, which was beginning to lighten and turn gray. Only when the fuel indicator clamored for his attention did he begin to acknowledge that he might have to surrender the chase. For reasons that he could not fathom— Did it have an extra tank? Did it run on something else?— the silver Phantom did not seem burdened by the need for fuel. Unfortunately, the same could not be said for his rattling Datsun.

Finally, at twenty minutes past six, Chan slowed, watching the Phantom vanish over the horizon, and pulled off the freeway into a truck stop to refuel. The sun was beginning to rise through the Cascades in the east. It had all the feel of being a damp and misty summer morning. After he filled up—spending all the gratuities he had earned that night—Chan sat in his car for a moment, feeling as if he were emerging from some impassioned dream. Then he got back on the freeway, heading south, once more toward the Royal, nursing the overextended engine of his car all the long drive home.

Lottery

BARBARA WAS LATE TO THE meeting, and she rushed to it directly from her job at the call center. It was only after she settled down in her metal folding chair next to the two newcomers that she noticed the socks under her slacks were mismatched: one was navy and one black, a difference she'd been unable to distinguish in the dark that morning. She crossed her ankles and moved them underneath the seat, next to her purse, and tried to pay attention to what Dimsberg was saying, but her mind was distracted by the discovery of the socks—and Chimsky's phone call that morning, out of the blue, asking her to meet for a drink. Could anyone be more dense?

As she pondered what she'd ever seen in her ex-husband—it had become Barbara's habit to regard Chimsky as the catalyst of her issues, although a year in the Snoqualmie Chapter of Gambling Help had consistently reinforced in her mind that she was their source—the newcomers sitting beside her suddenly rose, startling her.

"Excuse me," mumbled the woman, aiming to get out of the circle by moving her chair. A man followed—her husband?

Barbara scooted aside several inches, and the couple had broken through and were mere steps from freedom when Dimsberg's voice ascended to arrest their escape.

"My friends!" he said. "Stay among us a while longer. You must've come for a reason—tell us your story." He opened his arms magnanimously. Dimsberg was not a charismatic person, with his long face and teeth like a rat's, but he seemed to have a way of making people do what he wanted, and the couple returned to their seats, although they remained standing.

"What are your names, my friends?"

They said they were Shirley and James Harris. Barbara joined with the rest of the group in welcoming them. "Welcome, Shirley! Welcome, James!" There was, of course, that perverse part of Barbara that wanted to whisper to get the hell out before Dimsberg could get his claws into them.

"We weren't sure, you know, if we belonged," Shirley said hesitatingly. "James and I—we don't gamble every day. Or even every other day."

"Shirley, one of our mantras is an addict is always an addict. Your very presence in this room is telling."

"Still—we aren't sure about this."

"Tell us why you came," Dimsberg said. "Why don't you let us decide?" Other people in the circle encouraged them, and Barbara again found herself in their number. She relished hearing first-timer stories—they satisfied to some degree her desire for action. She admired those in the circle who'd lived through worse than her; conversely, there were some in the circle whom she did not respect for what she felt were minor problems made major. Barbara was curious where this new couple would fall.

It was the woman, Shirley, who spoke. She explained that she and James never went to casinos, and before this past year had never gambled outside of occasional forays into the state lottery, when the amount of the jackpot was too large to resist. They never won anything. Still, they were doing fine. They had enough coming in from their jobs as math teachers to survive, and the children—there were several, Barbara couldn't tell how many—were out of the house. The mortgage was paid each month, et cetera. They were nice, unassuming people. Everyone in the circle was waiting, like Barbara, in anticipation of some more tantalizing morsel.

"Our youngest, Julia, was always the lucky one in the family," Shirley said. She placed her arm around her husband's waist. Sitting so close to them, Barbara could see his neck muscles tense at his wife's touch. "She kept track of the jackpot religiously, and would let us know whenever it hadn't been hit in a while. She was always winning small amounts—a hundred here or there, sometimes even a thousand. We dabbled, but she played every week, twice a week, like clockwork. We'd chide her about it. Just as a joke.

"One day," she continued, "ten months ago this week—we received a phone call from the police. There had been an accident downtown. Julia was walking with her friends. They were celebrating—she'd just found a job. Some maniac drove up on the sidewalk. She—Julia—was pinned underneath the car." She stifled a sob. "They rushed her to the hospital, but it wasn't any use."

Dimsberg told Shirley to take as much time as she needed. Barbara glared at him.

"I don't even remember what happened the rest of that week," Shirley said. Her voice grew quiet. "There were arrangements made on our behalf." She broke down again.

This time, Dimsberg had the sense to keep his mouth shut.

When she resumed, Shirley's voice was measured. "We thought we wouldn't be able to go on. But you know, life makes you. One day, about two weeks after the accident, we were filling up at our normal place. James went inside to pay, and when he came out he had the strangest look on his face. Like he'd heard something wonderful and awful at the same time. Do you want to tell them about it, honey?" He shook his head. His eyes never left the ground. "Okay, I will, then. But stop me if I get anything wrong.

"Apparently, there was a bit of a commotion in the shop. The jackpot had been hit the previous Tuesday—a dozen people had hit it. One of the twelve winning tickets had been purchased from that gas station! Everyone was talking about it. But no one knew who it was, because no one had claimed the ticket yet.

"Like I said, James had this strange look in his eyes when he got in the car and told me. He said he knew who had bought that ticket—Julia—and at first, I told him he was crazy. I didn't want to believe it. But the more I thought about it, the more it made sense. That was where Julia always bought her tickets. And why wouldn't someone claim their share of the jackpot? No one forgets to redeem $1.7 million. Unless they couldn't. Unless they were dead. We never wanted to forget about what happened to Julia— that lost ticket became a symbol to us. It was like a gift she'd left us, James said. It was our responsibility to find and redeem it."

The woman paused to take a drink of water from a bottle that Dimsberg handed her. Barbara looked around, and everyone was waiting on her next words with rapt attention.

"We started by searching her apartment," Shirley said. "All her old rooms. We became obsessed with finding that ticket. Pretty quickly, things started to get out of hand. We bought an X-ray detector, an infrared camera. We tore the furniture apart. Pried open the floorboards. We looked every-where a ticket could be. All of Julia's dear clothes—we ripped open their seams and pockets. But we found nothing. We were sitting in the kitchen one morning, drinking coffee, and James was saying we'd looked everywhere.

"Suddenly I remembered Julia lying in her coffin at the wake, in the suit she'd been wearing the day she interviewed for her new job. It was her only suit. Could she have bought the ticket the same day as her interview? Could the ticket still be inside that suit? I said it was at least possible. I looked over at James and he had that strange look in his eyes again. I was afraid to ask, but I already knew what he was thinking. It was the same thing I was thinking. Forgive us, dear Lord, we've both gone a little crazy since Julia left us. James said her spirit was not at rest. Was it possible that we could desecrate our own child's grave to find that ticket? I firmly believed she wanted us to." Shirley looked around the circle. "I know how all this must sound to you—!"

"You're among friends," Dimsberg said. "There's no judgment here."

The husband continued staring down, unmoving. There was only a slight ripple along his jawline as his wife spoke, as if he were grinding his teeth. Shirley held onto him tightly. "That night," she began—she was almost whispering, and Barbara had to strain to hear—"James and I went back to the grave. We had a bag of tools in the back of our pickup. There were two of us shoveling, but it still took hours. Finally, we got down to the coffin. I remember the sound of James's spade scraping against the wood, and it seemed to snap me out of my trance. Suddenly, I felt that we shouldn't be doing this—that what we were doing was wrong, horribly wrong.

"But James said we had gone too far already. I said all right, but you have to do the rest. I turned away and I heard him grunting and prying open the lid of the coffin with the crowbar. I heard the snap as it opened. James was shrieking, and I covered my ears and shut my eyes, and I shouted at him to grab the ticket, grab the ticket! It seemed like hours before I finally heard the noise of the lid slamming closed. When I opened my eyes, James was standing there. He could hardly speak.

"'Did you get it?' I said. I could see in one hand he was still clutching the crowbar—and in the other he was holding a slip of paper. It was the ticket!"

Someone in the circle audibly gasped. Barbara realized she hadn't taken a breath in several moments. She had never heard a story such as this.

"Go on," Dimsberg said.

"We went back to the gas station the next afternoon." The life had drained from Shirley's voice now. "The ticket wasn't the winning jackpot ticket after all. We told him to check again, and he said that he was absolutely certain that it was not the winning ticket. Julia had only gotten two of the numbers right—but it was still worth fifty bucks."

The way the woman said "fifty bucks" made Barbara cringe—like they were all victims of some sick joke.

Shirley closed her eyes for a moment. "James hardly speaks anymore, since that night. But I know we're on the same page. Fifty dollars is far from enough. We play every drawing now, for Julia's sake. We started buying seven tickets a time, because that was the day she was born. Then we bought seventeen every time, because that was both the month and the day she was born. Then thirty-seven every time, factoring in her birth year and age. Still, we haven't won. But we know we will if we can just find the right number to buy. Julia is worth more than fifty goddamned dollars."

Here, the woman fell silent.

"Hey, at least she won," Dimsberg said. "Lucky Julia, you know?"

Quickly, Barbara rose—feeling everyone's eyes turn to her—and left the circle. She nearly ran.

Once outside, Barbara leaned her head against the cool brick of the Community Center, smoking a cigarette. No one else came out. She couldn't believe they could all still sit there, after hearing a story like that. What she needed was to get away from them for a moment. What she needed was a drink, she thought, recalling Chimsky's offer. She ground the butt to ash on top of the trash bin, and stepped across to the pay phone beside it.

"Okay," she said into the receiver when he answered. "One drink. Meet me in half an hour at Rudy's."

WHEN SHE ARRIVED, CHIMSKY WAS already waiting at their usual spot in the back, a small booth for two underneath a mounted moose head, a drink in hand. He was dressed in his dealer's garb. He rose to meet her, extending his arms in an awkward attempt at a hug, but she patted his arms away gently. "No, Chimsky," she said. "Sit down." She pulled out her chair, collapsed heavily on it, and sighed. He looked at her with unconcealed delight.

"Hi, Barbara. I was so thrilled when you called."

"I see you've started without me."

"I was a little nervous," Chimsky said. "I'm really glad you called, Barbara—but I said that already. How are you doing?"

The waiter came by, a young man with wet, spiky hair, and Barbara asked him to fetch her a gin and tonic. After his departure, she sighed again. "To be honest, Chimsky, it's been hard, fitting everything in. I'm working full-time now. And then going to the meetings."

"Are they still making you feel terrible about yourself?" Chimsky said. "I never liked—"

"Please," she broke in. "Don't start. They provide structure in my life. I was out of control for a long time."

"But we had a good time," Chimsky said. "We were good for each other."

"Stop, Chim. You know that's not true." Barbara's drink was placed in front of her on a tiny napkin; she thanked the server, and he nodded and left. "Let me enjoy this, will you?" She sipped it, relishing its smoothness. "Why don't you tell me what's been going on with you?"

Barbara listened to her ex-husband's recap with only half an ear. Rudy's was loud at that hour, and Chimsky was describing a series of events that she did not have the desire to understand completely. She looked him over as he spoke, noticing how he had aged, growing thinner, more lined. He was ten years her senior, but the difference had scarcely been noticeable when they'd been married—now, however, she thought he looked in his sixties, despite being fifty-two. No, fifty-three. Chimsky was fifty-three, because she was forty-three. He was explaining to her a hand of Faro, a game she never played, and an old woman who tipped him $5,000—

"Wait, did you say five grand?" Barbara asked.

"Yes."

"How much of that is left? I'm afraid to ask."

"At least twelve hundred," Chimsky said. "Business has been slow at the Royal lately, but we still have good nights. You should come by—"

"I told you I hate that place," she said. The waiter returned, and she ordered noodles—she hadn't eaten all day, she realized. Chimsky ordered another whisky sour. "Do you ever play the lottery?" she asked after a moment.

"The what?"

"The lottery. The state lottery."

"I've bought a ticket or two," Chimsky said. "Why?"

"Do you ever win?"

"Of course not," Chimsky said. "You know how much of a scam those tickets are—on average, they return sixty-two cents on the dollar."

"Never mind," Barbara said. "Someone was testifying

about it tonight in my meeting, and I guess it's on my mind. I can't tell you about it, of course."

"You've been thinking about playing it?"

"No. But the new people were so odd and sad. She said they play thirty-seven tickets at a time."

"They're wasting their money. They'd be much better off coming into the Royal once a week and betting it all on red."

Barbara laughed. They ordered another round of drinks, and then settled into light reminiscing. Her noodles were delicious. She hardly knew what Chimsky was saying while she ate and listened to the music, which seemed softer now that she'd been drinking, but she found his idle chatter not unpleasant to hear again, after things had been so brutally quiet recently.

At midnight that night, before separating outside Rudy's— Chimsky wanted to escort her home, but she said no, firmly— they agreed they should get together again sometime in the vague future. She was too unsteady to drive, so she began to walk in the rain, only about twenty minutes through the silent, wet streets to her apartment. Along the way, she passed a gas station, and she went inside to warm up and get a cup of coffee. In the line at the counter, Barbara broke her usual practice and glanced at the dazzling array of state lottery tickets in the display case. The ingeniously designed Changing of the Card caught her eye. A dealer was depicted with a white-gloved hand poised over a playing card. From the left, the card was the 7 of Diamonds. From the right, it was the Queen of Spades.

She hesitated when it came her turn in line. She could break her rules once. No one was watching. She turned to double-check. Then she pulled a five-dollar bill from her purse and bought her coffee, her gum, and one Changing of the Card. She folded the ticket and slid it inside her purse, into the side pocket, and walked home quickly, humming a faint melody underneath her breath.

BOOK TWO: SNOQUALMIE

In the last decade of the nineteenth century, the town's saloons became known for their notorious all-night poker games, in which new settlers faced off against unscrupulous sharps over property deeds and entire inheritances' worth of cash.

—*Untold History of Snoqualmie*

Changing Room

AT THE BEGINNING OF THE year, Mannheim had ordered the Countess's black high-backed chair moved to her spot at the Faro table, where it stood dark and hulking. The Countess had been adamant that she needed it on the premises while she gambled in the High-Limit Salon, for it was, as she explained to Mannheim and Lederhaus, her equivalent of a severed rabbit's foot. The patterns she had expected to see in the Faro deck had not shown up for over three years now, she told them, and she felt her charm so close might attract a different vein of luck. It was a testament to how much she had grown to be a fixture at the Royal that her wishes were accommodated, and soon, the high-backed chair became nothing more than a curiosity to the other players in the high-limit room, and a common sight to the staff, who moved it to the corner during the daytime.

And in fact, on Saturday evening, the Countess had won the largest hand dealt at the Royal the entire year. Mannheim heard the commotion from the pit, and upon inquiry learned that she and the new customer from Florida, Mr. Murphy, had together both successfully called the last turn and won

almost two hundred thousand dollars in sum total. Chimsky
had been the dealer. Mannheim had not thought much more
about this coincidence, the Countess and the stranger winning simultaneously, except to consider the possibility that
the presence of her chair had played some incomprehensible
role. Still, Mannheim had witnessed countless big hands at
the Royal over the years, and this was another one that he
filed away in his memories with the intention of quickly for-
getting about it.

Therefore, he was surprised several weeks later to receive
a call from Gabriela. She wanted to see him in her office before
his shift began, for a private meeting—just the two of them.
Mannheim, who had always harbored the slightest hint of an
attraction for his boss, ironed a white shirt and gray slacks
and selected a red tie with a striking impressionistic pattern.

When he arrived at her office, she told him to shut the door.

"You're looking better these days, Mannheim," she said
pleasantly. "Have you been exercising?"

"Well, I started seeing someone," Mannheim said. He took
the seat facing her across the desk. "To help me sort out a
few things."

"You mean a therapist?"

"Someone like that."

"Good for you. I'm a big believer in taking care of every
side of ourselves."

Mannheim coughed nervously and nodded.

"Remember that big Faro hand from a few weeks ago?"
Gabriela said.

"Do I. I was in the pit when it happened."

"I always thought there was something fishy about that
hand, and I think I've figured out why. I want you to take a
look at this." Gabriela turned the television monitor on her
desk so that they both could see. "This is the tape from surveillance of the table that night."

The video was gray and grainy, with no sound. It was a bird's-eye view from atop the Faro table, and showed Chimsky gathering the deck and washing it, shuffling it, and inserting it into the shoe.

"Do you notice anything unusual?" Gabriela asked.

Mannheim asked her to play it again. After another look, he said, "No, it looks all right to me."

"This is the deck previous to the one where the big hand was dealt," Gabriela said. "I timed it, and the entire shuffle takes fifteen seconds. I timed the deck before and it took fourteen seconds, essentially the same amount of time."

"Okay," Mannheim said.

"Now watch this." Gabriela fast-forwarded to a point in the tape where Chimsky handed over an old deck to Lederhaus, who was standing behind him. He received a new setup in return, which he removed from the box and fanned out over the felt. After confirming the fronts and backs, Chimsky scrambled the cards together and performed his standard shuffle. But Mannheim could tell that this time, something was different.

"How long did that take?" he asked.

"Twenty-three seconds, from the first wash to putting it in the shoe," Gabriela said. "And this was the deck where the last three cards were called in order, not only by this stranger with the beard no one's ever seen before, but also by a customer who almost never bets."

"Could it have been the new setup?" Mannheim said. "Sometimes they come out of the box too slick."

"It could," Gabriela said. "Do you think that's the reason?"

Mannheim watched the replay again. "Well," he admitted, "if you just look at the deal in isolation, it seems okay. But with the other two—something smells fishy."

"Indeed," Gabriela said, reclining in her seat and regarding Mannheim carefully. "There's no hard evidence.

But something happened between the other two decks and this one. It might just have been the new setup. But then again, it might not."

"I think we should keep an eye on Chimsky," Mannheim said. "Maybe we should ask Lederhaus?"

"Lederhaus is seventy-five," Gabriela said. "He's already halfway out the door. If something crooked did happen, anyone who's in on it will cool out for a while—at least three or four months—before they try it again. You're next in line—I'll lay you 3 to 2 you'll be in charge of the high-limit room by then."

Mannheim had not thought about his place on the seniority list for a while, and the news surprised him. "I understand," he said.

"What about the Countess? Do you think she was in on it?"

"I don't think so." They watched the tape again. "She makes her bet after Murphy does, right before Chimsky is about to deal. I wonder if she picked up on something and was just taking advantage of it."

"Right. Maybe somebody should talk to her."

Mannheim understood that Gabriela meant himself. "I'll see what she says," he said.

"Wonderful. Let me know what you find out."

Mannheim said good-bye, rose from the chair, and left Gabriela's office, heading downstairs toward the changing room. Chimsky cheating? And then there was Gabriela's implication that Mannheim would be supervising grave-yard shift in the High-Limit Salon soon, sooner even than Dr. Sarmiento's timetable for his demise. This was a position Mannheim had always believed he wanted, and it seemed like a symbol, holding a new kind of meaning for him now.

His instinct to seek professional guidance had been right, Mannheim thought—his life had become richer since he'd started seeing Little Theo and Dr. Eccleston. Something was happening in his life—something remarkable, according to Eccleston and Theo—and this idea delighted Mannheim, so much so that several of the dealers he passed on the stairs commented, as Gabriela had done, on his seemingly improved appearance and mood.

Once in the changing room, Mannheim stood in front of his locker, combing his hair and humming an old tune, "I'm Forever Blowing Bubbles." The Royal was in mid-shift, and no one else was around. After he finished grooming, Mannheim returned the comb to its spot on the top shelf and was about to close the locker when he stopped short. He smelled something coming from within the locker. The scent of skin dried in the sun, Mannheim thought. Or old, thinly shaved wood. He sniffed at his clothes and shoes—was it coming through the locker from the other side? Mannheim shut his own and slowly walked over to the next aisle.

He approached the locker opposite his, counting each intervening door with a tap of the hand—one, two, three, four lockers from the end of the aisle. With each the smell grew more powerful, and Mannheim covered his mouth—it was pungent, murky, and made him feel short of breath. He heard voices in the hall outside, faint and distant. Was there a wetness in his ear? The lights were growing dimmer and Mannheim placed both hands on the locker to steady himself. The metal felt warm. He could scarcely make out the name on the door of the locker—CHAN—before he fell on his side, and everything became dark.

A Mysterious Caller

A MONTH AFTER HIS FRUITLESS night on the interstate, Chan received a phone call in the early evening, while he was sleeping. Emerging from a dream set in his old Westchester high school, it took Chan a moment to differentiate the reality of the rings from the agitated school bells of his reverie. He pressed the receiver to his ear, catching a sharp intake of breath.

"Hello?" he asked.

There was silence—a pause as a decision was made. Then a click and the buzz of the dial tone. Chan hung up. His first thought was that someone had discovered what he'd done, following the Countess, and this idea persisted in his mind as he slowly dressed for work. He'd taken a month off from investigating her further, just in case. But had someone finally found out?

In the pit that night, Chan felt unseen eyes upon him as he dealt, scrutinizing his movements. He forced his hands to go slower, in order to commit no errors. Mannheim was acting distant toward him, and this coolness only served to increase Chan's unease. On his first break, instead of kibitzing with

Leanne and Bao in the lounge, he wandered the periphery of the pit, surveying each aisle of slot machines for he knew not what.

Eventually, he found himself drifting down the long entrance vestibule and stepping outside. The Countess's Phantom was there in its usual spot in the valet line, gleaming almost phosphorescent in the moonlight and the heat from the high-wattage bulbs under the casino awning. A thin line of vapor rose from the hood of the car. Chan ran a finger along its edge, and it came back moist and warm.

After admiring the car a moment longer, Chan went back inside, and for the rest of his shift, he dealt precisely, painstakingly.

Later, in the hour before dawn, he was walking out to the employee lot when he saw someone leaning against his pock-marked Datsun, a man with his arms folded across his chest, his legs casually crossed. As Chan neared, the man rose from the car, and Chan recognized him. It was J. P. Dumonde. A battered red leather suitcase stood by his former boss.

"I see you're still driving the same reliable car," Dumonde said, smiling and revealing a pristine row of white teeth Chan did not remember him having. The man patted the hood of the hatchback. "Same old Chan, I take it?"

"Hello, Dumonde," Chan said. "What are you doing here?"

"I was just passing through. The casino was in the guide-book, and you know me. I can't pass up a good gamble. And to my delight, who do I see dealing at the $5 Blackjack table but none other than my old friend Arturo Chan?"

"Did you call me yesterday?" Chan asked.

"Of course not," Dumonde said. "You know I prefer the direct approach."

"So you're just dropping by to say hello. Well, I'm happy to see you too, Dumonde. We'll have a decent meal, catch up on old times, and then you'll be on your way?"

Dumonde stepped aside as Chan unlocked his car door and opened it.

"Not exactly," Dumonde said. After Chan got in the car, he stared at Chan, his arm on the door. His breath was minty. "You might say the tables have turned on your old friend. It's I who need your help now, Chan. Remember," he added, smiling apologetically, "you are under an obligation to me."

"Climb in," Chan said finally. "I know a good place for breakfast." Dumonde closed Chan's door and walked around the front of the car—for a half second, Chan imagined gunning the engine and flattening his old boss underneath the wheels—and then Dumonde was sitting in the car beside him, filling up the small space of the vehicle with his minty breath.

"I can't wait," said Dumonde, rubbing his palms together. He seemed to relish Chan's discomfort. "You can't believe how hungry I got waiting for you."

CHAN DID, IN FACT, OWE Dumonde. Twelve years ago, when he'd first started dealing, Chan had allowed a customer, an old woman who reminded him of his grandmother, to become too familiar.

When the customer had been caught stealing other players' chips at the table, Chan's close relationship with the perpetrator made him look especially bad. There was a question whether he'd been complicit in the customer's actions over a prolonged period. He'd done none of the pilfering, nor had he facilitated it—but he'd witnessed it, his friend's hand sliding a red chip or two down a sleeve from a tall stack, where their absence would be most unnoticed. But Chan had said nothing—he did not want to inform on her; she was not a bad person but a horrible addict, working odd jobs at the age of seventy, sleeping in parking lots in the back of a station wagon.

Chan's superiors were certain he must have known—the

surveillance video showed the acts of stealing to be crudely executed, easily discerned even on black-and-white video. A report was filed with the West Virginia Gaming Commission, and Chan's license was suspended indefinitely—he was called in unceremoniously on a Tuesday morning and fired. Chan had nowhere to go, now that the only thing he was qualified to do was closed off from him—suspension in one state meant suspension in all.

Chan started appearing at the neighboring Blackridge Casino daily, whiling away his hours at the Blackjack table as a player. His life was well on its way toward becoming much like his unfortunate friend's, a miserable progression-less grind. Dumonde, the pit boss at the Blackridge, knew Chan and was surprised to see the clean, austere dealer from their rival casino slowly transform before his eyes into one who flitted away his life on arbitrary turns of the card. One night, Dumonde took Chan aside and told him he knew some people on the commission—knew them well enough to be aware of professional secrets they would not want divulged. He would try to pull some strings for him, on two conditions to which Chan readily agreed, despite reservations about Dumonde's oily reputation. First, 25 percent of his tips at the Blackridge. Second, future considerations that could be called upon. At any time.

When Chan had headed west, he'd believed he would never see Dumonde again—after all, Dumonde had a good job, with obviously many important connections. But now, he had come calling—and as Chan drove through Snoqualmie in silence, his old boss snoring softly in the passenger seat beside him, he found that the wet, darkened streets were imbued with a fresh sense of dread.

AT THE DINER, DUMONDE ORDERED a six-egg omelette and ate voraciously, wielding the knife and fork to great effect and refusing Chan's pointed looks for an explanation as to his appearance until he was entirely done. Chan himself had just a cup of coffee and a plain, buttered roll. Pushing the empty plate away from him, Dumonde wiped his mouth with his napkin and folded it neatly before fixing his eyes upon Chan.

"You wonder why I'm here. It's simple," said Dumonde. "I require a temporary resumption of our arrangement."

"What do you mean?" said Chan. "As far as I'm concerned, that's finished."

"Times change, Chan. As I see it, you owe your current dealing job—and really, any dealing job you've had since the Blackridge—to me. So I'm only asking for what I'm owed: twenty-five percent of your tips at the Royal."

"What if I say no?" Chan said. "I've held gaming licenses in four different states since West Virginia. I doubt you have the power to revoke my current one."

Dumonde smiled and held up his hands. "You're right, Chan. But I know you. You're like me—a man of your word, as they say. A man of honor. The worst thing in our field is a welcher, and that you are not. The Chan I know would never renege on a promise made to an old friend, one who aided him in a time of crisis."

"As you say, times change."

"Have you?"

"I feel under no great obligation to you, Dumonde—not anymore. But you're right. You helped me out and I am willing to return the favor—within reason. How much money do you need?"

"More than you have." Dumonde glanced around before resuming. "I'm not merely drifting, Chan. You might say I'm on the run from my past. You know how I pride myself on knowing things—information that could be dangerous."

"Did you finally pick the wrong person to blackmail?"

"Extortion is a delicate matter," Dumonde said. "I've

learned my lesson. But I can't take a job now because I'd have to use my name, and that would make my whereabouts known. I just need to survive until my present situation resolves itself."

"I can't afford to supply you with money indefinitely," Chan said. "I'm working graveyard shift—as you know. And rent is far from cheap here."

"I can see why you like Snoqualmie." Dumonde looked around at the tastefully decorated diner, its wooden walls lined with ancient logging implements. "It's the perfect setup. Far off the beaten path. Good weather. Good food. Maybe I should settle down here."

Chan cringed. "As I said, I am happy to supply you with a one-time payment," he said. "I can give you five hundred to get started—somewhere else."

"Five hundred!" Dumonde scoffed. "That won't last two weeks out here. I need to disappear for a while, Chan. And a way to pay rent for a few weeks, a month. Two months at the most."

"That's impossible," Chan said. "I can barely make my own rent, much less pay yours."

Dumonde swirled a spoon in his mug of coffee, thinking. Chan was afraid of what he might suggest. "Well," Dumonde said after a while, "how about if I stay with you until I can figure out my next move?"

"No," Chan said. "Absolutely not."

"It would only be a month—two at the most."

"No," Chan said again. "I'd rather give you money than have to live with you."

"I appreciate the force of that remark, Chan. But I plan on staying, whether it's with you or not. I can be at the Royal every night, like a festering sore. Watching you— bothering you."

Chan thought about his paranoia earlier that night—

how discomfited and distracted he'd felt. And there was the matter of his interest in the Countess. He wanted Dumonde far, far away from her.

"Of course," Dumonde said, "I would consider your obligation entirely satisfied if you would allow me to stay with you." When Chan continued to maintain his silence, Dumonde added: "I'm a very clean person, Chan. You'll hardly know I'm there. You may even grow to like having me around."

Chan felt himself caving. "And you would promise—on your word of honor—to never come to the Royal while I'm working there?"

"Cross my heart," Dumonde said, smiling and showing his dazzling teeth.

"And not a day over two months."

"I promise I'll be gone by Thanksgiving," Dumonde said, extending his hand across the table. Against his will, Chan allowed Dumonde to shake his hand.

The server passed and refilled Dumonde's coffee, while Chan declined another cup. His roll lay half-finished on the plate, and the server took it away. Chan's stomach churned at the idea of living with Dumonde. But he couldn't have Dumonde coming to the Royal! Chan wanted to deal in peace, and this was the only way he could ensure that. When the server returned to ask if it would be one check or two, Dumonde told him that Chan, perfect gentleman that he was, had been kind enough to offer to pick up the whole thing.

Hair & Now

AFTER SCRATCHING OFF ALL THE spots with the edge of a dime, the happy outcome was indisputable. Beat the dealer's hand, the card read, and win the prize indicated. Under his gloved fingers, the dealer showed two Kings for a 20. Barbara's own hand revealed itself as an Ace and a Queen, for 21. Underneath, she scraped at the prize amount until there was no silver left, until there could be no doubt about the amount. A thousand dollars! Barbara was so thrilled she almost called Chimsky to tell him, but she restrained herself. She knew him well enough to know he would want to take credit for encouraging her behavior, when it had been completely her own decision, and a one-time thing. In her mind, the reason for the unforeseen win was clear: she had abstained from gambling for almost two years, and the gods of chance were rewarding her for her chastity. Tomorrow, she would return to her seven p.m. meetings at the Community Center as if nothing had happened, and her sober life would resume as usual.

The next morning, Barbara woke up half an hour before her alarm, still buoyed by the knowledge of the win. She lay

in bed the extra time, stretching and luxuriating in her delicious little secret. A cool grand, from nowhere. Afterward, she
took a long, hot shower and carefully applied her makeup in
the mirror—the lips proved especially difficult because she
couldn't help smiling—before drinking a cup of coffee and
heading to work at the call center.

It was a month until the election. Barbara was supervising over a dozen temps in polling for the upcoming
Washington gubernatorial race, and they were entering
their final stretch of calling. When she arrived, many of her
workers were already on the phones, and a pleasant buzz of
excitement filled the room. Barbara went to her office and
closed the door. For the next several hours, she pored over
the raw data coming in, in an effort to come to some sort of
conclusion she could deliver to her client.

Based on her calculations, both the incumbent, John
Spellman, and the new candidate, Booth Gardner, had a
good chance of winning—her estimates were 45 percent for
Spellman, 43 percent for Gardner, and the rest undecided.
But the more she examined the numbers, the more Barbara's
instinct led her to disbelieve them; she had followed both
their campaigns closely, and thought Gardner, the younger,
more charismatic Democrat, would win the election with
room to spare. The report to the client had to be based on statistics, though, and not the kinds of hunches that had gotten
her in trouble in the first place. Against her own judgment,
Barbara spent the afternoon carefully composing a memo
stating that entering the election's final weeks, the incumbent Spellman was the favorite to retain the governor's office.

At six p.m., as she was finishing up, there was a knock on
her door. A group of her employees entered, telling Barbara
they were going out to celebrate a colleague's birthday, and
invited her to join them. Remembering her nightly appointment at the Community Center, Barbara declined, but they

persisted. The project was almost finished. This would be the last time she would see two of her temps, who had found permanent positions elsewhere. As they pleaded this case, Barbara weighed the ebullience of her young staff against the pale and sickly flesh she would see at Gambling Help— their sad, dull stares. Where was their enjoyment of life? Wasn't that at least as important as sobriety? She decided that yes, she *could* miss tonight's meeting.

While Barbara sat at the bar, however, she found that her thoughts kept wandering from the conversation of her employees, whose exuberance over the latest fashion trends (a shirt that changed color when you touched it!) she did not share, to the image of the thousand-dollar ticket resting snugly in the side pocket of her purse. For an hour, Barbara shifted in her seat, offering only the most perfunctory remarks for the sake of cordiality, and twice left on the pretense of smoking, although the second time she just stood outside and watched the stars emerge overhead.

On her way home, Barbara stopped at the gas station to redeem the ticket. The cashier snapped out each crisp twenty on the counter: one, two, three, four, five, six, seven, eight, nine, ten, and so on. One thousand dollars. The cashier slid the entire fat sheaf across to Barbara, and it felt wonderfully substantial in her hands. She folded it twice over and carefully placed the tight roll inside her purse. She couldn't resist touching it, squeezing it, as she walked back to the car.

Barbara did not make it to the seven p.m. meeting at the Community Center the next evening, either.

She began taking the scenic route home from work to her apartment in downtown Snoqualmie, which took twenty minutes instead of the usual twelve. One day not long after, she noticed in passing that the old Snoqualmie Theater, which had lain dormant for over a dozen years, was now undergoing a renovation. A banner hung over the awning proclaimed:

ARRIVING NOVEMBER 15
THE MOST INTENSE EXPERIENCE OF YOUR LIFE

After parking the car in the lot at her building, Barbara walked the three blocks back to the site, and peered through the windows that had remained dark so long. They were covered from the inside by a sheer material, like drapes made of hose, and revealed to her what looked to be an array of plush salon chairs surrounded by sinks, trolley carts, and a tall, imposing stack of loudspeakers.

The door jangled open beside her, startling her. An enormous head covered with red hair emerged. "Want to take a look inside, ma'am?"

"What is this place?"

"We're a full-service, members-only salon," the man said. "And much more." He stuck out a massive hand, which Barbara shook. "My name is Simon. Allow me to tell you a bit about ourselves. We're also an aerobics studio. We guarantee the most intense aerobics classes in town. And we also have a private cafe upstairs. Do you want a tour? I promise we're not like any club you've ever seen."

"All right," Barbara said. "What are you called?"

"Hair & Now. Do you like it?"

Barbara did. Simon opened the door wider to allow her to pass into the space. The floor was covered in sawdust, and the whole place smelled of fresh pine. A thin man with a clipboard was directing another man, one even more massive than Simon, in the construction of a counter. "Those are my partners," Simon said. "I'm just showing a potential member around," he shouted to them.

Barbara turned and faced the entire wall of loudspeakers, black-carpeted cabinets with deep, menacing subwoofers. "Excellent sound intensifies the experience," Simon said. "Studies show." He walked her through a carpeted entryway to the hair salon. "The salon will be open the same hours as the rest of the building," Simon said. "From six in the morning until midnight, seven days a week except Christmas and Thanksgiving."

"Impressive," Barbara said.

Simon asked her to follow him upstairs. She climbed the wide, hardwood staircase, and soon found herself in a large room that overlooked the studio. It had all the makings of a pleasant cafe, with shiny parquet floors, a bakery display case, a counter behind which stood several espresso machines, and a large chalkboard for the menu, which was currently blank.

"Looks like a great place for coffee."

"We import beans from around the world and roast them right here," Simon said. "For members only."

After Barbara had finished looking around, Simon tapped the glass wall separating the room from the gym floor below. "Soundproof," he explained. "Check this out." Simon flipped a switch and the room glowed a warm, dark red. Barbara heard a faint noise, like the sound of a stream. "Obviously," Simon said, "it looks better in the dark."

Simon handed her a flyer, pointing out "Individual Memberships." The "Body & Soul" package was $250 per month, or two grand for the entire year. Each month, this included two salon visits, twelve classes in the aerobics studio, weekly sessions with a personal trainer—"That's me and Quincy," Simon explained—and unlimited use of the cafe, plus classes that would educate her on the best diet and nutrition for her hair.

"I'll have to think about all this," Barbara said. "It's a little overwhelming."

"Of course. I'll show you out."

They returned downstairs, and Simon said they hoped to see her again. After she said good-bye, Barbara exited the building and, instead of walking across the street toward her apartment complex, she went around the block. The autumn air was crisp, and Barbara savored it, breathing deeply. Unbidden, a smile crept at the corner of her lips. Life was mysterious after all, wasn't it? She had had no plans to join a gym. Now she was actually considering it—the idea of meeting people who were improving themselves in a way that wasn't completely demoralizing appealed to her.

Her steps were light as she entered her building, and she was halfway across the lobby before Barbara saw him.

Dimsberg, of all people, was standing by the elevator.

"Oh, hey, Barbara!" he said. He took off his hat. "I was just coming up to see you."

"What are you doing here?"

"Well, we've missed you the past couple weeks," Dimsberg said, smiling. "As your chapter leader, I feel like it's my responsibility to see if there's anything we did that made you stop coming. Or anything we can do that will make you come back quicker."

"I haven't been feeling well, Dimsberg. I'll come back when I'm better."

"We're very sorry to hear that, Barbara." The elevator doors opened, and he held them for her. Then he followed her in. She pressed her floor and they rode up awkwardly. He continued looking and smiling at her, and she felt obliged to invite him in.

"Please stay for only twenty minutes," she told him. "I need to get some rest."

"Thank you, Barbara. I don't want to be a nuisance."

In her apartment, he sat down on her couch, crossing his legs.

"Do you want a glass of water?" she asked from the kitchen. "I don't have anything else, unfortunately." She moved the bottle of red wine on the counter behind a houseplant.

"I'm fine," Dimsberg said. "It's you we're worried about." He patted the space next to him on the couch.

Barbara sighed and sat down, as far from his hand as she could without being impolite.

"What's wrong?" Dimsberg said. "We only want to help."

"Nothing is wrong. Things couldn't be better."

"We're so glad to hear that, Barbara. You've missed some pretty interesting meetings." When she failed to respond, he continued. "That new couple—Shirley and James—they're doing really well. Since the night they came, they haven't bought a single ticket."

"I'm glad for them," Barbara said.

A long, painful silence ensued. Finally, Dimsberg cleared his throat. "I apologize for asking, Barbara, but I feel I must. Are you gambling again?"

She shot him a look. "Of course not. What makes you say that?"

Dimsberg wrung his hands. "You understand I had to ask."

"Once an addict, always an addict, right?" she said.

"Precisely."

Another silence passed while Dimsberg drank his water. Barbara watched his pronounced Adam's apple go up and down as he swallowed. "I appreciate your concern, Dimsberg—I really do. But I must ask you to leave now. It's election season and I'm swamped at work. I have to be there first thing in the morning."

"Can I get you to promise to see us at the Community Center as soon as you're well?"

Barbara said, "Of course," although she crossed her fingers behind the cushion. "Once I'm over this bug."

Dimsberg rose and tried to take her hand. "Be well, Barbara."

"We shouldn't," she said. "I'm sick after all."

Dimsberg doffed his hat again and finally—mercifully—

exited. Barbara waited until she heard the bell from the elevator in the hallway. Then she peered through the fish-eye lens to make sure he was not still standing there, looking in sorrowfully.

Two Conversations

MANNHEIM LEFT THE ROYAL ONE evening at half past five
in the morning, spent from a particularly trying night in the
pit. There were two customers he'd had to order security to
remove, one for swearing at the dealers and the other for
making aggressive advances toward the female staff. Both
were drunk, and the latter had told him to go to hell. As he
drove home, Mannheim saw their red, angry faces superim-
posed on the windshield over empty residential streets and
dark houses shuttered against the cold. Suddenly, an animal
darted in front of his headlights, its white fur and long tail
illuminated for a brief moment. He swerved to avoid it, his
car fishtailing in a wide arc, nearly ending in a ditch, facing
the other way. Mannheim had to pause to collect himself.
Then he got out and inspected the tires.

It was the first time that year he could see his breath.

After satisfying himself that the car was undamaged, he
returned to the road, driving deliberately now, and eventually reached a three-way junction. The near accident had
severely jolted him, and to his dismay, Mannheim found he
could not recall which arrow on the sign to follow. He turned

left, creeping along, looking for his street. Its name remained just on the tip of his tongue—he thought it contained at least three syllables and began with an *S* or a *Z*. From afar, several houses looked like they might be his, but every time he neared, he found a different name on the mailbox, a car he did not own in its driveway.

After twenty minutes of circling, Mannheim, growing agitated, pulled his vehicle to the curb. He could feel he was close. He cut the engine, opened the door, and pulled the collar of his gray coat tight around his neck. The stillness of the night accentuated the pulse of blood in his ears. Mannheim walked briskly in the autumn chill.

Dr. Sarmiento had told him the incidence of a person dying in his manner was one in a million, and Mannheim pondered this most unlikely of hands as he walked. Both his body and his memories were being effaced off the physical earth, a day at a time. But there was a freshness to much of his experience now, like old streets turned new. Did he have any regrets? He didn't know.

After several minutes of walking, Mannheim finally saw his house—47 Severance Lane—that was the name! He was certain he'd passed it earlier, in a distracted state. Now Mannheim climbed the graduated series of stone steps that led to the front door, an entrance he normally never used. He tried the knob, and the lock clicked and gave easily, the door swinging inward of its own accord. It might've been unlocked for months. Shaking his head, Mannheim stepped across the threshold and pressed the light switch several times in succession, but nothing happened. He stepped carefully into the kitchen, his arms out, fumbling in the drawers for a flashlight or candles, but all they contained were old batteries, business cards, and untold numbers of receipts he'd failed to organize.

Giving up, Mannheim dragged his body up the stairs in the dark, his head drowsy with images: a red face, white fur,

a long tail. He collapsed into bed still wearing his gray coat
and shoes, and for the first time in months, Mannheim slept
soundly and dreamlessly for eleven solid, end-to-end hours.

THE LIGHTS WERE ON IN the house when he awoke. His clock
had stopped, at three fifteen. But Mannheim knew he was
very late for his weekly appointment at Dr. Eccleston's—the
sun was already well along its western descent in the sky.
He brushed his teeth quickly. Then, by the time he found
the car—it was up on a curb, three blocks away—and finally
appeared in Eccleston's shop, there was hardly any time left
in the appointment. Both Theo and Dr. Eccleston were sitting in the waiting room, the younger swinging his heels. Dr.
Eccleston glared at him.

"I'm so sorry," Mannheim said. "It seems I'm having a
harder time conducting my affairs these days."

"It's all right. That's why you're seeing us, after all.
Unfortunately, you've come very late."

"I understand," Mannheim said.

"Let's speak inside for the time remaining," said Dr.
Eccleston as she rose. "On practical matters." She and Theo
led Mannheim into her office, a large room where they each
sat in tall armchairs around Dr. Eccleston's impressive desk.
The room felt cool and dim, and Mannheim began to relax.

"The reason I've asked us all here today," Dr. Eccleston
began, "is that Theo and I conferred, and we believe the most
effective way to guide you in your journey is by working together.
For instance, you and I talk about your job, Mr. Mannheim,
but you and Theo talk about your childhood—what you can
remember of it. We both want to know everything."

Mannheim nodded. "Yes, I agree. I depend on you both.
I lost my way home last night—I couldn't for the life of me
remember which house was mine!"

"Let's hold hands," Theo suggested.

Mannheim took the boy's hand in his right, and Dr. Eccleston's in his left. "I feel like my reality is—how should I put this—becoming unreliable. Sometimes, I feel like I've already lost my place in this world," Mannheim said. "Other times, I feel very present. Everything is more vivid."

"You are undergoing a painful process, Mr. Mannheim. But the process of dying can also be profound—in a better way."

"And you are not totally gone yet, sir," said Theo.

"I think I'm getting closer. When I finally found my house last night, the lights were out and everything felt empty, like no one lived there anymore. I became tired—so tired and heavy I could hardly move."

"Have you ever played Sandman, sir?"

Startled, Mannheim looked at Theo, and the boy repeated the name. "The game, Sandman. Your body gets filled with sand, and you feel so heavy you can't move."

"Yes," Mannheim said after a moment. "I think I have."

"I think we should play Sandman."

"Is it that important?" Dr. Eccleston asked.

"I think so," Theo said. He squeezed Mannheim's hand. "He wants to play it too, don't you, sir?"

"Yes," he told Theo. "I believe you're right."

"Very well," Dr. Eccleston said. She released his hand. "I will confer with Theo about this game and we will prepare to play it the next time we meet. On that note, we both agree— your time is short, Mr. Mannheim—we should begin meeting twice a week."

Mannheim said he thought that was an excellent idea.

HIS NORMAL ROUTINE RUINED BY his late start, Mannheim did not get a chance to eat before appearing at the Royal prior to his shift that evening. He arrived two hours early, and it was only when he entered the bright casino that he began to feel hungry. He ordered the special, a pimento cheese sandwich, from the kitchen, and ate it with relish sitting by himself in the lounge. Chimsky was there, talking to some of the pit dealers, and his presence reminded Mannheim of Gabriela's suspicions. Mannheim had promised her he would speak with the Countess about the Faro hand, a task he'd neglected for many evenings now on account of its awkwardness. But tonight, Mannheim resolved to speak with her.

At ten, when he saw her entourage entering the casino, Mannheim left the safety of the pit and joined the old woman's escort, making his way to her ear. "Madam," he whispered into it. "A moment, please."

She stopped, as did the whole train surrounding her. "What is it?" she asked.

"Can we speak sometime this evening? In private?" He eyed the driver, who was standing close beside them.

"What do you have to say to me that you must say in private?"

"I apologize, madam. It's of a delicate nature."

The Countess's left eye flickered with annoyance. "Fine. Come see me at one. I'll take my break from the Faro table during the first change of the shoe."

Mannheim thanked her and bowed as her train resumed its passage. Then he returned to the pit. At midnight, Chan's shift came in, and Mannheim felt heartened, watching over his regular crew for several downs. Leanne and Bao were their usual chatty selves, and Mannheim asked them about a weekend trip they were planning to Crater Lake. At other moments, he watched Chan deal: the smoothness and ease with which Chan slid cards from the shoe and revealed them imbued Mannheim's observations with a kind of meditative quality, and he lost himself in the minute and discreet movements of a wrist here, a finger there.

Before he knew it, it was one. Mannheim told Dayna to stand watch and crossed the casino floor, entering the

High-Limit Salon. The Countess was still engaged, and Mannheim sat at one of the unused Baccarat tables near the entrance. While he waited, he observed her in her chair, watching the cards but not making any wagers. At 1:07, the current shoe completed, she rose and signaled to her driver. He aided her across the ornate rug to where Mannheim was sitting, and then stood several feet away, out of earshot.

"Well?" the Countess said. She remained standing. Behind her, Lederhaus was overseeing the new setup. "I don't like to make the table wait."

"I apologize, madam. It is one of my unfortunate duties to have to occasionally speak to customers about their gambling. There was a Faro hand played over a month ago now, when you and another player called the last turn and won."

"I know the hand," she said. "What of it?"

"It has come to our attention that there was something unusual in the betting before the hand."

"Are you accusing me of some impropriety?"

"No, madam. Please don't misunderstand me. I am just interested in whether you noticed anything about the other player. Lederhaus said that you followed his bet—"

She stopped him short. "Is it not customary," she said, "when a stranger appears and makes a large bet, for it to draw one's attention?" She raised a finger and tapped it on the arm of his chair. "Is that not customary?"

"Certainly it is."

"And isn't it true that your high-limit players are allowed to wager any amount, in any manner they see fit?"

"They are."

"That is all I have to say on this subject," she said. "The next shoe is ready." Her driver appeared, standing beside her. "Is there anything else?"

"What about Chimsky?" Mannheim said.

The name elicited a scoff from the Countess. "I do not make it a habit to follow the affairs of your employees." With these words, she turned around very quietly, and walked with a shuffling gait toward the waiting table.

The Unwanted Houseguest

TWENTY-ONE DAYS HAD PASSED SINCE Dumonde moved in, and each day, Chan asked how things were progressing, how long it would take before he would leave. Dumonde assured Chan he was doing everything in his power to resolve his situation and spent many mornings out of the apartment making calls from a pay phone on the corner, next to a convenience store. Still, there was no indication Chan's houseguest would be gone soon. In fact, by the second weekend, Dumonde succumbed to allergies and was laid up in Chan's bed for several days, sniffling. Chan tended to Dumonde as best he could given his dislike for the man, administering heavy doses of antihistamine along with strong black tea, while secretly stewing over how to get rid of his former boss, short of poisoning him.

Chan had less than $700 in his checking account, and every day he stayed, Dumonde was sapping these meager resources. After seeing how Chan had been eating—"worse than a convict" as Dumonde described it, often just instant noodles or rice—his old boss insisted on buying the groceries and preparing their meals. The elaborate dishes pained Chan greatly, yet he had to grudgingly admit after supping on steamed legumes or fried clams that Dumonde's way of eating was far superior. But after Dumonde had gotten sick with allergies, they often resorted to even more expensive take-out.

Dumonde began spending every moment of every day at home, resting on the couch and perusing Chan's library of gambling. "Ah!" he would say when pulling out a particularly choice volume, like the Rocheford. "One of my favorites. You have excellent taste, Chan." Dumonde said that he was writing a gambling text of his own, a memoir he wanted to call *My Life in the Pit*. It would not be a tell-all, he told Chan. He would air no one's dirty laundry. Instead, it would be a work of fiction, and its point would be to glamorize the world of gambling, to elevate it out of the muck.

"The more I'm away from the casino," he told Chan one day as they ate, "the more I miss the old milieu. It makes me sick not being around it."

"Go ahead," Chan told him. "There are plenty of casinos around here. Just stay away from the Royal."

"Why don't we go together, Chan? You have the car, remember? It'll be like old times."

"I have no interest in reliving old times."

"We could go on a rush. We could win enough money for me to leave."

"No," said Chan. "And that's final. That's not part of our deal."

They ate their soup in silence. Then Dumonde said, "We could do it with a single hundred-dollar stake. We've done it before." He smiled winningly. "We're good gamblers, Chan. You know that. We don't even have to go to a casino. For example, I hear Snoqualmie Downs is beautiful this time of year. We'll go on your next free day."

"No. But if it'll make you feel better, you can take my car on Saturday, when I'm off."

"A hundred-dollar stake," Dumonde said. "That's all it ever takes."

Chan winced at the paltry amount. He thought of the Countess who bet $25,000 or more—on a single turn of the card. His own smallness of means irritated him, and he pushed his bowl away. "The soup's fine," he said in reply to Dumonde's questioning look. "I'm just not hungry."

"You're thinking about the track," Dumonde said. "We'll go Saturday. I promise we'll have fun."

For the next several days, Chan noticed Dumonde poring over a book from the gambling library that had lain unshelved at the bottom, a ratty paperback of Michael Goodman's *How to Win*. Dumonde took notes on a small pad he kept in the front pocket of his shirt. "There's a system in here," he explained to Chan, "for the Daily Double. Snoqualmie Downs has two of them. If we can hit them both, you can say good-bye to both me and this apartment."

Like many in the industry, Dumonde had formed his own philosophy on gambling, one that proved immune to Chan's arguments against going to the track. "I don't believe in long-term statistics," he explained. "They're for the losers who go every day and bet every race. We're going for one day. Those numbers don't apply."

Chan tried his best to ignore Dumonde's imploring. But on Friday afternoon, Dumonde interrupted Chan's nap and insisted on showing him two pages of math he had carefully performed in his ledger. "Look, Chan. If we had followed Goodman's system the last two days, we would've turned a hundred dollars into over six thousand."

"Can't we talk about this later? I'm trying to get some rest."

"Look at the math, Chan. Please. If the numbers are not legitimate, I promise I won't ever bring it up again."

The new note of desperation—an uncharacteristic crack

in Dumonde's veneer—drew Chan's attention. "All right," he said. He sat up in bed and took the ordered notes. The numbers were meticulously rendered, and he looked them over while Dumonde explained his calculations.

The next morning, gray and drizzling rain, Chan and Dumonde drove to Snoqualmie Downs in the old hatchback. Dumonde seemed delighted by the miserable weather, and drank the entire thermos of coffee after Chan said he wouldn't be having any. The rain would make the track slow and muddy, Dumonde said, causing havoc with the odds. "Heavy variance plays directly into our hands," he told Chan. Chan, for his part, did not care to interrogate Dumonde's reasoning now that they were on their way. It *was* possible they could get lucky. Chan saw it happen every night, to both the deserving and undeserving alike.

There were two Daily Doubles at Snoqualmie Downs: the Early Double in the first and second race, the Late Double in the twelfth and thirteenth. Michael Goodman's system was simple. They would spread Chan's meager hundred over every horse in the first race, doubled with a single lone winner in the second race. If the first Double came through, Chan and Dumonde agreed they would parlay their winnings by similarly spreading it over every horse in the twelfth race coupled with a single lone winner in the thirteenth. Chan had to acknowledge that the system simplified the often Byzantine betting options available at the teller window. There were only two questions to consider: who would win the second race and who would win the thirteenth?

They arrived at Snoqualmie Downs early and, after parking the hatchback, walked around the paddock in the drizzle. The crowd was sparse due to the weather. Only the desperate and the degenerate would be out on a day like today, Chan thought. All the while Dumonde spoke energetically. "I like Charlie's Kidney in the second race. He's the second favorite, and that's what Goodman recommends. Runs good in the muck. Comes from an excellent lineage. Comes from a very respected stable." Chan only half listened. He was looking at the tote board, estimating the various payouts they would win in each of the instances of the number six horse, Charlie's Kidney, winning the second race. Dumonde's pick was currently at 7 to 1, a very attractive number.

At ten minutes to post for the first race, Chan and Dumonde went to the two-dollar bettor window and spent all five twenties Chan had earned during the week on ten bets: every horse in the first race coupled with Charlie's Kidney in the second. Chan clutched the tickets to his chest as they climbed the wet, misty grandstand. The horses were mounted and being led around the track by their handlers while a desultory voice introduced each over the loudspeaker. Chan and Dumonde found an empty spot in the middle of a scattered patch of spectators, and Dumonde immediately began chatting with their neighbors about the rain and its effect on their picks. Chan was only mildly interested in the outcome of the first race, as they had all the horses, but he knew they would prefer if a middling choice came in rather than one of the favorites. Unfortunately, at the conclusion of a slow-paced mile and a quarter, Centaur, at 5 to 3, finished first by two-and-a-half lengths.

Chan tore up the nine tickets that did not have Centaur's number on them, leaving only the single live ticket. According to the board, it would pay off at $660 dollars if Charlie's Kidney won the second race. A jumpy Dumonde left to get them more coffee in the twenty minutes before post, and Chan watched with some amusement his old boss weaving through the crowd, talking with strangers all the while. More people were arriving now, filing in and distributing themselves in the grandstand. Suddenly, Chan thought he recognized one of them, a man bundled in a heavy brown parka. The man looked like Chimsky—he felt he could hardly mistake the high-limit dealer's long, extroverted gait. It was the same way he walked around the Royal, lording over the pit dealers. Thankfully, the man chose a section far from where Chan and Dumonde sat, at least a dozen rows away. When Dumonde reappeared with two cups of coffee soon after, Chan gratefully accepted his, drinking it entirely in the last nervy moments as the horses lined up in the gate for the second race. Chimsky's presence receded in his mind, replaced in Chan's thoughts with the more pressing concern—if Charlie's Kidney did not finish first, it would be an early afternoon indeed for him and Dumonde.

After what seemed an interminable pause, the shrill starting bell rang out over the grandstand. The gates opened, and the field of horses jostled down the track, laboring in the thick muck. To Chan's dismay, Charlie's Kidney was pinned on the rail as the horses rounded the first bend and vanished into a dense fog. Dumonde was shouting incoherently beside him, but only the voice over the loudspeaker seemed to know in what order the field was running. Chan strained to hear mention of the number 6. When it sounded like Charlie's Kidney was struggling to negotiate his way through, Chan closed his eyes and focused on the number 6, imagining it getting larger and larger, the glowing digit filling his entire range of vision. His surroundings faded away—he no longer heard the announcer, nor Dumonde next to him: he focused only on the shape and sound of the number. It wasn't until he felt the small crowd rising to its feet around him that Chan opened his eyes. Miraculously, when the horses emerged from the fog, Charlie's Kidney held the lead, and was widening it with every stride!

"Didn't I tell you?" Dumonde was shouting into his ear. "Didn't I tell you?"

Chan trembled with excitement as the horses thundered

down the stretch. Throwing up huge chunks of mud in his wake, Charlie's Kidney streaked across the finish line, clear by four lengths. Dumonde clapped Chan on the back and almost knocked him over. Chan was too excited to care.

After collecting their breaths, they walked to the teller window to cash the ticket. They were paid $660 in twenties, and Chan held the money. Now came the waiting: there were nine more races to sit through, almost three hours, before the Late Double. Chan was adamant in refusing Dumonde's appeals to bet at least a little something—even as small as a $2 Exacta Box—on each race just to pass the time. Instead, they used some of their winnings to have a light lunch in the pavilion.

After eating, they were returning to the grandstand when a voice hailed Chan from behind. "Chan! Over here!"

Chan ignored the voice, but Dumonde halted. "There's someone coming," he told Chan. "A dealer if I ever saw one."

Chan groaned. He turned and saw Chimsky, dressed in his black dealer pants under the brown parka, walking toward them, smiling. His manner was magnanimous, and Chan guessed that Chimsky must be winning too.

"Hello, Chan! Imagine running into you here!" Chimsky shook Chan's hand with one arm and clapped him on the back with the other. "I didn't know you liked to play the horses. Too bad the weather isn't cooperating."

Chimsky was acting far more familiar with him outside the Royal than in it, and Chan did not appreciate this. "Hello, Chimsky," he said.

"I don't believe I've met your friend."

"My name is Jean-Paul," said Dumonde, extending a hand when Chan made no move to introduce them.

"Sam Chimsky. The pleasure is mine. Chan and I work together at the Royal, you know." He nudged Chan's shoulder. "A fine dealer. One of our most promising."

"I see you have an excellent eye for dealing," Dumonde said. "I wholeheartedly agree."

"Likewise, sir," Chimsky replied. "Most people don't give the dealer a second thought." He turned to Chan. "Having a good day at the track?"

"We're up."

"We just hit the Early Double," Dumonde interjected. Chan cringed at the needlessly offered information. "For nearly seven hundo."

"Ah, that's fantastic! That's a wonderful hit. Let it ride, I say. If you get a little bit more money, come see us in the High-Limit Salon at the Royal."

"We really must be on our way," Chan said.

But as he stood there, the two men continued to converse for another half hour. Two entire races came and went as Chimsky and Dumonde debated their preference for big or small horses in the rain. Chan was only able to draw Dumonde's attention by pointing out that it was now twenty minutes to post in the twelfth race. Chimsky appeared to want to join them, but Chan felt secretive of the system they were playing.

"There's an item we must discuss in private," he told Chimsky.

"Might I suggest Pinchbelly in the thirteenth," Chimsky said, tapping the side of his nose with an index finger. "Take my word for it."

After they said good-bye, Dumonde and Chan returned to the grandstand to handicap the thirteenth race. Dumonde was leaning toward the number 3 horse—Josephina, a filly. "There are five horses who could win this," he grumbled as the minutes steadily ticked off the board.

With five minutes left, Chan demanded that they come to a decision. "It's now or never," he said. "Are we betting or not? We can always leave with the six hundred."

"No," Dumonde said. "We must play the system." He eventually selected the number 8 horse: the enormous, coal-black Pinchbelly—Chimsky's recommendation.

Chan rushed to the window to bet their $660 spread over every horse in the twelfth race coupled with Pinchbelly in the thirteenth. He got back to his seat just as the twelfth race went off. It was an unremarkable contest. The second-favorite at 3 to 1, Yankee Doodle, won wire-to-wire. Chan tore up the losing tickets. According to the tote board, their lone remaining live ticket—the Late Double of Yankee Doodle and Pinchbelly—would pay off at over $7,000 if it came through—$7,162 to be exact.

The two men said nothing to each other during the twenty long minutes until post time for the thirteenth and final race. Neither wanted to jinx the outcome by making a foolhardy remark. Much of the crowd had departed already, leaving behind in the damp, gloaming dusk only the unregenerate few. Even Chimsky appeared to have left. The atmosphere was gloomy in the grandstand, but Chan could hardly contain his nerves as he sat on his cold hands, shivering.

The track had turned into absolute slop after twelve races. To Chan, the delay as the horses were led around the track and loaded into the starting gate was excruciating. Finally, all was at the ready. Chan quieted himself. Then the bell rang and the gates exploded open. Three horses fought their way through the melee to the front of the pack: the number 7, Gentleman Jim, got to the rail first, followed by the number 3, Josephina. The number 8, Pinchbelly, was close behind. The fog had lifted, and Chan could see the entire track—around the first turn, it was Gentleman Jim, Josephina, and Pinchbelly still running 1-2-3, leading the chasing pack by two good lengths. Their pace was measured and deliberate. At the farthest point from the grandstand, on the other side of the track, Chan could dimly make out their forms as they exchanged order. Josephina made her move on the outside and seized the lead; Gentleman Jim was beginning to fade. Pinchbelly's stride remained restrained and relaxed. When would the jockey unleash him?

All the while, Dumonde whispered encouragement to the jockey: "Steady, steady, steady."

As they entered the back turn, Josephina opened a two-length lead on Pinchbelly and was striving to increase it. Gentleman Jim had fallen back, and the chasing pack closed on him and would engulf him in a matter of seconds. There were only two furlongs left and it was a two-horse race—the dashing Josephina, now a full three lengths ahead of Pinchbelly, still being held in reserve.

Chan closed his eyes, and visualized the number 8, Pinchbelly's number, getting larger and larger, as he'd done before. He focused on the number 8 until he could see or feel nothing else. "Number eight," he whispered. "Number eight, number eight..."

"Go now!" Dumonde shouted next to him. "Now!"

Chan opened his eyes. With a mere furlong left, Pinchbelly's jockey finally let him run. The number 8 horse uncoiled his massive stride, eating up the distance between himself and the leader at an astonishing pace. Josephina still held the advantage, but she looked nearly spent. Her jockey was urging the gallant horse on. The lead was now down to two lengths, then one and a half, then one, then only a neck. Less than a hundred yards remained. Pinchbelly was running beside Josephina, still behind by a nose with hardly any track left. They thundered across the finish line amid the flashing of camera bulbs and raucous cheers from the sparse crowd.

Chan and Dumonde did not look at each other. Their eyes remained fixed on the tote board, breathlessly awaiting the results to be confirmed and posted. It had been a photo finish, and would take time to decipher. Meanwhile, the announcer was thanking the exiting crowd for attending another great day of racing at Snoqualmie Downs. Soon, only Chan and Dumonde were left in their section.

Finally, the numbers flashed on the board. Three in second—eight in first!

Pinchbelly had won in a photo finish. Chan and Dumonde began jumping up and down, hugging each other. On the massive video tote board, the finish-line photo showed Pinchbelly edging Josephina by the merest pixel of a nose. The forgotten Gentleman Jim wound up finishing dead last.

Sandman

EARLY IN THEIR RELATIONSHIP, DR. Eccleston had told Mannheim she'd never encountered an aura like the one that surrounded him: it was radiant yellow, and streaked through with deep scarlet and lime, like veiny fingers. She said it reminded her of the organ of some ancient beast—the worm-ridden heart of a saber-tooth. Little Theo recognized the singularity of Mannheim's aura as well. It was growing, enlarging slowly, as his mind and body failed to contain it.

"It's preparing," the child stated solemnly.

Mannheim himself did not know what it was his aura was anticipating. He had never married or sired children, nor could he remember ever having held any sort of ambition other than to perform his job at the Royal competently and without fuss. He understood his subconscious was a sort of blank wall, its repression complete. But Mannheim wanted to break through. On the other side was an understanding that eluded him: why had he arrived at this late point in life, having hardly made any impression at all on the world around him?

On a gray, rainy afternoon, Mannheim arrived at Dr.

Eccleston's and was ushered by the child directly into the spacious office. The desk at which they usually sat had been pushed against the wall. Mannheim was made to take off his jacket, shoes, and socks and lie down on the dark leather divan that now occupied the center of the room.

As before, Dr. Eccleston connected diodes leading from his temples and his wrists to the intaker machine. Once this was completed, Little Theo dimmed the bulb and lit a tall, tapered candle. Dr. Eccleston placed a heavy black pillow over Mannheim's eyes. The smoke was musky and sweet, and soon his nerves calmed. As in their first interview, Dr. Eccleston sat beside him.

"Fifty years ago," began Theo, "there was a mother. She had a young son. One night, he was sleeping. His mother walked into the room quietly." Mannheim heard him blow out the candle. Dr. Eccleston breathed nearby. He sensed her close, hovering over his shoulders.

"She cut open her son's arms," Theo said.

Mannheim felt something sharp penetrate his shoulder—a nail?—and he jumped. But there was no pain. The nail—if that was what it was—scored its way down to the elbow, bisecting the vein, and then to the wrist. It moved to his left arm, again starting at the shoulder, scoring the middle of it, all the way down.

"Then she put sand inside," said Theo.

Starting at the wrist, Mannheim felt Dr. Eccleston pressing on his right arm vigorously with her palms, working their way up to his shoulder—she did this several times, each time increasing the pressure with her palms. Then she did the same with Mannheim's left arm.

"She cut her son's legs open," said Theo.

The nail scored Mannheim's right leg from the top of the thigh to the knee, splitting the shin, all the way down to the ankle. Then the nail moved to his left leg, again scoring the middle of it to the knee, through the shin, all the way down.

"Then she put sand inside."

Dr. Eccleston circled her palms around Mannheim's right calf, kneading upward to his thigh—each time increasing the pressure. She did the same with his left leg. Both these sensations and the boy's excellent reading served to hypnotize Mannheim, and he was already feeling very heavy, and faint of breath. He knew what came next.

"She cut open her son's stomach," said Theo.

Mannheim felt the nail cutting open his belly, starting underneath his bottom rib, circling down below the navel to his pelvic bone, and then back around to the hollow space below the sternum.

"Then she put sand inside."

Dr. Eccleston opened the flaps into his stomach, pushing his guts upward toward his heart to make room. He felt the muscles giving way, opening itself for the filling sand. Dr. Eccleston packed in more and more—by the time she finished, Mannheim's belly was full, the skin over it re-sewn and taut as a drum.

"Her son woke up in the morning," said Theo.

A candle was relit. The smoke was strong and pulled him back to the divan in Dr. Eccleston's office. With both hands, she gently removed the pillow from Mannheim's face. His eyes fluttered and opened.

"I can't move," he whispered. "Am I dead?"

Theo looked at Dr. Eccleston. "Is he dead?"

"Your vital signs are fine, Mr. Mannheim. You're just getting readjusted. How do you feel?"

"Heavy," Mannheim said. He hadn't budged. "So heavy."

"That's because you're filled with sand," Theo explained.

Slowly, Mannheim raised himself on an elbow. He tried to draw a deep breath, and was racked by a series of dry hacking coughs. A substance that looked like dust came out

of his mouth. Dr. Eccleston ordered the child to fetch a glass
of water.

"I was somewhere else by the end," Mannheim said. "It
was the changing room at the Royal. I was lying on a long
table. The door to the casino was open. Outside, there was
a party, people dancing. I could see couples in formal dress
waltz by, right outside the door. The music was too loud. How
could they dance to it? I thought.

"Then a tall woman entered the room. She had short
hair—nearly white—and her shoulders were stooped. She
was dressed like some kind of doctor. I had collapsed during
the dance, and they had brought me into the changing room
to recover. I was trying to tell the woman that I was all right,
but my mouth was full of pebbles. My throat and lungs were
full of pebbles, and I couldn't move!"

Eccleston finished recording his statement, and then
tried to soothe him. "You've experienced something trans-
formative, Mr. Mannheim—a privileged glimpse into
another realm."

"Is that my future?" Mannheim asked. He turned franti-
cally. "Why is everything still dark?"

Dr. Eccleston signaled the child turn on the lights, and
they withdrew to the waiting room, allowing Mannheim to
put his socks and shoes on in private. By the time he emerged,
he could see again, although his peripheral vision remained
blurred. He felt slightly embarrassed, and apologized if his
behavior had been untoward. Dr. Eccleston assured him that
on the contrary, his intense vision proved that the measure had
been a success, and whatever its meaning, it should be taken
quite seriously. "I looked over the results from the intaker, Mr.
Mannheim. You had the strongest reaction when you described
seeing the dancers waltz by right outside the door."

"That's when you were the most scared," Theo explained.

• • •

LATER THAT EVENING, WHEN MANNHEIM arrived in Gabriela's office—she'd asked him to come in early again—she remarked that Mannheim looked a little peaked. "Are you feeling all right?" she asked.

"I'm fine." Mannheim tried to smile and ran a hand through his thin hair, over his nose and ears. His fingers came back dry.

"Good. So what did you learn from the Countess?"

"Nothing," Mannheim said. "I do believe she knows something. But she's not telling."

Gabriela sighed. "I've gotten nowhere on Chimsky's end either. I've looked through every surveillance tape since that night, and he's been dealing straight, thirteen or fourteen seconds per shuffle, like a machine. We're stuck for now." She spun a pencil in her hand as she spoke. "We need something—a witness, an informant. Something that will make him talk, and won't get us sued."

Still parched from the afternoon in Dr. Eccleston's chamber, Mannheim told Gabriela he would remain vigilant and rose to leave. But she detained him a moment more. "On an unrelated note," she said, pulling a file from a drawer underneath the desk. "One of yours—Arturo Chan, pit dealer. I don't believe I've ever met him. Anyway, he's been with us almost six months now. Anything I should note in his review?"

"He's an excellent dealer," Mannheim said.

"Any complaints? From either staff or the clientele?"

"None that I know of."

"Do the customers like him?"

"He's quiet and polite. Many of our players prefer a serious dealer. And he's actually very funny when you pay attention. He won't say anything for twenty minutes, and then he'll make some sort of remark that will leave you wondering."

"Good. We'll say he's passed his review with flying colors. Do you think he's going to stay with us?"

"Yes," Mannheim said after a moment. "I think he likes it here—I truly believe so."

Gabriela shut the file. "Great. Go ahead and let him know he's through his probationary period."

Mannheim nodded and left the office. As he walked down the stairs toward the casino, the intricate spiral pattern on the carpet, which had never before affected him, made him feel queasy. He stopped and gripped the railing to catch his breath, and unbidden, he recalled something he'd unconsciously withheld from Dr. Eccleston and Theo that afternoon. During his vision, the tall woman in the gown had leaned close to his ear, so close that Mannheim could feel her breath tickling his earlobe. Her face was Gabriela's. Mannheim thought she was about to whisper a name, a secret, something that would illuminate his situation. But instead, her tongue had issued out and entered his ear, inserting a hot, hard little kernel of something in the canal, a small pebble or pill of paper that remained there after her tongue withdrew.

Downstairs in the casino, the music from the pit grew louder and louder. Like circling tongues, the spirals in the carpet swam under his feet, and Mannheim cried out, shutting his eyes. He seized the railing with both arms and blindly staggered down the stairs.

Barbara Makes a Bet

WHAT BARBARA DESIRED WAS TO never see Dimsberg again, but the more time she spent away from Gambling Help, the more persistent he became, calling her every couple days to "check in." She even told him she was changing her number, but to her chagrin, Dimsberg refused to believe her, saying she was just confused, that she would come to realize this was one of those times that try all recovering addicts.

"We're all praying for you, Barbara," he kept saying. "Remember that."

Barbara tried once to go back. She arrived twenty minutes late, so as not to run into anyone in the parking lot. She got as far as the front door, but stopped herself when she imagined the gruesome welcome she would receive upon entrance: how they would embrace her and rub her hand, nod at her knowingly, and try to make her feel as miserable and guilty as they did.

Since the night she'd bought the lottery ticket, there were two things driving Barbara's new state of mind. The first was the pleasant idea of becoming a member at Hair & Now, which seemed like the direct obverse of Gambling Help.

The second was related to her work at the call center. The election was days away, and the polling numbers from her company were being paraded on the news as evidence that the Washington gubernatorial race was a fifty-fifty toss-up. Yet despite having been in charge of collating these statistics, Barbara's hunch that Gardner, the challenger, would prevail had grown stronger in the last week, coupled with a resulting notion that—once it gained entry—refused to exit.

The Monday evening before the election, she remained in her office until everyone was gone. Then she closed the door and placed a phone call, dialing the number from memory.

"Hi, Chimsky," she said. "It's me. I have a favor to ask."

She waited for him sitting in their old booth at Rudy's. A whisky sour was already in front of his seat when Chimsky arrived. His hair was slightly disheveled, as if he had rushed to the meeting. Although Barbara could not admit to harboring any residual romantic feeling toward her ex-husband, it moved her a little to see how excited he was over her invitation.

"So?" he asked. "I'm all ears."

"It's a gambling matter, actually. I remember a couple months ago, you said you lost a bet on a boxing match."

Chimsky winced. "Thank you for reminding me, Barbara. But yes."

"Does your bookmaker take other sorts of bets? I mean bets on things other than sporting events."

"For example?"

"Who's going to win the Oscar for Best Actor, say."

"The Oscars aren't until March."

"Or who's going to win the election tomorrow."

"I see. And who do *you* think is going to win the election tomorrow?"

"I asked first."

"I suspect," Chimsky said, "my bookie would take a bet on just about anything. Tomorrow's election included."

"Can you tell your bookie I'd like to place a wager?"

Chimsky was thoughtful for a moment. Then he smiled. "You know, Barbara, you almost had me believing you would never gamble again. Hold on a minute." He left his drink on the table and strode toward the back hallway. Barbara watched as he inserted a coin into the pay phone and dialed a number. As he waited, he smiled and winked at her, and Barbara waved. Then he began talking, turning his back to her, the cord of the phone coiled around his neck. He talked for less than five minutes. When he returned, he was beaming. "It's all set." He wrote down a phone number on the back of the happy hour menu and slid it across the table to her. "His name is Fong. Call him tonight. Just tell him who you are. I've explained everything."

"Thank you," Barbara said. "I mean it."

"I miss you, Barbara," Chimsky said. He held out his hand, palm up in the center of the table. "Can't we be friends now?"

Barbara laughed. She placed her hand over his and squeezed. "Of course, Chimsky. Of course."

"Can I ask you to do me a small favor in return?"

Barbara stiffened. "What is it?"

"Whoever it is that you're betting on—would you mind playing $500 for me as well?"

"Can't I just tell you who I'm picking?"

"No," Chimsky said. "I don't want to know. I trust you."

ON HER WAY HOME THAT night, Barbara passed her lucky gas station, and she pulled over to have another look at the state lottery display case. Changing of the Card was no longer available, she noticed, replaced by a seasonal one entitled Thanksgiving Jackpotpourri. Barbara was debating whether or not she should buy the new card when she felt a presence sidle up beside her.

She turned. To her utter disbelief, it was Dimsberg.

"What a happy accident, Barbara," he said, smiling. "Bumping into you here of all places." His shirt, with its single vertical beige stripe, looked brand new.

"Are you following me?" she asked.

"What? No. It's pure serendipity, Barbara." He glanced at the display case. "Anything catch your eye?"

"It's none of your business," she said, turning away. She was fuming.

"Barbara, your gambling *is* our business. We're Gambling Help, after all. We're here to help you."

"If you continue to harass me, I'm going to file a police report."

She tried to walk past him and out the door, but he held out an arm to detain her.

"Barbara, please don't act this way. We all care about you a great deal."

"Move your arm, Dimsberg. Or so help me God, I'm going to belt you in the mouth."

For the first time she could remember, Dimsberg appeared nervous. His arm lowered. "If that's how you feel, Barbara—"

She barged past him. Without looking back, she got into her car, locked the door, and turned the ignition. The radio came on, startling her—an animated DJ was introducing a new hit single called, bizarrely enough, "The Glamorous Life." Barbara quickly switched it off. Then she calmed herself and drove off quietly, making sure there was no one in her rearview mirror.

When she got home, she poured a glass of wine, lit a cigarette, and dialed the number Chimsky had provided. She asked for Fong, explained she had been referred by Chimsky, and placed her bet on the election for governor. She chose Booth Gardner at 6 to 5, for $1,500—a thousand of her own money, and five hundred of Chimsky's.

• • •

ON THE NIGHT OF THE election, Barbara stood inside her place of polling, the auditorium in a local grade school, watching the results coming in along with a small crowd gathered for the event. A few snacks and coffee had been provided by volunteers, and she nibbled at a cookie absentmindedly. Its frosting had grown a crust, sitting on the tray. Like the others, Barbara fixated upon the updates from the various precincts—but she also wanted to be in a public place if Dimsberg "accidentally" ran into her again.

The early numbers were too close to call. Nervously, Barbara finished the cookie and started on the platter of crackers. She had hoped for a blowout, with the outcome all but confirmed by eight p.m., but now she knew she was in for a long sweat. When she was younger, she would've found that prospect exciting—she almost felt cheated if a win came too easily. Now, she wanted the evening as free from stress as possible, and the updates did not suggest that would be the case: a fifth of the precincts were in, and the race was dead even. "It's anybody's election," someone next to her said. She looked up and it was a policeman, smiling at her. She laughed politely, grabbed a handful of crackers, and edged away.

At ten p.m., the same policeman directed everyone to leave the building as the polls were closing. The election was still too close to call. Barbara walked out in the middle of a group of seven or eight people and hurried to her car. She saw no sign of Dimsberg. She parked in the alley behind her building just in case, and entered through the service entrance, to which only residents held the key. Avoiding the lobby, she climbed four flights of stairs to her floor, and once inside her apartment, bolted the front door.

Immediately, she turned on the television, opened a bottle of wine—a nice Merlot—and settled into the couch. With over eighty percent of the precincts in, the tide was finally swelling in favor of Gardner—this news awakened Barbara, and she couldn't sit still, her fingers and toes tapping in anticipation. It was a feeling she'd grown unaccustomed to, these last two years she'd spent in purgatory. But the tables were finally turning. At half past one in the morning, when the outcome was officially confirmed in her favor, Barbara, moved to excitement, applauded Spellman's stirring concession speech. She knew that luck, good or bad, arrives in streaks, and she had always been among the streakiest gamblers she knew. Now Barbara could tell she was getting hot again, and she wiped grateful tears from her eyes.

Thanksgiving Dinner

CHAN AND DUMONDE DIVIDED THEIR winnings from Snoqualmie Downs unequally—Chan was happy to give Dumonde the lion's share so long as that meant his old boss would be leaving town. Still, Dumonde lingered, saying he wanted to spend Thanksgiving, what he claimed was his favorite holiday, with his friend Chan before striking out on his own. Chan, who had become used to Dumonde puttering around the apartment, agreed he could accompany him to the unofficial Royal Casino Staff Thanksgiving Dinner, annually hosted at the home of Leanne and Bao. Chan learned from his colleagues that it was an intimate affair, with never more than seven or eight attendees, including Mannheim, a fact that gave Chan pause. But Dumonde promised Chan he would not mention any of their past dealings together. He would say he was an old friend from their school days in Westchester, out for a short visit. In addition, Dumonde swore to Chan he would leave Snoqualmie immediately after.

This last condition was one Chan insisted upon. The Tuesday before Thanksgiving, Chan had arrived at his door from grocery shopping and heard the phone ringing inside the apartment. He thought Dumonde might be home, but the rings continued unabated, and when Chan unlocked the front door and picked up the receiver, he was surprised to hear a female voice greet him.

"Mr. Chan? This is Faye Handoko. We spoke previously at Scribes, several months ago."

"Yes," Chan said, immediately alert. "Please hold on a moment." He put the phone down and quickly scanned the apartment to confirm Dumonde was not hiding somewhere. Then he said, "Sorry, Ms. Handoko. Go on."

"We talked regarding a story my late father had written."

"I remember."

"I've discovered some information you may be interested in. About the car."

"Her car?"

"Possibly," she said. "I thought you'd want to know."

"I do. Very much so."

"Good. Let's meet to talk about it. How about on Saturday, after Thanksgiving—around two?"

"At the same place?"

"Let's meet somewhere a little more quiet this time."

ON THANKSGIVING DAY, DUMONDE SPENT the better part of the afternoon in Chan's small kitchen, fussing over a curried pumpkin pie. Chan was worried they might be late, but when they arrived at Leanne and Bao's attractive apartment, they found themselves the first guests. Two bottles of wine were open—one red and one white—and after a glass of each, Dumonde regaled their hosts with fictitious stories about high school life with Chan in Westchester. Mannheim and the other guests trickled in—a cashier and a poker dealer, neither of whom Chan knew.

Chan had only ever seen Mannheim at work, and was surprised how pale his boss looked outside of the Royal's warm glow. There was a kind of ghastly, unfocused energy to Mannheim's behavior as he greeted Chan, shook hands with Dumonde, and inspected the foods, all the while saying how delighted he was they were all together. While Leanne and Bao prepped the mushroom-and-barley casserole in the kitchen, and Dumonde was explaining himself to the cashier and the poker dealer, Mannheim touched Chan's sleeve and pulled him aside.

"Chan, you've been with us for six months now. How do you like our neck of the woods?"

"I've greatly enjoyed my time at the Royal, sir."

"Call me Stephen," Mannheim said. "We're not in the pit, are we?" He was drinking a glass of wine with one hand and waving an empty glass with the other. "Gabriela wants you to know you've passed your probationary period. We both think you're doing a fine job."

Chan laughed nervously. "Thank you, sir—Stephen."

"I hope you stay with us for a very long time," Mannheim said. Then he paused, sighing. "Like you, I have spent a large part of my life in casinos, Arturo. I feel at home inside them. The constant atmosphere of uncertainty, of unknowing, appeals to me. Oddly, I am less interested in gambling. I will dabble, of course—who doesn't?—but I play the basic strategies and never vary my bet. I used to play more, but once, I suffered a very bad loss. . . ." Mannheim paused again, and appeared puzzled. "I swear I can't remember the details. But it was very bad, very substantial."

Chan wondered about this old bet. Was Mannheim even talking about gambling?

Placing his glasses on the sideboard, Mannheim looked around before leaning closer to Chan. "I prefer being behind the ropes, you see, watching the action from a safe distance. I have the final word without incurring any of the risk. And I always back my dealers, Chan, one hundred percent. You can deal with perfect confidence on my watch."

Chan nodded. "We appreciate your support, sir."

"We do have a good crew, don't we?" Mannheim gazed around the living room. "I like that we can come together outside of work and enjoy one another's company so. Excuse me for a moment—I have something important to tell you, but first I must refresh my glass."

Chan leaned against the wall to await his boss's return. He could hear Dumonde in the kitchen, talking with Leanne and Bao about the preparations for dinner. Several minutes passed, and he began to wonder if he'd been abandoned. The other guests were spread around the couch, laughing about something the cashier had done at last year's event, and he considered approaching them. Then Mannheim appeared, holding drinks for himself and Chan.

"I was told by those in the know," Mannheim said. "Only twenty minutes more."

For a minute, they chatted politely about their respective states of hunger. Then, when no one had said anything for too long of a time, Chan reminded Mannheim: "I'm curious about this matter you wanted to tell me."

"I have been following a couple of mentors, so to speak," began Mannheim. His voice lowered to a whisper. "We discovered something important together. Let me pose the question: where is time at its most relative?"

"I can't say, sir."

"In a casino! Yes? That's what we realized, Chan. The body wears itself thin from the tension and nerves of not knowing. But most powerfully, the mind, body, and soul are devastated by losing, Chan. Prolonged losing crushes the spirit. And I have spent more than half my adult life in casinos—despite being a mere observer, this continuous, terrible agony of losing has taken its toll. In my case, it is slowly destroying my mind."

Chan was startled. "I beg your pardon?"

"In other cases, it's the lungs. Or the legs. But there are those who seem unaffected by all this anguish. These are the real lucky ones. Some even seem to grow younger, while the rest of us speed to our graves." He peered at Chan closely. "Are you one of these? You've worked in casinos for twelve years and yet you don't look a day over twenty-eight."

"That's very flattering, sir. But what do you mean about your mind?"

Mannheim looked around, and then whispered very gravely: "This is my last Thanksgiving, Chan. I'm dying from dementia of the brain."

Chan was dumbstruck. Haltingly, he began, "I'm sorry, sir—I really am. How—?"

"I've only got a few weeks left, according to the medical authorities. I'm telling you because I don't want this secret between us. I know you won't make a commotion out of it, like the others would, Chan—they would only pity me, and throw parties on my behalf. As much as we all like one another, they see me as their boss, outside of their experience in some way. But we can trust each other, Arturo."

"Certainly, sir." Chan was moved by the request. When Mannheim extended a hand, he quickly took it. "I promise to never throw you a party."

Mannheim smiled and released Chan's hand. When he spoke again, his tone was more measured. "Is there something in your locker? In the changing room at work?"

"What? No," Chan said. "I usually dress at home." Neither spoke for a moment. Then Chan said quietly, "You're holding up commendably well, sir. All things considered."

They were interrupted by a loud clamor from the dining room. "It's almost time!" Leanne said with glee.

"I'm going to put in a good word for you, Chan, before my time is up. I know you're interested in Faro."

"I am." Chan felt urged to reciprocate Mannheim's openness toward him. "I would like to deal to the Countess."

"The Countess!" Mannheim laughed. "She hasn't aged the entire time I've known her."

Chan's reply was forestalled by the voice of Dumonde, exhorting the guests to gather around the banquet table.

"Oh, by the way," Mannheim added before the two men rejoined the others, "who is this Dumonde fellow? I like him."

AFTER EVERYONE HAD SETTLED INTO their seats, Bao rolled a large silver platter into the room. The guests applauded as Bao and Dumonde lifted it and placed it in the center of the long table. Then Leanne rose and asked if anyone wanted to lead them in an interdenominational prayer of gratitude. Chan avoided eye contact in the silence that followed, and was hardly surprised when he heard Dumonde's voice beside him: "I'll say a few words if you'll allow me."

Chan bowed his head and hoped for the best.

"I am thankful to you, Chan, for introducing me to your friends, and I hope I am not being too presumptuous in calling you all my friends as well. I suspect we have been brought together today for a very important reason. Yesterday we were strangers, and now we are united, the oddest of families.

"We give thanks for this past year—an eventful one, hopefully, full of the unexpected turns that make life strange and delightful. We give thanks for the bounty laid upon this table, under whose hand no poor creature was hurt. Thank you, Leanne and Bao, for inviting us together on this worthy occasion and preparing this wonderful feast." He raised a glass toward them, and Leanne beamed. "Finally, on behalf of us all, I would be remiss in not thanking you, Lord, for your most baffling creation—the world of risk. The bet, and the free will with which to exercise that option. Thank you,

God, for coolers and heaters—the devastating loss and the miraculous win!"

"Hear, hear," said the poker dealer, whose name Chan had learned was Rumi. The cashier, Max, began applauding, and everyone joined in. "To luck!" they cheered, and drank heartily, before descending upon the meal.

By half past nine, the guests had made their way to the living room and were sprawled out on the sofas in various stages of fullness. Dumonde's pie had been completely devoured. Rumi looked like she could hardly move, and Max was yawning. Mannheim was drinking with Dumonde, exchanging stories from their respective pit careers. Chan glanced at his watch, wondering if it was time to leave, when a knock came at the door. Bao answered it, and Chan heard him exclaim, "Why, hello there!" Looking up, he saw over Bao's shoulder that Chimsky and someone else had arrived. They were ushered in, and Chimsky introduced her as Barbara, "the ex-love of my life." Both seemed in excellent spirits. Bao and Leanne brought the newcomers plates of food, and they ate while chatting. Chimsky was going around the room with Rumi, polling the various parties on some idea he was proposing.

"Arturo," Chimsky said. "Just the man I wanted to see. Rumi has been kind enough to agree to deal us a true Thanksgiving treat: a dealer's choice poker game. I'm seeing who wants to participate. Max is out. He hates poker. Bao's going to bed, but Leanne says she's in. Mannheim says he'll play, believe it or not. Barbara's in, of course. Dumonde says he's willing if you are. So how does a game of poker sound to you?"

"I don't know," Chan said. "What are the stakes?"

"We're playing five-dollar antes. The rest is up to the dealer."

Dumonde came up to them, holding a drink. "Come on, Chan," he said, placing his arm around Chan's shoulders. "It's my last night in Snoqualmie."

"It wouldn't be much of a game with just four," Chimsky said. "We need you two."

"Exactly," Dumonde said. "Let's make the best of it."

Chan looked over at Mannheim, who was now sitting alone by himself on the couch, lost in his thoughts. Then he considered his own wallet in his back pocket, still plushly lined with the winnings from Snoqualmie Downs. "All right," he said finally, to their grins of approbation. "I guess we can play for a bit."

Dealer's Choice

A SURFACE OF BLUE FELT was unrolled, pulled taut, and clothes-pinned to the legs of the dining room table. Rumi, the dealer, sat in the middle on one side. The players drew cards for the seating arrangement, and around Rumi, clockwise, sat Mannheim directly to her left, then Barbara, Dumonde, Chimsky, Leanne, and finally, to Rumi's immediate right, sat Chan. A dealer button rotated in the same order around the table, with the person governing it calling the game. Rumi dealt the cards, in return for which she was toked from each pot by the winner—"the only person in the room guaranteed to walk out ahead," as she happily described her situation.

During the first orbit, Leanne rolled a joint from materials she removed from a compact wooden box on the sideboard. Chan was surprised Leanne could be so open about smoking in front of their boss, but when the joint reached Mannheim, he took several puffs himself. "Why not?" Mannheim said. "We're all friends here." Chan decided to follow suit when the joint reached him. Several of the other players were already deep into their glasses—Mannheim and Chimsky, specifically—and he did not want to be the only sober player

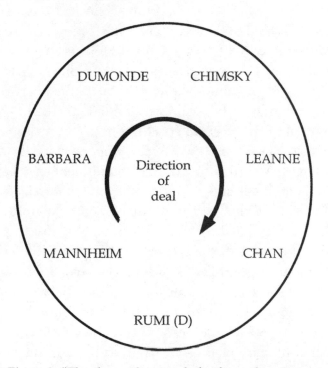

*Figure 2. "The players drew cards for the seating arrange-
ment and around Rumi, clockwise, sat Mannheim directly
to her left, then Barbara, Dumonde, Chimsky, Leanne, and
finally, to Rumi's immediate right, sat Chan."*

in a game that would most assuredly be marked by reckless play. Chan had not gambled since Snoqualmie Downs, and he felt overdue.

The session began with a series of small uncontested pots. Chan did not receive a playable hand until the dealer button settled on its second orbit in front of Leanne. She called Deuce-to-Seven Lowball. Additionally, she established that the hand should be played Pot Limit—"to spice things up." After tossing in his $5 ante, Chan squeezed out his hand and was delighted to find Rumi had dealt him a pat—though not great—hand: 9-8-6-5-3. He bet $20 into the pot and was raised to $50 by Chimsky. Everyone else dropped. Chan eyed Chimsky and immediately did not trust him. He watched Chimsky fiddling with his chips and made the call.

Chan told Rumi he was standing pat.

"In that case, I'd better draw," Chimsky said. He elected to exchange one card with Rumi. Chan immediately bet $200. He was hoping Chimsky would fold, but instead, Chimsky reached for his chips and lined up the call—then, disheart-eningly, he continued to add even more chips to the wager. Chimsky pushed a towering stack into the middle of the table, announcing a raise the size of the pot—$500.

Chimsky, of course, could be bluffing. He was chatting with Leanne about last night's shift, but Chan thought he was trying to appear more casual than he was feeling.

After waffling ten seconds, Chan said he would call.

"Good call," sighed Chimsky. He flashed an Ace sarcasti-cally. "Thanks for the brick, Rumi."

Courteously, Chan fanned his hand face up on the table and gathered in the sizable pot Rumi was pushing toward him. There was over $1,200 in it. Chan stacked the chips deftly with both hands, sharing twenty of it with Rumi. Chimsky, acting none the worse for wear, pulled out his wallet and rebought another $500.

Thereupon, the game grew wilder in complexion. Glasses were refilled, a fresh joint rolled, and dwindling stacks were replenished with ready cash. In this atmosphere, the button fell to Dumonde, and to Chan's annoyance, he called Five-Card Stud, Deuces Wild, a game Chan had never known anyone else to enjoy.

He surrendered his hand—a Jack with a 7 in the hole— very early, then watched as the pot ballooned to $1,000 between Dumonde and Mannheim. On the last street, Dumonde bet $900 with four Hearts showing, and the action fell to Mannheim and his two Aces. Chan saw Mannheim was almost undoubtedly beaten, and he hoped to see his boss fold—quickly. But instead, Mannheim appeared to be preparing his remaining chips to call. "I've gone this far," Chan heard him say.

No! Chan thought emphatically. *Fold!*

Mannheim was in the act of pushing his chips across the line. But just as he was about to, he paused, cocking his head slightly, as if he sensed Chan's mental remonstrance. But then he sighed, and pushed his chips in anyway, all in a heap. "I'll pay to see it," he said.

Dumonde smiled, his white teeth gleaming. He turned over the Ace of Hearts in the hole. "I never bluff," he said politely as he gathered in the rest of Mannheim's chips.

To Chan's dismay, beginning from this mistake, Mannheim's self-control steadily eroded over the next hour. Chan watched his boss go on tilt, playing every hand to the end, splashing in pots when he should have long given up. Equally erratic was his behavior. When it was his turn, Mannheim repeatedly called Sandman, a nonsensical variant of Guts that Chan was sure his boss had made up on the spot. On another occasion, after losing a large pot to Barbara, Mannheim began to mutter a rhyme under his breath.

"Excuse me?" Barbara asked.

"I was just saying," said Mannheim, "'No one knows where the hobo goes when it snows.'"

"What's that supposed to mean?"

"Years ago, customers would say it after they lost a big hand."

"It sounds unlucky to me," Barbara said, and Chan silently agreed. But he could only bite his tongue as he saw—hand by hand—Mannheim losing and rebuying twice more, for $500 each time, now repeating whenever he lost the unpleasant incantation, which appeared to draw nothing but further misfortune to him.

NEAR THREE IN THE MORNING, Leanne was felted by a cruel river card in a Hold'em hand, losing all her chips to an apologetic Barbara. Because Leanne was the host and no doubt desired to see the game conclude now that she had busted, the remaining five players agreed they would play just one more hand. Leanne remained in her seat, consoling herself with a nightcap. The button sat in front of Chan.

"Well?" Rumi asked. "What shall it be?"

Chan thought back to his favorite game, playing penny ante with schoolmates. "How about Lowball?" he said. "We'll each ante fifty and play for table stakes."

Dumonde whistled. "Nice, Chan. Ending with a bang."

"What about wild cards?" Chimsky said. "It's the last hand."

Chan turned over the possibilities: Deuces, one-eyed Jacks, suicide Kings. But none of them felt right. Then the image of a card occurred to him. "Rumi, please put the Joker back in the deck."

Chimsky's eyes lit up. "Perfect, Chan."

Rumi dealt the cards, five to each player. Chan inspected his hand, and his spirit rose when he saw that it contained so many of the little cards he'd hoped for:

Chan looked up, and Dumonde, sitting directly across the table, winked at him, before opening for $200.

Chimsky immediately called.

It was now up to Chan. He threw in the $200, and so did Mannheim and Barbara. With the antes, the pot now contained over $1,200.

Starting with Mannheim and proceeding in turn, every player exchanged one card with Rumi except Mannheim, who drew two.

Chan discarded the Deuce of Diamonds, all the time watching the other players' reactions. Mannheim appeared annoyed as he checked. Barbara's check, on the other hand, looked determined, like she held some sort of middling calling hand.

When it came to Dumonde, though, he did not hesitate. "I'm all in," he announced, moving at least $2,000 into the pot.

Chimsky had over $1,300 in front of him. Quickly, he counted everything up and pushed his chips in next to Dumonde's. "You can't have it every time," he said as he called.

The action fell to Chan. He placed his left hand over his new card, and, very slightly, he lifted the edge off the felt with his thumb, revealing the corner a millimeter at a time. The first thing he detected was the color of it. Red. Then, that it was a small card. Chan's heart leaped. It was the Six of Diamonds! He'd made the second-best possible hand!

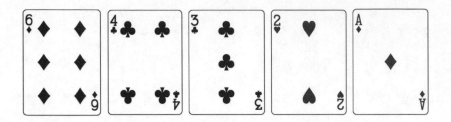

Chan was now confident the pot was his. Surreptitiously, he eyed his stacks—in three neat rows, Chan estimated he had nearly $1,700 in front of him. He looked at the huge pot in the middle of the table and was about to join his money with the other players' when his gaze passed over Dumonde. His old boss was carefully inspecting the fingernails of his left hand, something Chan had never seen him do before.

Dumonde caught Chan's gaze and quickly lowered his hand. "So Chan, you look like you're at least thinking about calling. But remember: I never bluff."

This statement gave Chan further pause. It began occurring to him that despite making a hand—the second-best possible hand—it still was not good. Dumonde was either warning him or trying to goad him into calling. Either way, Chan knew he should fold. For a brief moment, he shut his eyes and focused on Dumonde's thin, white set of teeth. They felt sharp to Chan.

Chimsky cleared his throat. "Chan, please—I hate to be impolite, but sometime tonight."

Chan apologized. After another moment, he silently folded.

"I'll join you," Mannheim said, pushing his cards into the muck.

Barbara passed as well. "I don't think my hand's good anymore."

At showdown, Chimsky promptly turned over his cards, revealing the 6-5-4-3-Ace. "I hope that's good."

Chan did not think so. Dumonde was grinning, showing his new set of teeth.

"Good hand, Chimsky—but you're not going to believe this." Dumonde fanned his cards elegantly on the table. "I'm holding the nuts."

Chan was elated—he had been right to fold!

Dumonde began collecting the massive pot Rumi was pushing toward him. Even as the others were rising and stretching, Chimsky fumed in his chair—"It's the story of my life!" he exclaimed.

"Come on, Chim, we're all adults here," Barbara said. "Let these poor people go to sleep."

Chan was still buzzing. He could hardly believe he had so narrowly avoided Chimsky's fate—by all rights, he should have lost all his chips. As they drove back to the apartment in an exhausted, post-haze glow, he could not conceal his glee from Dumonde, and they chatted amiably about the last hand. "You're getting sharper, Chan," Dumonde told him. "Still," he added, smiling, "I wouldn't have minded if you'd called."

The next morning, Chan awoke past noon, bleary of eye and slightly nauseous, to find, to his immeasurable relief, his apartment vacated as promised. The events of the previous night—his talk with Mannheim, the poker game—were already fading in his memory, like a dream. On the coffee table was a note, written in Dumonde's fine hand. It thanked Chan for his graciousness, and promised a "significant" mention in his book, *My Life in the Pit*, in a chapter about Daily Doubles. Sitting on the couch in the living room, which felt larger now without Dumonde's presence, Chan carefully folded the note and placed it in the flyleaf inside the Goodman book, which had been Dumonde's favorite, as a kind of souvenir of his stay.

That night at the Royal, Chan dealt freely and easily for the first time in two months, and throughout his shift, his tables stayed full and lively, many of the players leaving substantial winners.

THE FOLLOWING AFTERNOON, FAYE HANDOKO told Chan it was the peculiarity of their first meeting that had drawn her interest. "My father was an investigative reporter when he was younger," she said. They were sitting at a small table in the back of a bar called Rudy's, underneath the shadow of a mounted moose head. "He met with informants fairly regularly. He called them work friends." She paused to sip her drink. "But nowadays, the paper prints mostly wire copy. You're the first person who's ever asked me about one of his stories."

Faye was, as in their first meeting, small, dapper, and this time, dressed more casually, in a sweater off one shoulder and jeans. "I'm glad you called," Chan told her. The bar was empty that afternoon, and they spoke softly.

"You said when we met previously that the old woman's car was a silver Rolls Royce Phantom," Faye continued. She pushed two documents across the table. "I took the liberty of contacting someone in the Department of Licensing who owed me a favor. It turns out there are only two vehicles matching that description in the entire Snoqualmie County database. The first is owned by a high-end limousine company. The second is privately owned." Before Chan could look at the faxed forms, she placed her hand over his, halting him. "Remember," she said. "This information is strictly confidential. My friend could lose her job."

"I understand," Chan said.

The Phantom belonging to the limousine company was a recent vintage, and not the one he was after. Chan flipped the page. This one described a 1965 model Phantom V, silver in color, registered to a Thomas Eccleston.

"Does the name ring a bell?"

"No—but the car is from the right time." The name puzzled Chan. Then something clicked in his mind. "Perhaps he's the driver."

"Recognize anything else?" Faye said, pointing to the place of residence listed for the vehicle—1442 Majestic Avenue. It was the address of the Royal Casino.

"What does it mean?"

"It suggests the owner has no permanent place of residence. My friend said that's what people sometimes do when they live out of an RV or camper. They make an arrangement with a relative or a business to collect their mail."

"What an odd notion," Chan said. "The Countess with no home." He imagined her and the driver living in the Phantom, stopping only to gamble at the Royal. No wonder no one knew where she lived!

Faye shrugged. "It's certainly unusual." She looked around the bar, before leaning close to Chan. "So," she said, "have you learned anything more about her system?"

Chan recalled the night of his pursuit and shook his head. "Only more questions. As far as I've heard, she hasn't played a hand in several weeks."

"What's she waiting for?"

Chan shrugged. "I've no idea." He placed his straw on the table, next to his empty glass, and glanced over at their waiter.

Chan had recognized him immediately. It was the same

spiky-haired boy he'd sat with at the public library, months ago. The boy's reappearance now, while he was chatting with Faye, served to raise in Chan's mind an odd sense of the connectedness of things. The coincidence wasn't surprising—Snoqualmie at its heart was a very small town. But it was the contingency of moments, of events, and of people that struck Chan. He took a deep breath, shutting his eyes momentarily, and when he reopened them, Faye was looking at him from across the table, a quizzical and bemused expression on her face.

BOOK THREE: HIGH-LIMIT SALON

There exist untold pathways that twist between the world of the infinite and the soul of man, most of which remain undiscovered. The three most direct are dreams, first and foremost; second, art; and lastly, the wagering of prodigious sums of money.

—Marquis de Rocheford, *Les Caprices du Hasard (The Vagaries of Chance)*

A Darker Luster

IN THE MIDST OF A heater, one with no sign of cooling, Barbara promised herself she would be smarter this time. After setting aside enough winnings to pay two months' rent, she estimated she still held more than sufficient funds to become a member of the unusual aerobics club in the old Snoqualmie Theater: the place called Hair & Now. She returned there the Monday after Thanksgiving and saw the large plate-glass windows were now draped in lavish, gold-tinted Grand Opening banners. An arrow lit by flashing bulbs enticed her to enter, and Barbara did, feeling both curious and apprehensive.

There were several young people chitchatting in the lobby—fit, dressed in chic leotards—and they looked up when she entered. Barbara smiled nervously and then saw to her relief that the enormous red-haired man, Simon, was working the front desk. He rose to greet her, saying "Hello! Welcome back! Barbara, isn't it? So happy you returned."

"I like what you've done here," she said. The lobby was freshly tiled in a lush green-and-white checkerboard, and tall houseplants surrounded the doorways leading to the salon and gym. "Nice touch with the ferns."

"My idea," said Simon, smiling. "Gets more oxygen into the air. I'm hoping you've returned to sign up?"

"I think I just might've talked myself into it." Barbara took one of the brochures from the reception desk and opened it, pointing at the Body & Soul package. "I want this."

Simon clapped his palms together. "That's fantastic, Barbara! That's our finest package. You won't be disappointed."

Barbara paid for twelve months up front, $2,000 in cash, counting out the twenty hundred-dollar bills on the counter quickly and efficiently. Simon respectfully watched as the pile accumulated in front of him and then, collecting them, he inserted the sheaf into a yellow envelope he placed inside his desk. He wrote out a receipt and handed it to her, along with a registration form attached to a clipboard. Barbara spent several minutes filling it out with her personal information.

"Your last name is Chimsky?" Simon said, looking it over.

"Yes. It's not my name—I'm divorced."

"Is your ex-husband a dealer? We may know him."

"I wouldn't be surprised," Barbara said. "He comes into contact with a lot of people. He works at the Royal."

"Yes, of course." Simon was silent as he perused the rest of the form. When he was finished, he initialed the bottom and then shook her hand gravely. "Welcome to the club, Barbara. We'll have everything in order for you by tomorrow."

The next afternoon, Simon escorted her to her personal locker in the spacious and carpeted changing room. The carpet was maroon, accented by overlapping gold circles. Imprinted on an embossed plaque above her locker was her name ("Barbara C."), followed by her membership number (17) and the current year (1984). Several of the lockers close by had plaques on their doors, but there were entire rows that were empty. Simon assured her word of mouth was quickly spreading through Snoqualmie, and that they would have a full coterie of members very soon—by the following spring.

"We only have room for two hundred," he said. "After that, we expect to have a very long waiting list."

In her first week of membership, Barbara spent much of her time on the second floor, in the cafe. She went there on her lunch break to take a light meal, a salad and half an avocado sandwich, and began meeting the other members as they trickled in. Member number one was a businessman who lived upstairs in the same building as the club, and Barbara rarely saw him. Member number two was an older, gray-haired woman named Frances Murphy, and they quickly hit it off. Frances told Barbara she was the mother of one of the primary investors in the club, a son she referred to as "my sweet Henry," whom Barbara did not know.

Dutifully, Barbara attended an aerobics class every third day, despite protests from her ill-toned body. Simon and Quincy were excellent instructors—Simon was effusive, while Quincy's style was more quiet and cerebral. Barbara also availed herself of her two salon visits per month, where she entirely gave her hair over to the whims of a talkative stylist named Monty. His thin, perfect eyebrows reminded her of a silent film actor. He convinced her to get a feathered perm with frosted tips, and Barbara hardly recognized herself in the mirror afterward, her face framed by the ghostly new halo. Her coworkers seemed genuinely impressed; in the weeks to follow, several of them got their own perms and dyes, and the office, which had previously looked like a relic from the seventies, was transformed into what one of her interns described in glowing terms as "very MTV."

Each day after work, Barbara returned to the club, and she and Frances Murphy went around introducing themselves to new members. She plunged into her life at Hair & Now as she had plunged into new endeavors in her past—with full vigor and intensity—and she soon knew most everyone. The people struck her so differently from the ones she knew at Gambling Help. They were vibrant, full of life, and passionate about things; she could tell by the way they moved and the way they spoke. They never seemed to be on the verge of tears, nor close to revealing a shameful secret, a fact which Barbara discovered she greatly appreciated.

ONCE A WEEK NOW, SHE and Chimsky met at Rudy's in their usual spot—they had settled into what Barbara felt was the most satisfying phase in their relationship thus far, including their marriage: a convivial care without, as she thought, any of the bullshit. Chimsky, of course, desired more, but their weekly drink would have to suffice. Inevitably, his talk would turn to his latest gambling venture, but Barbara did not allow herself to be drawn back into his web, no matter how certain he was of this or that outcome.

She did not tell him about Hair & Now until she had been a member for ten days, after she had gotten her hair styled and was confident she had not made a mistake. Chimsky was obviously taken with the new look, complimenting its fresh style, and Barbara mentioned where she'd had it done. Chimsky, who had been eating, immediately set down his spoon.

"You said it's run by a couple guys," he said. "Simon and Quincy?"

"Yes. They said they know you."

"Well, I come into contact with a lot of people—"

"That's what I said. Anyway, what's their story?" It was a chilly Tuesday in early December, and quiet at the bar. As was their normal practice now, they were sharing a large bowl of noodles with their drinks.

"Do you have any idea where their money comes from?" Chimsky said after a moment.

"Will it affect my opinion of them?"

"It could. That's why I hesitate to say."

"Is it something illegal?"

"Nothing too untoward," Chimsky said. "But remember my little trouble with the bookmaker a few months ago? Remember how I put you in touch with someone to place your election bet?"

Her winnings from the election had been delivered in a stuffed envelope—Chimsky had picked it up for her, at his insistence that he was going over to Fong's anyway. Now she pushed her chair back from the table and crossed her legs. "They're bookmakers?"

"Not them exactly," Chimsky said. "But the person who's bankrolling them—his name is Fong. Or sometimes he goes by Murphy."

It was Barbara's turn to be surprised. She imagined the polite, older woman—Frances Murphy—and all her talk about her "sweet Henry." Could it be the same person? She couldn't see why not. "That's very interesting. But no, I've never actually met him. I'm friends with his mother."

"Really? That guy has a mother? Anyway, I just thought you should know what you're getting yourself into."

"Well, I've got nothing to do with any of that. The club is legitimate, which you would see if you drop by. As for the bookmaking, I only intend to ever make that one bet."

"I didn't mean to alarm you," said Chimsky. "I'm sure it's all above board."

"It's beautiful inside—very tasteful. You should drop by, like I said," Barbara added politely, although she was unsure whether she really wanted her ex-husband in that part of her life.

Thankfully, he seemed dismissive of her suggestion. "That's your thing, Barbara. I'm not exactly the gym type, if you haven't noticed. I'm just happy you're happy." He raised his glass and drank it in one gulp. "I'm especially glad you're no longer going to that other thing."

"Chim," Barbara said. "Please. I needed Gambling Help

once. But this is what I need now." She smiled and leaned back in her chair. It was interesting news, what Chimsky had told her, but she found that, if anything, it made Hair & Now and its owners more appealing than before. The idea that they were secretly engaged in the underground world of gambling seemed to her, in her new state of openness, to be a fact loaded with meaning—it was as if all her interests in life, past and present, were converging at this one point, and in her mind, Hair & Now shone with an additional, darker luster now.

THE NEXT DAY, BARBARA ENTERED the club doors, and Quincy, who was sitting behind the front desk, flagged her down as she headed toward the changing room.

"New members?" she asked.

"Several," Quincy replied. "It's been a good week. But one in particular—a man in rather poor health. He put you down as a referral."

Barbara had told her coworkers about the place, and wondered if one of them hadn't decided to enroll. Or had Chimsky changed his mind? "Who? Let me see the name," she said.

"It's right here." Quincy shuffled through the paperwork on the desk. He pulled out a form and turned it so that it faced her on the counter. "He came in this morning."

For a second, Barbara scanned the page without its information registering. Then she saw the name signed at the bottom of it, and her blood froze. Written in jagged block letters was Arthur Alan Dimsberg. He was forty-eight years old, lived in East Snoqualmie, and had listed as his reasons for joining, "exercise, healing, and the company of close friends."

Another Audition

AFTER HIS MEETING WITH FAYE, Chan began driving to the Royal two hours earlier than was required for his shift in order to espy the Countess and her driver as they arrived for their nightly engagement with the Faro table. Chan did this even on his off night, loitering at the boundaries of the casino entrance, dressed in his dealer garb so as not to draw undue attention. Regarding the Countess, Chan noticed only the slightest deviations in time and dress from evening to evening. Sometimes, the Phantom was a minute early or late, which Chan attributed to traffic. Despite the color of her gowns changing, the cut remained the same, as if all her dresses had been made by a single hand. He noticed both he and the Countess preferred rich, deep hues, shades of red in particular.

Her driver—Thomas Eccleston, Chan assumed—appeared to have only one outfit: a gray chauffeur's jacket with two columns of brass buttons tapering from the shoulders down to a thin waist, and gray blousy pants stuffed into shiny black calf-length jackboots. Over the period of Chan's observation, a thin, black mustache was starting to form on the driver's upper lip.

The driver went outside twice an evening, to have a smoke and look over the car. The rumor was that he was mute, and Chan saw no one attempt to converse with him at any time, although he was cordial with the valets, inclining his head in passing.

During this period of observation, Chan carried a note he'd composed to the Countess, using one of the blank sheets left behind by Dumonde. After several attempts, the letter of introduction read simply:

> *Esteemed Madam,*
>
> *I am interested in learning your system at Faro. Would you consider teaching me?*
>
> *Signed, Arturo Chan, Pit Dealer*

Chan was not used to obtruding, making himself a nuisance (or worse) in a stranger's eyes, and for two nights, he failed to deliver the note, excusing himself for the reason that it was a particularly busy time in the pit. But when he carried the message with him to the casino on the third night, he was determined to convey it at the first opportunity. He knew the driver's pattern: the man would go outside at one a.m. for a cigarette and to check on the Phantom, and Chan made sure to engineer his downs with Mannheim so that his break corresponded with this time.

At five minutes to one, Chan sat on the couch in the lobby, vaguely flipping through the pages of a recent *Casino Times*. His eyes were on the entrance vestibule, a high arch surrounded on either side by a suit of armor. Several minutes passed before the driver emerged. Chan watched him walk by, then rose from the couch and followed him through the revolving doors. He saw the driver standing several feet away, underneath the awning, his back to the casino, smoking. Chan steeled himself and made his approach.

"Excuse me, sir," he said. The driver did not turn around, and Chan plunged on: "My name is Arturo Chan. I'm a pit dealer. I have a note I would like conveyed to your madam."

Still, the driver smoked calmly, appearing not to hear at all.

"Sir?" Chan tried again. "Mr. Thomas Eccleston?"

The name did the trick: the driver gave a little start, and turned to look at Chan, seeing him for the first time. He extinguished the cigarette under his heel, parted his lips, and spoke very thinly and softly: "How is it that you know my name?"

"My apologies," Chan said. "I discovered it through your vehicle's registration."

"It's not my vehicle," the driver said. He looked around to ensure no one was near. "What is it you want?"

"I would like to learn from your mistress," Chan said. "Her system of gambling."

The driver's thin mustache twitched. "You've made some sort of mistake," he said. "She has no students."

"Nevertheless, could you pass along this message on my behalf?" Chan held out the note. "I would like her to decide if she will speak with me."

The driver looked at Chan again. Then he took the note and put it in the front pocket of his jacket. "You can be assured she will hear about this, although I can hardly vouch for a favorable response—or any response at all."

"Thank you, Mr. Eccleston. That's all I ask."

The driver turned and walked away without closing remark, the heels of his boots resounding hollowly against the pavement. Chan watched as he slowly circled the Phantom, buffing small spots on the tire well and bumpers with a handkerchief. When it seemed like he wouldn't be done soon—perhaps he was purposely delaying—Chan returned inside.

THE REST OF THE WEEK, Chan made it a point to make himself available at the Royal at one a.m. At that hour, Eccleston would stride through the lobby and go outside to smoke and inspect the car, but there was no indication he was aware of Chan's presence on the couch, much less that he had any information to pass along. Watching him come and go, Chan wondered whether he shouldn't inquire as to the effect of his note, and was beginning to entertain the idea it had been for naught—maybe the Countess had read and dismissed it. Or she hadn't read it at all.

Sitting in his usual place, Chan was mulling over these possibilities one evening—a strangely quiet Friday, the last day of November—when, at five minutes to one, a shadow passed over the couch. He looked up, and the driver stood over him, hands on hips.

Outside, the driver indicated with his head.

Chan silently obeyed, following him through the doors, and when they were alone under the awning, the driver said to him, "Please listen carefully. My mistress has read your message. After several days of consideration, she has decided to offer you—against my urgings—a one-time audition."

Chan was unsure if he'd heard correctly. "An audition? What kind?"

"A dealer audition. She would like to play a hand on your deal."

"When? Where?"

"Sunday night," the driver said. "In the pit. At two a.m., when we leave the casino. We will stop by your Blackjack table."

"But what is this about?" Chan asked. "What happens if I pass? And, for that matter, how do I pass?"

"Your first two questions I cannot answer," the driver

said. "As for your last question, the answer should be fairly obvious. You will deal her one hand, and of course, she must win the hand."

During the rest of his shift that night, Chan could hardly keep his attention on the paltry five-dollar bets the players at his table were making. Finally—finally!—he'd created for himself an opportunity—a dealer audition, no less, something he had never failed to pass before. Yet, this audition had to result in a victory for the player, and this was a factor that, by all logic, was beyond his means to control.

Or was it? Recently, Chan had perceived inklings that there *was* some aspect of influence that was within reach: at Snoqualmie Downs with Dumonde, he'd seemingly willed Charlie's Kidney and Pinchbelly to triumph; then in the Thanksgiving poker game, on the last hand, he'd seen through Dumonde's normally unflappable stare.

Could this influence translate to the dealing of cards? It never had before, and Chan had stopped trying long ago to will winners and losers into the hands of his customers. Invariably, the smiling, the most generous would be the ones to whom he administered horrible, improbable beats, while the angry players, the ones who entered casinos with chips on their shoulders, would not lose for an entire shoe, building tall stacks they would cash out without tossing him a single dollar. And so it went that evening, despite Chan's renewed attempts to visualize the next card in Blackjack for the benefit of the players he favored.

Undeterred, Chan tried again when he got home. He showered thoroughly, then turned off the lights and lit a pine-scented candle. From the book shelf, he removed a deck of cards and fanned it face up on the coffee table. He closed his eyes and meditated on each card, visualizing its face, the arrangement of pips, the particular shades, the suits. When he was confident he knew the exact appearance of each

card, he began dealing out hands of Blackjack. The player—
he imagined the Countess with her driver standing close
behind—received a 9 and an 8 for 17. Chan had a 10 showing.
Chan closed his eyes and concentrated on his second card,
visualizing it as a small card, a 5 or 6—no, Chan had to be
more precise. He focused on a 6 of Diamonds. He turned it
over and it was a Deuce of Clubs. Not bad. He hovered his
hand over the next card in the deck, imagining it as a bust
card. The Jack of Spades. He imagined it until he could see
it clearly: side-profile, one-eyed, brandishing a scepter. He
held the vision for as long as he could. Then he flipped the
card over: it was the 7 of Clubs. "Player loses," Chan muttered.

He dealt the rest of the deck this way, focusing on specific
cards he wanted to appear. Most times, a completely different
card would turn up, making his hand instead of the player's, or
busting the player instead of him. He was close on several occasions: a pip or two off, or the right color but wrong suit. Chan
decided he would continue until he achieved a perfect match.

It took four times through the deck before it happened.
Chan visualized a 5 of Diamonds, imagining it getting larger
and larger, until red drowned his entire field of vision and
his hands felt warm. He slipped the next card off the deck,
gently turned it over, and there it lay:

TWO NIGHTS LATER, AT THE appointed time, Chan saw
them approaching, the Countess and her entourage. There
were only two players at his table, the mother and daughter—both regulars—and Chan watched over their shoulders

as the retinue slowly wound its way through the casino and
toward the pit. Dampness formed on his brow as she neared
and eventually halted several yards from the table. A buzz
arose over this detour from the Countess's pattern—Chan
could not hear them, but he saw her signal to her driver, and
the two broke off from the party, shuffling toward him.

"Welcome to the table," he said, as heat colored his cheeks
and neck. Chan could feel Mannheim hovering behind him,
watching.

In her gloved left hand, the Countess grasped a single
black $100 chip. Everyone watched as she placed it in the
betting circle, and then looked at him expectantly. "Please
proceed," she said. Her voice was powerful and undisturbed,
and fuller than Chan had imagined.

Nonplussed, he quickly dealt out the hands. He had an
Ace showing. Playing ahead of the Countess, the mother and
daughter received a 17 and a 19, and both stood pat. The
Countess held a 10 and a 5 for 15, but she did not even pause
when the action fell to her. She immediately waved off the
offer of an additional card.

Instead, she stared at Chan, as if saying, what now?

Chan slowed his breathing. Inhaling, he turned over the
card beside his Ace: it was a Deuce, giving him 3 or 13. Chan
exhaled—now he had a chance.

He closed his eyes and imagined a bust card, the King of
Hearts. Face-on, long locks of hair, sword in hand, plunged
into the skull. He pushed out the next card in the shoe and
flipped it over. It was a 9 instead, making a hard 12.

Again, Chan paused. He looked at the Countess regarding him across the table—standing behind her, exactly as he'd envisioned during his practice, was the driver, one hand on the back of her chair, the other hanging loosely at his hip. Chan closed his eyes and moved the next card out of the shoe by feel. Once more, he focused on the King of Hearts: the long, flowing locks, the sword, the suicide. He opened his eyes at the same moment he turned the card over, and saw paint first (!), then that he'd dealt himself not the King but the Jack of Hearts.

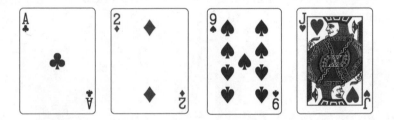

"Dealer busts!" Chan announced proudly, relieved.

The mother and daughter high-fived one another, while the Countess hardly reacted at all, though she continued to stare intently at the cards on board. Chan paid them, the mother and daughter winning ten and fifteen dollars, respectively, and the Countess a hundred. The old woman picked up her two black chips from the felt and slowly rose from the chair, whereupon the driver gave her his arm to lean against.

In one deliberate, agile movement belying her age, the Countess flicked one of the black chips toward Chan, and he watched it turn end-over-end through the air, bounce once off the felt, and come to rest a mere inch from his toke box.

"Thank you, madam," Chan said. He bowed his head slightly as she and the driver rejoined their retinue. Meanwhile, at his table, the small crowd gathered around them began to disperse, and Chan could plainly hear their gossiping.

"How old do you think she is?"

"A hundred."

"At least!"

"She must be worth five million."

"Easily—I heard ten."

"Strange," uttered Mannheim behind him. "You think you've seen it all, and then something comes along and shatters all your pre-established notions."

"Sir?"

"The Countess. As far as I know, she's never placed a bet in the pit before—until now. I think she's taken a liking to you," Mannheim said, eyeing Chan peculiarly, before walking away to tend the other tables.

Fugue

IT WAS WINTER NOW—WET, UNCEASING—AND only inside the walls of the Royal did Stephen Mannheim continue to feel like himself, alive and whole, and certain he was both. His dealers, suspecting nothing, treated their boss as they always had, with a casual cordiality expressed through inside jokes and similar benign remarks. Chan remained deferential and polite, never bringing up the subject of his impending death again. Mannheim felt solid and substantial standing in the center of the pit, where time passed with no reference to the world outside, where no difference existed between living one or a thousand days more.

Whenever he exited the casino, however, Mannheim felt himself splintering—physically and psychically. He had begun relying on extensive notes, directions, and lists he wrote reminding himself how to get home, his schedule for the day, when and what he'd eaten so as to not forget a meal. It was in these lost moments when he would emerge into consciousness in some strange location that it was becoming more and more clear to Mannheim he was nearing the end.

These moments—what Mannheim called his own private

fugues—had begun more than a year ago. Through his work with Dr. Eccleston and Theo, Mannheim could now remember two of these episodes vividly—he "came to" once sitting in an empty, darkened movie theater, the end of the credits scrolling on the screen, an usher with a broom gently nudging his shoulder, saying, "Sir? The show's over, sir." Another time, he awoke in a nightclub, music blaring and drink in hand, his wallet gone. Everyone seemed to know his name—and called him Steve!—slapping him on the shoulder even as he was trying to exit and regain his bearings.

Mannheim would find all kinds of detritus in his pockets—torn halves of tickets, matchbooks, receipts, business cards. He would deposit these in a drawer in his kitchen to forget about, despite his intention of eventually piecing them together to form an idea of his whereabouts during these lost moments. From the places he'd visited, like the theater and the nightclub, Mannheim discovered his "fugue self" was far more social than his real one, as if a complete lack of memory allowed him to be a person he wasn't, but perhaps could've been.

The morning after the Countess played a hand of Blackjack in the pit—an event so remarkable it left the Royal buzzing in its wake—Mannheim arrived at Dr. Eccleston's in the afternoon carrying his entire junk drawer in both arms. Dr. Eccleston had promised (for an additional fee) she would work alongside Mannheim to aid in deciphering his mysterious movements. In a previous life, she said, she'd been an accountant, and the beginning of their task that afternoon proved little more than the sorting and categorizing of each item into date and kind.

Little Theo quickly grew bored watching this. Seeing the child's dissatisfaction, Mannheim explained that he was only weeks from the end, according to both the doctor's timetable and theirs, and it was time to get his affairs in order. In the past several days, he told Theo, he'd visited his bank and several lawyers, as well as Snoqualmie's two leading funeral parlors.

"What did you find out, sir?"

"Yes," Dr. Eccleston enjoined, peering up from a stack of receipts. "What did you find?"

"Well," Mannheim said, "even though I have hardly any assets to speak of, the lawyers still encouraged me to write a will for the disbursement of my personal effects."

"May we have some of your stuff, sir?" Theo asked.

Mannheim laughed. "Of course. What would you like?"

"Surprise me," Theo said after a pause.

"I'll have to think about it," Mannheim said. "In the meantime, Theo, the funeral parlors—you can't imagine all the options! Oak, mahogany, pine, metal—whatever I want, the man said. The interior lining in any color and any pattern, satin or silk. The shape of the handles, whether they're silver or bronze. Did you know you can even get an outer casket to contain the coffin, in order to slow decomposition of the body?"

The child seemed entranced by this array of funereal possibilities, and Mannheim did not disclose to them the disagreement he'd had with the first undertaker about the cost of the burial, nor the fact he'd gone with a much cheaper, nondescript aluminum model at the second place he visited. During the past few months, Mannheim had carefully winnowed his bank account down to the bare minimum, most of it going toward his extravagant dining practices and to Dr. Eccleston, but he'd squandered most of his remaining funds in the Thanksgiving poker game, and he did not want this information coloring their opinion of him.

Instead, he redirected their attention to the task of sorting. "Have you discovered anything?" he asked Dr. Eccleston.

She raised her glasses to her forehead and leaned back.

"As far as I can tell, these papers suggest you've had at least four of these episodes." She indicated the piles in front of her, neatly ordered on the table. "In addition to the cinema and the discotheque," she said, "we also have evidence you went to the museum one afternoon, and to a comedy night at Rudy's on another occasion. You may have just wandered in—there's a receipt from a gas station next door, where you purchased some gum, and here is a matchbook from a bar located right next door. Does any of that ring a bell?"

"Somewhat," Mannheim said. The recollections were faint. As with his first two episodes, Mannheim knew of the locations, although he hardly frequented them. They were all within a twenty-minute walk of his house. "What I'm most afraid of," he said, "is that I'll die while I'm in the middle of one of these things."

Dr. Eccleston reassured him. "We will be extra watchful, Mr. Mannheim—Theo and I—from now on."

Then the child spoke: "Why don't you live at work, sir? Don't you say it's the only place where you feel whole? Why don't you live there instead of your house?"

Mannheim laughed. "I can't do that, Theo. Where would I sleep? It's a casino, not a hotel."

"A casino is better than a hotel," Theo explained.

THEO'S IDEA, THROWN OUT SO peremptorily, began to gain traction in Mannheim's thoughts. After all, it did make perfect sense: there was no building more familiar, more comforting to him than the Royal. When he clocked in that evening, just in case, he carried a duffel bag filled with toiletries, several changes of clothes, plus a blanket he put in his locker at the beginning of his shift. Then he went to see Gabriela to inform her—although she must've heard from day shift already—of the incident of the Countess playing a hand of Blackjack in the pit. Mannheim told her he couldn't make heads or tails of it, other than perhaps the Countess had taken a liking to Chan. "And I believe the feeling is mutual," he said. "I think she's fascinated him."

"She has that effect," Gabriela said. "On a related note," she told him, "changes in the High-Limit Salon are imminent. I spoke with Lederhaus on Monday. I offered him general manager of day shift, getting him out of the High-Limit Salon. The hours will suit him better. He said he would think about it, but I'm going to press him. You'll move right into his spot."

"Thank you," Mannheim said.

"Consider it an early Christmas present. This way, you can keep a closer eye on Chimsky. I trust you," she added with a conspiratorial wink, and Mannheim smiled, blushing.

Several hours later, his shift over, Mannheim returned to the changing room. No one else was around in the predawn hour. He began inspecting the doors inside the changing room, the ones reserved for the use of the custodial staff. The first opened onto a closet, where brooms and mops hung on a rack over a sink. The second opened onto another closet, this one containing shelves of folded staff uniforms, vests of various shades, and a stack of pointy celebration hats reaching all the way above the doorframe.

The third door, located in the far corner behind a row of long-unused lockers, was locked. Mannheim tried each of his master keys, and after several attempts, one succeeded in releasing the bolt. Carefully, he pushed the door open and was enveloped in an ancient pungency—he had to cover his mouth. It was the smell of old pulpy paper, returned and intensified fourfold. There was nothing else he could distinguish in the darkness, except for several cardboard boxes stacked just inside the door on either side, forming an entranceway. Mannheim reached out with both hands and felt along the walls for a light switch. Then he remembered seeing a row of flashlights in the first closet. After retrieving one, he returned to the room and crossed its threshold, brushing aside several lush layers of spider-webbing in order to do so.

Eventually, Mannheim discovered that the boxes contained hundreds of flyers printed on cardstock, advertising a Grand Re-Opening and Winter Solstice Ball at the Royal Casino, dated December 21, 1971. The scene depicted knights and ladies of the Arthurian court, dancing and celebrating under a banner that read "Drink, Revelry, and the Pursuit of Chance." Inspecting the drawing, Mannheim realized he'd worked that night, so long ago. He remembered his first boss, Kowalski, remarking at the time that Mannheim was the spitting image of the harpist in the picture.

Figure 3. "Mannheim discovered that the boxes contained hundreds of flyers printed on cardstock, advertising a Grand Re-Opening and Winter Solstice Ball at the Royal Casino, dated December 21, 1971."

The Trouble with Dimsberg

BARBARA KNEW IT WAS ONLY a matter of time before she ran into Dimsberg at Hair & Now, yet it still surprised her to enter the cafe one morning and see his long body folded over a chair, a mug of coffee in hand. She almost didn't recognize him. Gone were his outdated hat and frumpy brown clothes. He had pulled back his stringy, gray hair into a bun, underneath a red sweatband that foregrounded the top of his head, which was completely bald except for a pair of headphones. A club towel was draped over his shoulders, and he was clad in matching tank top and shorts shaded in light pastels, white athletic socks pulled up to the knees, and a pair of shiny white sneakers. His bare thighs, which were extremely thin and hairy, repulsed Barbara, and her instinct was to turn and go back down the stairs before he saw her.

Yet, she stopped herself. *This club is mine,* she thought defiantly—*I'm not letting him scare me off.*

Instead, she walked up to the table, startling Dimsberg by dropping her workout bag next to his chair.

"Barbara!" he exclaimed. He scrambled to shut off the

Walkman pinned to his waist. "Please, sit down."

"Don't bother. I'm only stopping by for a moment before my class."

"Which one is that? Maybe I'll join you—"

"I prefer that you don't, Dimsberg." She glared at him. "And to be honest, I don't appreciate your joining this club. What happened to Gambling Help? I thought you were committed to that."

"I can't do both?" he asked. A dark shade passed over his eyes. "The last time I checked, Barbara, this is a free country. I have as much right to be a member here as you, don't I?"

"Of course," she said. "You're free to do whatever you want, that's true."

She turned to pick up her bag, but Dimsberg kept talking. "And please don't think that your being a member had anything to do with my joining, Barbara, other than making me curious in the first place." He paused, and when he spoke again, his voice was edged with stone. "You're flattering yourself if you believe anyone would pay $250 a month just to see you."

He switched on the Walkman and returned to his coffee. Barbara felt chastened standing there, staring at the back of Dimsberg's bald head, before retreating down the stairs with her bag. She could not believe the encounter had gone so poorly—she hadn't wanted to give him the upper hand— especially not on what she felt was her territory—and yet he had gained it so easily.

As she walked downstairs, Barbara glanced at herself in the wall-length mirrors that lined the stairwell, and her pallid reflection seemed to reinforce Dimsberg's harsh closing comment. She passed by the front counter, ignoring Quincy's farewell, and exited the club, sitting in her car for several minutes before driving away, still steaming.

· · ·

DURING HER NEXT PERSONAL TRAINING session with Simon, who was encouraging her while she performed a set of squats, he remarked on her newfound fury and intensity. "What's gotten into you?" he asked. "You're not just doing your work today—you're attacking it. I like it."

Barbara wiped the sweat from her face. "Can I be honest with you?" she said. She and Simon had grown close over her sessions, and she felt open discussing private matters with him. "Something personal?"

"Of course."

"It's the new member. The one who put me down as a referral."

"Tall, skinny guy?"

"Yes. His name is Dimsberg. We share history. He was the leader of a support group I was in. For gamblers."

"I see."

"I quit the group a couple months ago. I didn't think I needed it anymore. But he doesn't agree."

"Did he follow you here?"

"In a way, yes. He says I'm not the reason he signed up. But I can't help thinking I am, at least partly. At first, I thought he was stalking me because he was interested in me—romantically. But now, I feel like he's here to ruin my time, the same way he feels I ruined his." Barbara hesitated. "I know this makes it sound like I think his whole world revolves around me. I just know I'm going to see him all the time. He's going to make sure of it."

"If I recall correctly, he's a monthly. Maybe he won't renew?"

"Don't take this the wrong way, because I want so much for this club to succeed. But I hope he doesn't."

"Well, Quincy's been working with him. He told Quincy he's very much into aerobics, but he's stiff as a board. Why don't you let us see how serious he really is about exercise?"

Barbara laughed. "Are you going to break him?"

"Maybe we will. Quincy isn't the biggest fan of his attitude either—he's only a monthly, but he acts like we're his servants."

Barbara did not encounter Dimsberg again for three days. The next time she saw him, they were crossing paths on the stairs—she heading down and he going up—and he looked twenty years older, stooped over and using a cane to support himself, although he was still garbed in athletic gear and wearing headphones. She attempted a wave. Seeing her, he stopped on the stairs, straightened as best he could, and glared at her unapologetically as she passed, offering no word or gesture of greeting in return.

Barbara had a very bad feeling about the encounter. "You guys sure did a number on Dimsberg," she said to Simon when she reached the front counter. "He can hardly walk."

"I was surprised to see him come in myself. Quincy told me he ought to be in traction after all the lunges and standing sit-ups he had him do."

She hesitated. Then she asked: "Does he suspect anything? I just passed him on the stairs, and if looks could kill—"

"No, don't worry about that. Quincy said he was completely gung-ho about accepting our Power Training Challenge. If anything, he'll blame himself for biting off more than he could chew."

Despite Simon's words, Barbara was not entirely consoled. After all, Simon hadn't seen Dimsberg's nasty stare, something she could not forget now that it was imprinted in her mind. She couldn't recall ever being looked upon with more venom, and she was dismayed to discover that even though she detested Dimsberg, she cared that his negative energy—now more than ever before—was permeating the fabric of the club, a place she had come to feel was her personal sanctuary, coloring it in lurid, ugly streaks.

What concerned Barbara even more, though, was that

this negative energy would serve to disrupt her recent run of good fortune, like an enormous wedge driven into a stream.

As she went through the motions in her Dance Aerobics class that afternoon, her mind drifted from Quincy's unflagging exhortations back to her life before she'd left Gambling Help. Barbara recalled the long, hapless nights, tossing in bed wondering if she would ever experience excitement and joy again, and she shuddered. Her new life, which a week ago had seemed like it would last indefinitely, now struck her as so much pretty window dressing, with a pane as thick as Dimsberg's enmity separating her from everything that was good and worthwhile inside.

DRIVING HOME FROM THE CLUB that night, Barbara pulled in to the gas station she usually bought her scratch tickets from, a sudden idea in mind. Ever since her encounter with Dimsberg, she was fearful her rush was over, and that she would start losing again. She would purchase a single five-dollar ticket and see if this were the case. But as she exited the car, money in hand, she noticed that on the curb outside the entrance, a group of young carolers had congregated, headed by a stout white-haired woman ringing a bell, wearing reindeer antlers, and a red-and-blue sweater trimmed in green. Beside them stood a cast-iron pot on a tripod with a sign over it that read "Goodwill to All," and as Barbara neared, she heard the woman's voice, loud and overpowering, over the children's:

> *Oh, tidings of comfort and joy*
> *Comfort and joy*
> *Oh, tidings of comfort and joy.*

Barbara listened for a moment—she had not heard this song for a very long time, and she was surprised to find herself moved by it. She had never been, after all, very religious: her father, a non-practicing Jew, had left when she was too young to remember, and she had been raised by a mother who'd been staunchly atheist. But now, listening to the soft melody, a calm slowly descended upon her. When they finished, she reached out and dropped inside the pot the five-dollar bill she had been clutching in her hand.

"Peace be with you," the stout woman said, smiling.

As the carolers began singing again—another song she remembered, "Silver Bells"—Barbara returned to her car, where it was still warm inside. Her errand no longer seemed as urgent, and she decided she would wait until tomorrow to see if her luck had changed. At least she could spend one more evening believing it hadn't.

Thirteen Thousand Years

THE GRAY, DREARY AFTERNOON FOLLOWING his audition with the Countess, Chan awoke with a start from a dream where he was sleeping in his childhood home. In the dream, the house was located in the hills, far from the murmur of crowds and casino lights, and in the silence and stillness, Chan had been frightened—there had been someone standing in the dark corner of the bedroom, shadowed by enormous, dead trees. The presence made him want to shriek, but he hadn't been able to turn his head, nor could he so much as lift a finger. The figure moved next to the bed, looming over his shoulder, just out of his vision. Somehow, Chan believed if he could just turn and see, he would find a person with his grandmother's face.

"It's a dream," Chan had told himself. "It will be over soon and you'll see, there's no one there."

Now, facing the window, he perceived a light through the blinds, the sound of a motor growing in intensity—the headlights of an approaching car. They bathed the wall in an eerie glow, punctuated by horizontal slits. Chan strained to listen as the groaning engine outside the window throbbed with the pulse in his ears. He thought he heard someone approach the front door, but he couldn't be sure, and no knock came. Then, after a moment, over the roar of the idling motor, he discerned quick steps retreating—a familiar clacking of heels—and a slam of a car door. The headlights receded, then vanished, and stillness returned. Chan wiggled his fingers and toes, then turned in bed, and saw in the corner the shadow of a swaying tree, its long, distended branches like icy fingers scraping the walls.

Chan slid his feet into slippers and padded down the hall to the kitchen, where he filled the teakettle and placed it on the stove. Then he walked to the front door and opened it. The parking lot was cold, a slight rain falling. There was only the mist—no person, no message.

Chan was off that day, and having heard no word from the Countess or her driver since his audition, he went to the Royal at 12:30 a.m. under the pretense of collecting his paycheck, after which he sat in the lobby to await Eccleston's break. The driver did not seem surprised to see Chan, and inclined his head as he passed. Chan waited ten seconds before exiting, and standing at a short distance, watched as the driver went around the vehicle with his handkerchief. The only difference in his routine was when he reached the trunk: taking out a key, Eccleston turned the lock, then looked at Chan knowingly before re-entering the casino.

After his departure, Chan's gaze returned to the Phantom. The long, silver limousine sat before him, glowing invitingly under the casino lights. He looked around to see if anyone was watching—the valets were all inside, warming their hands. Very quietly, Chan lifted the lid of the trunk, revealing inside a vast, empty space that could very comfortably and safely fit a human body.

· · ·

CHAN AWOKE SEVERAL TIMES DURING the journey—each time, the car was moving smoothly around him, and each time, for some unknown reason, he could not stay awake. There was such a luxurious, spacious quality inside the padded leather walls of the trunk—it was far more comfortable than the bed he spent afternoons tossing in—that the effects of the insomnia of the past six months, since he'd started working at the Royal, seemed to overwhelm him. He took a kind of delicious comfort in knowing that he was within a few feet of the Countess; he could feel the warmth of her body as he passed his hand over the barrier that separated them. And there was something else, too, some sort of spell woven around the car. Every time Chan felt that he could almost reach out and place his finger on it, his mind became dull and his eyes heavy.

Once, forcing himself to stay conscious, Chan carefully undid the latch that held the trunk in place. Holding the lid fast so as not to inadvertently fling himself out onto the road beneath like so much excess baggage, he raised it and glimpsed in the glare of the Phantom's rear beams the white lines of the highway disappearing behind them. He lowered the lid back into its housing and upon its closing almost immediately fell back into a dreamless stupor.

Hours later, Chan awoke and realized the car had come to a rest. There was light—bright sunlight—shining on his face. The interior of the trunk was lit through an opening into the car itself; a section of the back seat was down, and Chan could see through the glare that the passenger compartment was enormous, larger than he could ever have suspected. He could see the legs of a table and a chair, and the lower part of the gown the Countess had been wearing that very night. She was waiting for him.

Carefully, Chan poked his head through the opening, and saw, across the table from him, the Countess sitting and regarding him with interest.

"Sit down," she said. Her voice was clear yet distant, like the toll of a large bell from miles away.

Chan struggled through the opening, for although he was thin, he was not a short man, and his limbs got in the way. The Countess watched his attempts with some amusement. Eventually, Chan managed to get through, and he rose and dusted himself off, pulled the chair opposite hers, and sat down. The sunlight through the car windows had the effect of expanding the space in the compartment, giving it the feel of sitting on a veranda, and if Chan closed his eyes, he could almost feel hard cobblestone beneath his feet.

The Countess was regarding him curiously. This close, Chan was struck by the intelligence in her withered face: her veined hands that sat one upon the other on the table, a magnificent lower jaw bespeaking centuries of royal breeding.

"You were waiting for me to wake up?" Chan asked.

"We were," she replied. "It is not every day we harbor a passenger. I've seen you—even before you gave your message to Thomas. You appear to have developed an unusual level of interest in our activities."

"I have," Chan said.

"Do you understand why?"

"No—not fully. But I am interested in your way of gambling."

"You are a dealer. So you must perceive more than most the vagaries of chance."

"I thought I did," Chan said. "But I've never heard of the way you play."

On the table, the Countess separated her hands, turning them palm up. "Show me your hands," she commanded. "I must examine them."

Chan complied, placing them on the table next to hers. Her bony touch was unaccountably warm as she took up his hands—Chan felt faint, as if he were crossing some ancient threshold. Images of gambling ritual—the drawing of cards, the rolling of bones, the turn of a wheel—swam before his eyes, and he felt slightly nauseous.

"There, there," she said. She stroked his hands with the nails of her fingers until the feeling passed. Then she turned his hands over in hers, probing, feeling along the soft webbing between each of his fingers. "You have excellent hands," she said.

"Thank you," Chan managed to say. "You must know already—but I would like to deal to you."

"You will. Soon." She relinquished his hands. "The moment will come when a particular deck will be dealt," the Countess said. "The game will be Faro. The location will be in the High Limit Salon at the Royal Casino. I will be one of the players. And you will be the dealer."

"How can you know all this for sure?"

"We can never know anything for sure," the Countess replied. "For what we speak of is gambling."

Chan accepted this. He understood any explanation that was more certain would be in some sense unsatisfactory—the bond of chance was what was now uniting him with this profoundly singular gambler.

"We will set into motion the necessary conveyances to bring you to the high-limit room at the appointed time," the Countess was saying. "All you have to do is submit yourself to a series of directives that many may find arcane—but I do not think you will find them so. I hope I am not mistaken in saying an understanding exists now between us."

She placed her hand on top of Chan's, and again he felt the odd sensation of being pulled by her through some murky psychic space. He arose from the chair and crossed to her side of the table, to sit next to her, and there was no going back now. Chan, with all the passion accrued from a lifetime of dallying, of waiting upon something that had now so unquestionably arrived, was ready. "Please," he said. "Tell me everything."

Over the following hours, he listened as the Countess related her tale.

"IN 1912, I GRADUATED FROM Göttingen University," she began. "I was the first woman permitted to receive a doctorate in Mathematics from that famous institution. All the great thinkers of Europe were there in those years before the war, and I learned at the feet of the greatest: Josef Kunst. Under his guidance, I began studying repetitive patterns and series, particularly of numbers, everything that is typically thought of as random and assigned to what we call 'chance.' This includes behavior as seemingly simple as Heads or Tails when tossing a coin, to the more complex fluctuations in stock markets and world currencies.

"What we think of as chance, or probability, has been grossly misrepresented by the standard statistical textbook in use today. We have taught ourselves that all we know in regard to a coin flip, for example, is that fifty percent of the time it will come up Heads, and fifty percent of the time it will come up Tails—this profound reduction does not even account for the 1 in 10,000 chance the coin lands directly on its side. This dismissal, that we have exhausted our knowledge of outcomes, is not 'true' in any sense of that difficult word—mathematically or otherwise. The standard explanation depends on a hypothetical point in the future called 'the long term' that is, in my experience, always ever unreachable, even for someone who has lived as long as I. What I have discovered is that specific and reliable patterns *do* emerge in situations when the potential outcomes are highly and artificially constrained, as with a deck of cards and its fifty-two possibilities, two dice and their thirty-six possibilities, or a coin, with its two—or even three!—possibilities.

"Let me provide a deceptively simple example, one based on what high-school math teachers might describe as the so-called 'gambler's fallacy.' A coin is tossed ten times, and it comes up Heads each of the ten times. The ignorant bettor, believing that Tails is bound to appear after so many consecutive Heads, bets Tails on the next flip and loses, for the coin comes up Heads again. The explanation provided by the high-school teacher is that each flip is an independent event, with fifty percent probability of Heads and Tails each time (excluding, of course, the minuscule likelihood of the coin landing on its side). There is a fundamental flaw in this logic, a gap between our knowledge and the laws of the universe that has served as the basis of my research.

"One important aspect of this flaw stems from the fact that no coin is exactly the same as any other coin, even when straight from the presses at the mint, much less after years of common usage, with its everyday scratches and discolorations—some sides are smoother than others, the weight is unbalanced, et cetera. No coin is a true fifty-fifty proposition. (This also holds, as you might suspect, for the ball and the wheel in roulette, a pair of dice in a Craps game, a deck of cards in Blackjack—any physical object that is supposedly 'standard.') The astute gambler, seeing a coin land Heads ten times in a row, knows instinctively that it is more likely to land Heads than Tails on the eleventh flip, both due to a bias in the coin, and also an understanding that patterns of outcomes always occur in streaks.

"For there is no such thing, mathematically speaking, as an independent event. Everything coheres with what happens before, and also *what happens after*. Time is a fluid substance, and can be manipulated to a certain extent by our physical bodies, despite our retention of memories and the fact that we decay. How much more true, then, is it for physical objects such as dice, coins, and cards, who do not have memory?

"Returning to our example, the fact is that it is just as likely, in ten flips of an unbiased coin, for the pattern of ten consecutive Heads to emerge, as it is for any specific pattern of five Heads and five Tails, as, for example, five consecutive Heads followed by five consecutive Tails, say, or five Tails followed by five Heads. But you are aware of this already, I am sure. What you may not be aware of, however, is that specific patterns appear more than others depending on what I can only call 'external agents.' The appearance and movement of every object or thing on this planet, from a paper clip to a locomotive train, is to a certain extent determined by the interaction between our planetary core's magnetism and the gravity exerted upon it by the various celestial bodies in our galactic vicinity. Different patterns emerge more readily under different conditions—in a deck of cards, for example, where each card's weight is unique due to the amount of ink imprinted upon it. The Ace of Diamonds is the lightest card, the Ace of Clubs the next lightest, and so on—the Queen of Spades is the heaviest."

"I have heard this mentioned before," Chan said.

The Countess reached behind her on a shelf, and removed a deck of cards from a small wooden box. Chan watched as she shuffled the cards with her long, spotted fingers—there was no sign of arthritis he could detect. She handed him the shuffled pack. "Deal these out face down into two piles," she said. "Based on their weight."

Chan closed his eyes and held the pack lightly in his left hand. He slid the top card off with his right, and weighed it gently in his hand, feeling it. Then he put it down, and slid the next card off, comparing its weight to the first. It felt the same, and he put it in the same pile as the first. The next card, the third, felt just the slightest bit heavier and he placed it on its own, in a second pile. Chan went through the rest of the cards in this fashion, steadily increasing his pace, until there were two piles on the table, the first with approximately three times as many cards as the second.

"Now let us see how you did." The Countess took each pile and fanned them face up on the table. Chan was impressed to find that the first pile contained all the cards from Ace through Ten. The second pile contained all the paint: the Jacks, the Queens, and the Kings. There was only one interloper in the second pile, the Ten of Spades.

"This card contains almost as much ink as the royal cards," the Countess said, holding it up. "If you can focus your concentration, you'll be able to tell the difference."

"I've never tried before," Chan said. "I'll be better."

"You wouldn't be much of a dealer if you didn't improve," the Countess said. "You handle cards daily, repetitively. For you to be insensitive to their weights would suggest you are not the kind of dealer I am seeking."

"Thank you," Chan said. "I'm glad I haven't wasted your time."

The Countess placed the cards back into the wooden box and closed the lid. "Let us get down to brass tacks, as they say." Her voice became low and serious. "Two weeks from Friday," she began, "on December 21, the winter solstice will occur at precisely 1:59 a.m. For a few seconds, our location on Earth will be at its farthest from the Sun, meaning the gravity exerted by that celestial body will be at its weakest.

"Moreover, this upcoming solstice is unlike the standard solstice. You may remember from astronomy class the phenomenon of celestial precession—the precession of the equinoxes. Not only is our planet revolving around its axis, its axis itself is revolving—one revolution every 26,000 years. We are in the middle of this revolution, in the thirteen thousandth year, so to speak. This upcoming winter solstice is a convergence of these celestial events, a moment when the Earth's gravity will be at its most skewed since 7000 BC.

"You could say," the Countess added with a slight touch of humor, "that I've been waiting for this solstice my entire life. Based on these celestial factors and the extreme patterns that are more likely to occur under these circumstances, I am predicting a very specific and particular pattern to emerge during the dealing of cards at that moment in time."

"I understand," Chan said. "What is the pattern you expect on December 21?"

"Around 1:59 a.m.—in the three minutes before and after—a new deck of Faro will be dealt. After seeing the first dozen turns in the deck, I should be able to ascertain the order the remaining cards will appear in, based on what has come before. As an example, one of the potential patterns— the simplest to grasp—is all fifty-two cards in order of their weight. I suspect the pattern that will emerge that night will be more complicated, for instance the series Ace-Trey-7 followed by Deuce-4-8, and so on. Mind you, these specific patterns will depend on the dealer as well. The more consistent the scrambling, shuffling, and cutting performed on the deck, the more likely the order of cards will conform to one of my calculated patterns."

"Consistent in what way?" Chan asked.

"Consistently random. You should know as well as I that many dealers are profligate in their technique—the cards become sticky and remain alongside one another even through multiple, inefficient shuffles. What I require of you is to perform your job as cleanly and precisely as possible. Make sure the cards are completely scrambled once you receive the setup. When you shuffle, one card from one hand must interlace with one card from the other. When you strip cut, you must remove thirteen cards at a time, each time. And the one-handed cut onto the cut card must be exactly twenty-six cards deep into the deck."

"I can do that," Chan said. "I will practice."

"Certainly you will," the Countess said. "But I hope I have not adjudged incorrectly in presuming your entire dealing life has been practice."

"I will do my best not to disappoint you, madam."

She waved off his remark. "It bears repeating, Arturo: this is gambling. We can prepare our best—my calculations can be as mathematically correct as possible, and your dealing can be as physically precise as possible, yet the outcome remains fundamentally unknowable." She smiled and looked at Chan. "I believe I have made everything clear."

"You have. Still, madam, as you know, I work in the pit—not the High Limit Salon. Nor have I ever officially dealt a hand of Faro."

"Those are my concerns—not yours. I am going to create an opening in the Salon for you. Focus on preparing yourself for that moment. When it comes, it will be quick."

Chan had more questions—many more—such as what she planned to do, how she lived in the car, and why. But these matters of curiosity did not seem necessary to raise at that moment. Instead, he nodded. The Countess pressed a button on the console and spoke into it: "Thomas, I believe we have come to a satisfactory arrangement. Please take us back to Mr. Chan's residence now."

The Sacking of Chimsky

AFTER SPENDING SEVERAL NIGHTS IN the secret room inside the Royal, Mannheim found he slept much better in his new quarters, which were quite cozy and comfortable. Perhaps due to the boxes of old cardstock, the space had remained very dry despite the natural dampness of Snoqualmie, and Mannheim only had to clear it of cobwebs and the undisturbed dust of years to reveal the immaculate surfaces underneath. He slept on a thick pallet laid on the floor in the center of the room, and when the door was shut, he was enveloped in utter darkness and the smell of pulp, an odor he now strongly identified with this last period in his life.

Little Theo was glad to hear of the move. Dr. Eccleston, on the other hand, seemed less enamored of Mannheim's decision. "Of course, I am primarily thinking of your comfort," she said. "And the maintenance of your hygiene."

"It's strange," Mannheim told them. "I sleep better in that room than I ever have in my house. And I wake up feeling refreshed and clean, not disoriented. The only time I leave the Royal now is to come here, and the experience of walking into the world is like I'm entering another realm, a murky swamp I have to wade through just to arrive here. Then I come inside, and I feel like I do at the Royal. Like I'm home."

"We're happy to hear that," Dr. Eccleston said. "It is true we have become close these past few months."

"I'm very grateful," Mannheim said. "I think of you two as my closest confidants."

Theo asked to look at Mannheim's hand again. Mannheim was surprised: the boy hadn't read his palm since their very first meeting. As before, Theo intently traced the palm with his fingers.

"What do you see?" Mannheim said.

"Your aura." The child turned to Dr. Eccleston for confirmation, and she nodded. "It's expanding as we speak."

ON WEDNESDAY EVENING, AS HER entourage passed through the pit, the Countess halted and sent her driver to inform Mannheim she would like a word with him in private. Mannheim was surprised by this request, and wondered what it could be about—they had not spoken since their previous meeting. As before, they met near one at an empty table in the corner of the Salon, but this time, she told Lederhaus to proceed with the next shoe instead of waiting.

There was another difference from their previous meeting. She was seated this time, an arm's length from Mannheim, and she leaned closer and said in her clipped, efficient tone: "I confess I was not completely forthright with you on the earlier occasion of our speaking. I told you your dealer Chimsky's affairs were not my concern."

"I remember," Mannheim said.

"Yet I omitted something that may affect how you conduct your business with Chimsky in the future." She looked at Mannheim gravely, and he nodded.

"Please go on."

"Chimsky has been dealing to me six nights a week

over a period of eight years, and I am observant if I am anything—it is in my nature," she said. "I believe I am as attuned to a dealer's normal rhythm of shuffling as they are themselves—perhaps more so, as I can merely watch, while the act for them has become automated. That night, Chimsky was not shuffling in his normal way—for one particular deck, the one that resulted in the winning hand. It was impossible not to notice."

"You saw him do this?"

"I felt something was different," the Countess said. "And it drew my attention."

"Did anyone else notice?"

"Lederhaus appeared to sense something too. But he allowed the hand to go on."

"What about the other player at the table—Murphy?"

"As I told you previously, he was a complete stranger to me. But it was apparent there was something going on between him and Chimsky. They were trying too hard to convey the opposite impression." The Countess looked toward the Faro table, and then back at Mannheim. "I have told you all I know about this matter."

"Thank you, madam," Mannheim said. "Your information is very important—critical, even—to our ongoing investigation. Would you be willing to sign a deposition we can forward to the gaming commission?"

"If it comes to that," the Countess said, "my driver will testify. He was standing behind me the entire time and witnessed it happen."

"Certainly," Mannheim said. "That should be sufficient."

"We will do as you ask on one condition." The Countess lowered her voice to a near whisper. "No doubt Chimsky will at the very least be fired from his position."

"Yes, and possibly jailed."

"There will be an opening in the Salon then." The Countess

pursed her lips. "I would like one of your pit dealers, Arturo Chan," she continued, "elevated into that position."

From her manner, Mannheim thought she was not used to asking for favors. "He's only been here six months," he began to explain. "And we have an established schedule of promotion based on seniority."

The Countess frowned and raised her hand as Mannheim spoke. "That is mere policy," she said. "Not law."

Seeing her displeasure, Mannheim quickly added, "But we will take your recommendation under advisement, madam."

"Please see that you do."

"May I ask why Chan?"

"He is a good dealer," she said, slowly rising from the chair. "And I trust him—as I suspect you do already."

Although it was quite late, Mannheim phoned Gabriela at home, waking her up to convey the information he had learned, although he withheld the Countess's last request. Gabriela asked if Chimsky was working that night, and Mannheim consulted the shift calendar and said yes. She told him she was coming in, and to let both Lederhaus and Chimsky know she wanted to meet as soon as possible, during the next dealer change.

After he hung up, Mannheim returned to the High-Limit Salon and told Lederhaus about the meeting with Gabriela. He seemed surprised, but nodded and said Chimsky was most likely in the break room. Mannheim found him there, scrutinizing a *Daily Racing Form* and circling entries.

"Am I in trouble?" he asked when Mannheim informed him of the meeting.

"I won't lie to you," Mannheim said. "You must be for Gabriela to come in so late."

"May I ask what about?"

"Sorry, Chimsky. I can't say. But we'll both find out in due time."

A half hour later, there were four people in the general manager's office: Gabriela sitting behind her desk, Mannheim standing beside her, Lederhaus in the chair across the desk from Gabriela, his head bowed, and the principal himself, Chimsky, standing with his hands clasped in front of him, prayer-like.

"Let's dispense with the preliminaries," Gabriela began. "The reason you've both been called in is due to a discrepancy in the dealing of a deck of Faro approximately three months ago. This discrepancy occurred while you were dealing, Chimsky, and under your watch, Lederhaus."

Chimsky smiled nervously. He folded and unfolded his hands. "Did you catch an error?"

"No," Gabriela said. "We noticed something deliberate. If you do not recall the hand, the Countess and a new player named Murphy both called the last turn and won."

"Oh?" Chimsky said. He wiped at his forehead with the palm of his hand. "Deliberate, you say?"

Gabriela leaned forward and placed a video cassette on her desk blotter, within reach of Chimsky. "This video tape contains evidence you preset the deck. Which, as I'm sure you're aware, qualifies as tampering. You may also be aware that this is a felony in the state of Washington. You can take a look at the video if you'd like."

"No," said Chimsky, swallowing hard. "That won't be necessary."

"We could send this tape to the gaming commission, Chimsky. The evidence is circumstantial, we admit, which is why we have waited. But tonight, an individual present during the hand came forward of their own volition, and stated to us they saw you intentionally set the deck. You can rest assured the commission will conduct an investigation, during which time you would be suspended without pay. You might be exonerated—but if you aren't, we would be obliged to bring criminal proceedings against you. Even if you avoided prison, you would never deal again."

"I understand," Chimsky said softly.

"The thing is, Chimsky, we like you. You've worked here for over eight years, and everyone testifies to how outstanding a dealer you are. We don't want to railroad you—we just want to know the truth."

"Will I still be able to keep my job?" he asked.

"Unfortunately, there is no possibility of that. It would send the worst kind of message if our staff ever found out, which as you know is guaranteed in a community like ours. But we might just allow you to resign instead of forwarding this information to the gaming commission. Things will blow over, and you may eventually be able to get a job somewhere else—far away. But only if you tell us what happened. For example, who is Murphy?"

Chimsky became agitated. "Believe me, I'll tell you everything I can. Murphy is a frightening man—I owed him money, a great deal of money. We worked out an arrangement."

Mannheim usually disliked Chimsky, but he found himself sympathizing with the dealer's sad recital of his gambling debt. The information Chimsky provided was sparse—he didn't seem to know much about Murphy, other than that he was a local businessman, a moneylender and bookmaker.

"Was there anyone else present when you spoke to this individual?" Gabriela asked. She was taking notes in the ledger.

"Murphy always has his bodyguards with him," Chimsky said. "He has two. You can't miss them."

"One's on the tape," Mannheim said. "He walks in with Murphy."

"What was this arrangement you had with him?"

"I guaranteed he would win," Chimsky said. "He was to come in and play with his own money. I'd set the deck and he was to bet everything on the final three cards in ascending order."

Mannheim watched Gabriela as she took down this information. Then, addressing him, she said, "Isn't setting the deck in the way Chimsky describes almost impossible?"

"Yes," Mannheim said. "It's virtually unheard of."

"Don't get me wrong," Chimsky said. "I can't do it with any reliability. And that night, it was pure luck the cards came out in the right order. A complete accident of chance. But it got me off the hook with Murphy."

"And what would've happened if the hand hadn't played out the way you promised?" Gabriela said.

"I would hate to speculate," Chimsky said, looking from Mannheim to Gabriela. "I just want to say that I appreciate the kindness and generosity you're showing me. Thank you for allowing me to walk away. You'll always have a friend in Chimsky."

"You're not out of the woods yet," Gabriela said. "What about the Countess? Was she in on it? She won more than Murphy, and tipped you five grand."

"She had nothing to do with the set deck," Chimsky said. "She picked up on what was happening and took advantage of it. 'Get a hunch, bet a bunch,' as they say." He laughed nervously, and paused. "I actually thought she was going to say something to Lederhaus that night—but she didn't."

"That jibes with her story," Mannheim said.

"All right, Chimsky. If we find out you haven't told us the truth, or you've withheld information, this tape is going straight to the commission." Gabriela tapped the cassette with her fingernail and leaned forward in her chair. "Consider yourself terminated, Chimsky. Effective immediately. You will be permanently barred from ever setting foot inside these walls again. Please remove our uniform now."

Mannheim saw that Chimsky was shaken, and his heart

went out to him as Chimsky began unbuttoning his purple vest. Chimsky carefully folded the vest and placed it on the desk in front of Gabriela. "Your name tag too," Gabriela said. Chimsky unpinned the glossy card that read *Sam Chimsky, High-Limit Dealer* and placed it on top of the vest. He looked naked in his plain white shirt. It was true—Chimsky had no identity but that of a dealer, and now he was stripped bare.

"I am truly sorry. But know that I loved the Royal and I have betrayed her trust, and for that, I will forever live with regret. Thank you again for allowing me the dignity of leaving."

"That will be all, Chimsky. Good luck."

Mannheim shook Chimsky's hand. "Best of luck, Chimsky," he said. They watched him leave, and Mannheim wondered if it would be the last time he would see the dealer—at least in this world.

"Now," Gabriela said, turning her attention to the cowed Lederhaus, who had been silent for the entire proceeding. "We have enough grounds to terminate you as well based on the fact you were Chimsky's supervisor. But I made you an offer in good faith on Monday and it still stands. How do you feel about moving to day shift now?"

By the time he left her office that night, half an hour later, Mannheim was officially in charge of the graveyard shift in the High-Limit Salon. When he asked Gabriela about who should replace the disgraced Chimsky, she told him to select whomever he liked from the pit—he was in charge now, and "I'm not going to be looking over your shoulder—unless you make me," she said with a smile. Mannheim told her he would think about it and inform her the next day, although when he returned to the secret chamber in the changing room that night, he already knew he would say Chan's name when the time came. It was with this thought, in the comforting embrace of the smell of old pulp, that Mannheim drifted off into a deep, uninterrupted slumber.

An Understanding
Is Reached

"I'VE BEEN FIRED—THEY'VE THROWN ME to the wolves!"

Barbara listened to her ex-husband's tale in silence. They were at Rudy's on her lunch break—he had called her at work that morning, saying he had something very important to tell her, something he could say only in person. Now, sitting across from him, she placed a hand on his wrist. "I'm so sorry, Chim. I know that job meant a lot to you. But something better will come along."

"Not anytime soon," he sighed. "No casino in this area will hire me now—no casino worth working at, anyway. I may have to move back to Vegas. Or even Reno." He shuddered at the mention of these places. Barbara knew Chimsky had previously worked in Nevada when he first immigrated to America, and that he detested it, "desert towns full of Neanderthals," as he would say.

Chimsky had often told her that when he arrived at the Royal in 1976, he considered the job and Snoqualmie his final destination. First and foremost, he enjoyed the clientele,

a motley collection of oddities and obsessives. They encouraged his wild stories and appreciated his manner of speaking.
Barbara met him there in the pit, one night in 1979. He was
dealing to her when she'd gone on a rush, turning a small
stake of forty dollars into over five hundred. She'd tipped
him generously and gone to the lounge to drink some of her
winnings, and on his break, he had followed her to exchange
numbers. Their courtship was brief and intense, fueled by
a common interest in gambling, and took place at Rudy's,
Snoqualmie Downs, and the Royal when they were in public,
and usually in his rooms at the Orleans when they weren't. He
had a Siamese cat, Rajah, they both doted upon, and within
two months, on the morning after a particularly exciting day
spent at the track—they hit the Daily Double!—they'd gone to
the old Snoqualmie Courthouse and gotten married.

Unbidden, these remembrances came now, while Barbara
looked at Chimsky across the table. He was nearly inconsol-
able, his head in his hands, looking nothing like the person
she'd married. "Oh my God," he cried. "What am I supposed
to do now?"

"Hush, Chim," she said gently. "Maybe it's a sign you
should try something else."

"I can't do anything else!" he said, suddenly furious.
"You're right, Barbara—you've always been right. Since we
split up, you've changed for the better. You've gotten your
life in order. Me, I'm still where I've always been at. Except
now, I don't even have a job. I need to be like you, Barbara. I
need to transform myself." He looked at her, his face twisted
with pain. "I can't believe I'm saying this—but gambling has
ruined my life. I can see that now."

Barbara stared at Chimsky as he concluded his pronouncement. She thought about how they started out gambling together as a team, how excited they got when they
won, how important gambling was to them both. It wasn't

merely a pastime—it had been their life-blood. She began to laugh. "Please, Chim. You, quit gambling? Get serious."

"Fine, fine," said Chimsky after a moment. "But at least a brief hiatus."

"That sounds much more judicious. You're just going through a bad patch, Sam. You're due for something good to happen."

"Do you really believe that?"

"Yes, Chim, I do."

He drank from his glass slowly, and then he set it down on the table. When he spoke again, he sounded more like himself. "Can I ask you for a favor, Barbara?"

"Of course, Chim. Just say the word."

"Can you go to the Royal in a couple weeks," he said, "and pick up my last paycheck from the cashier's cage? I don't think I can stand showing my face in there, with everyone seeing me and talking about me behind my back."

"No problem," Barbara said. "It's the least I can do."

"The next time you see me, I'm going to be better. I promise."

He was silent again, staring at his glass. Barbara watched him carefully—he seemed to be deciding something for himself. Then his face became less strained, and a playful smile appeared on his lips.

"What did the Chimsky say to the Royal after he was fired?"

"I give up, Chim."

"I can't deal with you anymore!"

Barbara chuckled. It wasn't a good joke, but it was a good sign. Chimsky was going to be all right.

AFTER WORK ON THURSDAY, THE twentieth of December, instead of going to Hair & Now, Barbara drove to the Royal Casino, a place she had not visited in the almost three years since the divorce. She entered the revolving doors, walked through the entrance vestibule, and emerged into the casino proper. Since the last time she had been there, a clear night sky, replete with constellations and a luminous full moon, had been painted on the tall ceilings, giving the room an impression of great vastness. There were several dozen customers in the place at the moment, milling about, sitting at machines. She walked across the floor, soaking in the quiet early evening buzz, feeling pleasantly enlivened.

First, she collected Chimsky's paycheck from the cashier's cage and put it in her purse, a task which took all of five minutes. Then Barbara looked around, and an old and familiar urge tugged at her. Shouldn't she place a few bets and see how her luck was running? She had refrained from any sort of gambling since Thanksgiving, and she felt she should have a look, at the very least. She began drifting through the aisles of slot machines, seeing if any caught her eye. Eventually, she found herself near the pit, where traffic was light. The Blackjack dealers, standing idly over empty tables, tried to make eye contact with her as she passed, and she diverted her gaze. She was drawn to the four tall rectangular Roulette boards at the end of the row of table games, two of which were lit at the moment. Roulette was one of her favorite games. She had always enjoyed watching the wheel, how you could place your chips even as it spun, how the dealer waved a hand over the board when your time had run out.

Approaching the two active wheels, she suddenly realized that seated at the closest one, with his back to her, was—of all people!—Dimsberg. She could tell by his head, its shiny bald top and the bun perched on the back of his skull. He was still dressed in his aerobics gear, as if he'd come straight from the club. There was an empty chair next to him, and Barbara, instantly desirous of making him feel uncomfortable, pulled it aside and sat down. So absorbed was Dimsberg in his play that he did not notice until Barbara lightly tapped him on the shoulder.

"Isn't it against the rules," she asked, "for you to be in a casino?"

He looked up, saw her, and then returned to the stack of chips in front of him—Barbara estimated around $300. "Who's following who now?" he asked, out of the corner of his mouth. "Like you told me, what we do outside the group is none of anyone's business."

"Once an addict, always an addict, right?" Barbara said in her most cutting manner.

"Aren't the seats for players only?" Dimsberg asked the dealer.

"Who says I'm not playing?" Barbara rooted around inside her purse, and fished out three crumpled twenties. "Just Reds, please," she told the dealer, a short, barrel-chested man whose nametag read *Derek*. "I'm only going to play the outside."

"Certainly, ma'am."

She received her twelve $5 chips—redbirds, as she fondly called them—and looked at the board. She saw Dimsberg had bet various numbers, and also had ten dollars on Even. She took two red chips off the top of her stack and placed them on Odd. He pretended not to notice. The wheel spun and they both watched intently as the ball rolled, then fell and landed in the slot for 27.

"Red 27," the dealer announced, and he took Dimsberg's bet and shifted the chips to her.

The next spin, Dimsberg bet twenty on Black. Barbara took four $5 chips and placed them on Red. This time, Dimsberg glared at her, but said nothing. The wheel spun and the ball fell.

"Red 19," the dealer said. Again, he took Dimsberg's bet and shifted his chips over to her.

"I see what you're doing," Dimsberg said, "and I don't appreciate it."

"Like you told me at the club, it's a free country. I can bet any way I want, and you're free to leave this table whenever you'd like."

On the next roll, Dimsberg waited as long as possible to make his bet, then slid fifty onto Red. Barbara just got in her bet on Black before Derek waved his hand over the board to stop the betting. The ball clattered from slot to slot, and finally settled on 13—Black 13. Dimsberg was nearly apoplectic watching his money change hands to her again.

Barbara knew her toxic presence was affecting Dimsberg's luck—he should have left, but pride was rooting him to the spot. "Let's see if you can hang with me, then," he said angrily, and pushed all of his remaining chips—over $200—onto Even. Barbara looked at the board and saw the last six rolls, including the three she'd won on, had turned up Odd—surely, an even number was due at some point. Yet she hardly hesitated in fading Dimsberg's bet once again, moving all her chips onto Odd.

She stared at the ball as it rolled around the spinning wheel—the ball one way, the wheel the other. Eventually, it lost its battle with gravity, rattling from slot to slot as the wheel began to slow. Barbara closed her eyes, awaiting the pronouncement from the dealer.

"Black 17!" Derek announced.

When she opened her eyes, she saw Dimsberg, chipless and red-faced, and he looked as if he were about to overturn the wheel. As she collected her money, he rose painfully from the table and limped off. She watched him head toward the lounge, his shoulders stooped and quivering with anger.

"Boy, you sure did a number on him," Derek said.

"Thanks. I think my work here is done. Can you color me up?"

"Of course."

While Barbara waited for her chips to be counted down, her mood of triumph began to dissipate. She had to admit she felt slightly guilty about what she'd just done to Dimsberg— perhaps she'd gone too far. No doubt he had come to the Royal expecting to remain unseen, to gamble his small stakes anonymously for a couple hours, enough to satisfy his craving without losing (or winning) very much, or drawing undue attention to himself. But then she had come along and their rivalry had caused him to bet recklessly—now he was out of money. She collected her three black $100 chips from Derek, tossed him two redbirds, and decided maybe she would head over to the lounge and see how Dimsberg was doing.

"Did you come to gloat?" he asked when she found him sitting by himself at the bar. He had a glass of soda in front of him, a forlorn, untouched straw in it.

"Actually, no," Barbara said. "I came to apologize. Can I sit here?"

"It's a free country."

"I seem to be hearing that a lot lately," Barbara said, climbing onto the stool next to him. When the bartender came by, she ordered a gin and tonic, but Dimsberg refused her offer to buy him a drink. "I'm sorry," she said after the bartender had left. "I shouldn't have sat down at your table. And I shouldn't have played against you the way I did. That was uncalled for."

"Really?" Dimsberg said. "Or are you here because you feel guilty?"

"I do feel guilty—that's true," said Barbara. "But I'm not as bad a person as you think I am. And I don't think you're as bad a person as you think I think you are."

Dimsberg looked at her sideways. "You certainly have a way with words."

She laughed. "You want to know how sorry I feel?" She

reached inside her purse, felt inside for the three black chips, and placed them on the counter. "Here's your money back, Dimsberg. Take it."

"No," Dimsberg said. "I won't. You won those fair and square."

"You won't take them?"

"I accept your apology," Dimsberg said. "But not your charity."

"Well, if that's the way you feel." Barbara took the three chips into the palm of her hand. "I don't know what I'm supposed to do with these now."

"I know what I'd do if I were you," Dimsberg said. "You're hot—obviously. I'd keep gambling and see how high I could go. Maybe you won't ever lose again."

Barbara laughed again, and this time Dimsberg almost reciprocated, although he restrained himself to a smile. "Thanks for the great advice, oh vaunted leader," she said. Then she added, more seriously: "And your advice has helped me a lot, Dimsberg—please believe that. I left Gambling Help because I was good again, and I wanted to feel that way on my own."

"Fair enough. I might leave myself one day—but I still have a long way to go, as you can tell."

"I wish you the best, Dimsberg, and I hope you get as clean as you want to be. I know we can't be friends. But we don't have to be enemies. Can we at least be cordial when we see each other at the club? I promise I will."

"All right," Dimsberg said. "It's a deal." He paused and watched her finish her drink. Then he said, "Are you a hundred percent sure we can't be friends?"

"Yes," Barbara said. "At least 97 percent sure." This time they both laughed. She left some money on the counter to pay for their drinks, then stood and hugged his bony shoulders. "Good-bye, Dimsberg," she said. "I'll see you at the club."

He doffed an imaginary cap to Barbara as she left the lounge. When she looked back, he was sitting straighter than before. Then he inclined his head and began sipping from the straw.

For the next several hours, Barbara prowled the tables, moving from game to game whenever she felt herself beginning to cool off. For the most part, she kept winning. From one Blackjack table, she won $350. From another, $220. She took these winnings to the Roulette tables and doubled them by betting exclusively on Odd. Then she began to play Baccarat, a game she hardly knew. Here, she won another $500. At this point, she was betting $50 to $100 per hand. Finally, with over $1,200 in front of her, Barbara decided it might be time to cash in. She kept $1,000 behind and, for the first time that evening, she placed a $200 wager. Impulsively, she bet on Tie—an outcome which had yet to come up during her play at the table—and then proceeded to watch as the Player's hand was flipped over to reveal a 7-Deuce for 9. Then the Dealer's hand was flipped over, revealing a King-9—another 9!

"Player ties," the dealer announced.

The unlikely 8-to-1 win increased her bankroll to $2,800. More than ever, Barbara felt she should leave. After losing two consecutive hands that whittled her chips down to $2,000, she forced her body to rise before she lost the rest. She tossed the dealer two $25 chips and left the table, heading directly toward the cashier's cage. The line was long, and as she waited, Barbara looked at her watch for the first time: to her astonishment, it was almost half past midnight! Over six hours had passed since she'd first entered the Royal. Dazed and still buzzing from her rush, she fingered the four purple $500 chips in her grasp, rolling them in her palm, relishing their feel. Her eyes roved over the casino floor, and eventually came to rest on the entrance to the High-Limit Salon. It

was a room she'd always ignored because she'd never possessed the means to enter it. But tonight, she had two grand
in her hand and the line was moving too slow for her liking.

　　Why not?

Cursed

TWO NIGHTS AFTER HIS PRIVATE conversation with the Countess, Chan appeared for work and was directed by Mannheim, who was wearing a new suit, to exchange his black vest and name tag at the cashier's cage for purple ones that designated his promotion to the High-Limit Salon. Chan was floored. Indeed, even as he pulled the new vest over his white shirt, Chan could hardly believe the Countess had moved so fast in fulfilling her promise. More than ever, he found himself convinced of her powers—mathematical and otherwise.

Chan's promotion drew the attention of his colleagues in the pit, and he was heartened to hear Leanne and Bao whistle, cheer, and applaud as he walked across the worn casino carpet toward the entrance of the High-Limit Salon. He turned and smiled at them, waving before he disappeared inside.

He had never before set foot in the room, and as he entered, his shoes sank into the rich, plush carpet. Compared to the brazenly lit pit, the room was dim, and the color of the carpet—deep burgundy—emphasized the impression of murkiness and bloodiness. It took a moment for his eyes to adjust. Then Chan saw there were three tables, separated by tall marble braziers. To his left was the Baccarat board. To his right was the wheel. And in the middle was the Faro table. At the last, Chan saw the Countess seated in her imposing chair with her back to him, the driver beside her.

Mannheim, who was standing behind the Faro table, excused himself and approached Chan. He was in an exceptional mood. "How quickly things change," he said. "Who would imagine you and me in the High-Limit room, just half a year ago?" He patted Chan's shoulder. "You'll split half your time between Baccarat and Faro. You've dealt Baccarat before, right? That's where you'll start."

Chan was glad to begin his shift dealing Baccarat, although it had been several years since he'd last dealt it. There were only two players at the table, a man and a woman, betting between $100 and $500 per hand in a very deliberate fashion, and Chan was able to settle into the game. On one hand, he earned himself a green chip when he drew a third card to Player, making a 9 to beat the Banker's natural 8. "Nicely done, new dealer," said the woman, who was dressed like an executive. She raised her glass toward him. "Welcome to High Limit."

At twelve thirty, Chan was tapped out, and he shifted over to the Faro table. He was extremely nervous as he sat down, with Mannheim hovering behind him and the Countess there, observing him closely, the slightest hint of a smile on her lips. His fingers trembled slightly. Mannheim handed him a new setup and Chan broke the seal on the deck, then fanned the cards face up on the table and counted them. Then he took the leftmost card, the King of Spades, and deftly overturned the entire deck in domino fashion, before counting all the backs. All the while, Chan could feel the eyes of the Countess on his hands, watching him wash, shuffle, and cut the deck, and slide it inside the shoe.

The deck went slowly, with a hitch or two when Chan struggled to remove a card through the thin slit in the top of the shoe. On the second occasion, Mannheim told him not to worry, that he would soon get a feel for the unusual device. The Countess did not make any bets during the deck, and the other players—there were two others, local retirees Chan had seen before—made only small wagers occasionally. Nobody offered to call the last three cards. After dealing the hock, Chan scrambled the deck, shuffled it again, and reinserted it inside the shoe.

By this time, his fingers had loosened and become supple, and he was mastering the amount of pressure necessary to issue a card through the small opening at the top of the shoe. Again, the Countess placed no bets during the deck, and wagering remained light throughout the deal, no more than $100 or $200 per turn. When Mannheim asked if anyone wanted to call the last turn, one of the players bet $100 on a final sequence of Ace-Trey-7; the first card was a 7, and the player, an old man, groaned and said, "Oh well."

It was now one in the morning, and Chan was tapped out by the next dealer. He moved back to the Baccarat table, where the same two players from before had been joined by a very young spiky-haired man in an enormous gray pin-striped suit, the shoulder pads prominent and misshapen.

Chan recognized him immediately.

The boy had about $1,500 in front of him in black chips, the room minimum, and he refrained from betting for an entire shoe, saying he did not like the way Chan looked and was waiting for the previous dealer to return.

As Chan reshuffled the shoe, the boy asked him to call for service, a request with which Chan was obliged to comply. A server came by and the boy ordered a Manhattan, to be made with a specific kind of vodka. At this unusual order, Mannheim, who was still shadowing Chan on his first night, cleared his throat. "Sorry, sir, but would you mind providing identification?"

The boy rooted inside his pockets. "I don't appreciate being treated this way," he said as he handed over a card. "Perhaps I should take my business elsewhere."

Mannheim did not hand the card back. "According to this license, Mr. Peterman, you are thirty-six years old. I have a hard time believing that."

The boy's face colored. "Are you saying I'm a liar?"

"I'm saying there's been some sort of mistake. Unfortunately, we cannot allow you to gamble here."

By this time, Chan noticed several husky security guards, clad in all black, appearing inside the threshold to the room. They drew the attention of the other players, but the boy remained transfixed in his chair. "Can I have my ID back?" he said.

"We are obligated by law to retain IDs we deem false."

"This is unheard of!" the boy exclaimed. "Please call the manager."

"You're speaking to him," Mannheim replied.

"Then call your boss. I would like to file a complaint."

Mannheim signaled to the security guards, and Chan saw them approach the table. Finally noticing them, the boy began grabbing at his chips. "This is an outrage!" he said as he shoved them into his pockets. "You will hear from my lawyers."

By this time, everyone was watching the altercation at the Baccarat table. The two security guards surrounded the boy, who was still seated, and the first lifted him bodily from the chair while the other held on to his legs. They carried him out, and by this time, he was screaming insensately: "I curse this room! And everybody in it!"

After this undignified departure, the room took several minutes to quiet down. "Another night in paradise, hmm?" Mannheim said to Chan, squeezing his shoulder, before leaving to oversee the Faro table. Chan dealt the next shoe of Baccarat, and it proceeded in a subdued manner, with the two players left still chatting about the incident, and not paying much attention to the cards.

THE CURSE OF THE SPIKY-HAIRED boy seemed to cast a pall over the High-Limit Salon for the next two weeks. On Chan's second night, he dealt two entire decks of Faro without a single bet winning, and some of the players joked he was the one who was cursed, since the boy had last sat at his table. The Countess laid no bets for an entire week, continuing to watch every movement he made carefully. Then, during Chan's second week in the Salon, she played one hand of Faro, betting a single $500 chip on an Ace to appear—and losing. Chan looked toward her for some sort of explanation— had she been merely bored?—but she regarded him sternly, as if the errant card were his fault.

In the afternoons at home, Chan continued to meticulously practice dealing from a makeshift Faro box he had constructed from a shoebox, focusing on the cards until his eyes watered and the images of the cards began to blur. But every night at the table, he continued to deal losing hands to the customers, and one evening, he overheard some players discussing how he was already getting a reputation as "the new cooler" of the High-Limit Salon, a moniker which mortified him. For her part, the Countess remained aloof, returning his looks with a studied insouciance that was hardly comforting.

CHAN'S CONFIDENCE WAS AT A low ebb when he clocked in for work at midnight on Friday, December 21, the night the Countess had calculated for the cosmological event. At home,

Chan had cleaned himself thoroughly and carefully styled his appearance.

"You look just like you did during your audition," Mannheim recalled when he saw Chan that night. "Positively severe."

Despite Chan's preparations, however, he still seemed poison to the players at his tables, who lost over and over, with only an infrequent win to stave off their exodus. And on his second down at the Baccarat table, between one and one thirty, Chan had to suffer the ultimate embarrassment of sitting the entire half hour with no players.

At one thirty, Chan was tapped out and returned to deal at the Faro table. Two players immediately left when they saw him sit down. At the end of his nerves from hearing himself talked about and treated in such a manner, as a kind of anathema to good luck, Chan again suffered issues getting the Faro box to comply with the actions of his fingers. Noticing this, Mannheim told Chan to calm down. "We're in no rush," he said, but Chan could not help feeling they were.

After three hands, he stole a glance at his watch. It was 1:32 on the twenty-first of December, less than a half hour until the moment the Countess had specified.

He resumed dealing the deck of Faro, and as before, there was very little action. Then Chan was momentarily distracted by the sight of a new player entering the High-Limit Salon. Her open face and manner struck a strong chord of recognition—had he played poker with her over Thanksgiving? He had. Her name was Barbara, and she was Chimsky's ex-wife. Chan watched as she approached the table, pulled aside one of the empty chairs, and seated herself.

"Welcome to the table," said Mannheim. "Barbara, isn't it? Chimsky's friend?"

"Oh, it's you two!" she said. She looked at their name tags. "Nice to see you again, Stephen. And you too, Arturo."

Chan smiled at her. She exchanged four purple $500 chips for twenty black $100 chips, and asked about the betting minimum. Chan noticed the Countess was regarding Barbara with some impatience, and he quickly said it was $100. Barbara nodded and began to play. Very soon, within a couple hands, she was betting $300 or more at a time in random, haphazard fashion. Her fast and loose style appeared to amuse the Countess, and Chan allowed himself to relax slightly, resulting in a more fluid dealing style.

The Changing of the Card

At 1:40 A.M., AT THE completion of the deck in play, the Countess tapped her fingernail against the edge of the table. "A new setup, please," she requested.

Chan collected the cards and passed them to Mannheim over his right shoulder, in exchange for a fresh deck. Chan twisted the pack to break the seal and removed the deck from the box. He fanned the cards face up across the blue felt in a perfect semicircle. Everyone at the table saw that the new deck was complete, and contained all fifty-two cards in the expected order: the Spades first, from King through Ace, followed by the Hearts, the Diamonds, and then the Clubs.

Lifting the leftmost card, the King of Spades, under his left pinky, Chan flipped the deck over, domino-style. Then he inspected the backs of the cards. All were identical—an intricate, interlocking fleur-de-lis pattern in light blue—and again, everyone present saw there were exactly fifty-two cards.

After Mannheim confirmed the deck was complete and ready to be played, Chan washed the deck thoroughly, scrambling the cards using wide circular motions of both hands, counter-clockwise with the left, clockwise with the right. When he was satisfied the cards were fully mixed, he collected and squared the deck.

The Countess had been exact in her directions: during the three riffle shuffles, each card under his right thumb must perfectly interlace with each card under his left. Chan carefully performed two riffle shuffles in this way. Then he squared the deck in preparation for the strip cut. Holding the edge of the deck in his right hand, widthwise, he stripped from the top of the deck three times, each instance pulling between the thumb and forefinger of his left hand exactly thirteen cards. Then he performed the third and final riffle shuffle and squared the deck again.

Now there was only the one-handed cut left to execute. Chan stilled his breathing and concentrated on the fleur-de-lis pattern on the back of the deck. Then, with his right hand, he nimbly snatched the top half off the deck, exactly twenty-six cards deep. He could tell by feel he had done it. He placed these cards onto his yellow cut card and then put the remainder of the deck on top. He squared the deck one last time and inserted it into the shoe.

By the time this entire procedure was finished, it was 1:41 a.m.

Chan began dealing the fresh deck. The first card, the soda, was an Ace, which Chan discarded. The players were then allowed to place their bets for the first turn. The Countess refrained, as she had informed Chan she would. Barbara, meanwhile, placed a series of $100 bets on twelve different cards, playing Faro much like she would play Roulette. The next card off the deck, the winner, was a Deuce, followed by the loser, a 7. Mannheim duly noted these events on the case-keep.

Overall, Barbara won $100 from her dozen bets. "That's it?" she asked. "I need to change my strategy."

"You should," offered one of the players, a white-haired

woman in a pink polo shirt, the collar up. "You're not going to win anything that way."

"Maud, let her play how she wants."

"No," Barbara said. "She's right."

On the next turn, Barbara changed her wagering to three $500 bets, on Trey, 5, and 7. Chan revealed the next card off the deck, the winner, and it was the Trey of Spades. Barbara clasped her hands in delight. Chan paid her $500 for her win, and she tossed him a $25 chip in return.

"Thank you," Chan said, inclining his head politely.

"There's plenty more coming," Barbara said. "I can feel it."

The Countess looked at her as if to say, *You cannot conceive the half of it.*

Over the next dozen turns, Barbara continued her hot streak, winning half the time, $500 each time, and losing only once. By 1:54 am, Chan estimated she had close to $8,000 in front of her, three towering stacks of black chips she shifted and reconfigured continuously.

Finally, on the fifteenth turn, the Countess moved her left hand slowly forward, pushing a stack of twenty purple chips into the betting circle, $10,000 total. She bet on the 7 to appear. Seeing this, Barbara quickly placed five $100 chips on the 7 as well.

Chan hesitated, glancing over at Mannheim's case-keep, but whatever pattern the Countess recognized eluded him— the order appeared completely random. He heard Mannheim behind him, breathing shallowly, expectantly. After the players finished betting, Chan slid the next card from the shoe and it fell to the table.

It was a 7—the 7 of Clubs. "Yes!" Barbara cried. The Countess calmly watched as Chan made the payouts from his tray, matching her stack of twenty purple chips and Barbara's five black chips.

On the sixteenth turn, the Countess declined to bet. The

other players, including Barbara, bet as they had before, this time on the 9. The first card out was the 9 of Spades, and they all hooted—but then the next card, the loser, was also a 9, the 9 of Clubs. Chan was obliged to take half their bets on behalf of the house. "Nobody told me this rule," Barbara said as she saw her $500 reduced to $250.

The player named Maud told her it was the house advantage.

On the seventeenth turn, the Countess resumed wagering, $20,000 this time, on the 6. Barbara followed her with $1,000, and Maud joined as well, betting $500. Maud's partner, an old man in an ill-fitting ball cap, bet on the 8 after an examination of the case-keep. Chan slid the next card out and it was the 6 of Hearts—the Countess was right again!

"I've learned my lesson," the old man said as he glumly watched Chan pay the other players. "I'm following your lead next time."

The pattern had been established. On the eighteenth, twentieth, and twenty-second turns, the Countess did not bet, and neither did the three other players. But on the nineteenth, twenty-first, and twenty-third turns, the Countess steadily increased her wager—from $40,000 to $80,000 to $160,000—and each time, she won, and so did Barbara, Maud, and the old man.

After the twenty-third turn, a flustered Mannheim asked the table to pause as he assessed the situations. Chan counted down the players' stacks in his mind—the Countess had $350,000 in plaques and assorted chips in front of her, Barbara had near $25,000, and the old couple had over $10,000 between them. Their winning had drawn the attention of the other customers in the High-Limit Salon, and the Baccarat and Roulette players had stopped their gambling and gathered around the table to watch the action.

"Is there a seat open?" several asked, including the woman

who had toasted Chan at the Baccarat table on his first night, but Mannheim told them to please wait until the completion of the shoe, which contained only two more turns. Chan could tell his boss was becoming discomposed—and perhaps excited—about the size of the bets and the strange pattern in which they were being wagered, with the entire table in unison.

The five cards left in the deck, according to Mannheim's case-keep, were as follows:

Chan invited the players to make their bets for the twenty-fourth turn in the deck. Everyone's eyes fell upon the Countess, but instead of refraining, as she had done on every even-numbered turn up to that point, she moved her entire stack, ten $25,000 plaques and an entire rack of purple chips—$350,000 in total—onto the 7. Pulled in her wake, the other players, Barbara, Maud, and the old man in the ball cap, all moved their respective chips onto the 7 as well.

The crowd held their breath. Chan placed his fingers on the top card in the shoe and slid it out, cleanly and without fuss. He was now confident it would be the 7 of Clubs even before he turned it over, and indeed it was:

The crowd roared. The next card off the deck was the meaningless 9, and then, unbelievably, Chan had to call for his tray to be refilled in order to pay out the extravagant sums just won. When the dust settled, the Countess had $700,000 in front of her, twenty oblong green plaques, milky like jade, rising to her neckline even as she sat erect in her high-backed chair. Her left eye glittered with the fever of gambling—or perhaps it was the effect of low gravity. No matter—there was no material difference between these concepts now.

Only a single turn—three cards—remained in the deck: the Jack, Queen, and King. It was a minute until two, and Chan thought he could feel some change—some sort of shift in the atmosphere in the room. It's gravity, he thought. Everything is gravity.

"Would anyone like to call the last turn?" Mannheim asked. His voice sounded distant and nervous.

Again, all eyes fell upon the Countess. "I would," she said. "I call the Jack-Queen-King, in that order."

"How much is your wager, madam?"

She waved her hands over her empire. "Everything," she said. Although Chan was hardly surprised by her bet, there were numerous exclamations heard throughout the crowd. When Mannheim hesitated, she asked: "Is the house able to handle my action?"

"Yes, madam." Mannheim's voice had grown very grave. "In this room, one can bet any amount at any time."

"I'm not stopping now," Barbara enjoined. "I call Jack-Queen-King, too. All fifty grand here."

"And us as well," said Maud and her partner. "Twenty grand total."

When the bets were arranged on the table, Mannheim told Chan to go ahead. His boss's voice was so solemn and quiet now that Chan couldn't be sure anything had actually been said. He shut his eyes and imagined the first card in the sequence, the Jack of Hearts, in all its emblematic glory: side-profile, blond locks, brandishing a halberd, getting larger and larger in his field of vision. Using just the tips of his fingers, Chan swept the top card through the slot, and it fell on the table:

It was the Jack!

The crowd erupted again. Then the old man pointed out that the hand was far from over, and a hush settled over the room. Chan steadied himself, gently placing his fingertips on the next card. He closed his eyes and imagined the Queen of Spades—her imperious eye, her hands clutching flowers. There was something unsettling in her expression, and Chan could not fixate upon her face without it changing, the eye winking at him, the chin turning away from him, ever so slightly. But it was too late to stop now—even the Queen could not resist the force of the cosmos, Chan thought, before he flicked the card out.

He could tell by the weight something was wrong. When he opened his eyes, the card that lay on the felt was not the Queen of Spades, but rather the King:

There was a sharp, collective intake of breath. Chan stared at the board, incredulous as the crowd began to murmur. He looked toward the Countess and she appeared as stunned, as stymied as he—the color had drained from her face and, for the first time, she looked all of her one hundred years.

"Are you serious?" Barbara said. The reality of her last bet—$50,000—was seeping in, and she slammed her open palm on the table. "Please tell me I didn't just do that!"

"We got exactly what we deserved," Maud said, disgusted.

"It's this dealer," the old man in the ball cap groaned.

Chan remained rooted in his seat. The King lay there on the table, plain as day. All the bets wagered and lost—he could clearly see the plaques and chips piled on the table before him. Yet as he continued to stare at the awful King, Chan began to disbelieve the reality of the moment—these are mere trappings, he thought.

"Come on, Chan," Mannheim said behind him. "Let's get this over with."

Mannheim's words sent a sliver of insight shivering through Chan—he distinctly felt the idea come from *outside of himself*. The hand was not over, not officially, until the last card, the hock, was dealt. If the card underneath his fingers was *not* the Queen of Spades—as it most assuredly was—this Faro hand would qualify as a misdeal.

All of the active bets would be returned.

Chan heard the Countess's words: *Focus your concentration.* Once more he closed his ears and his eyes, and the murmuring around him slowed, calmed, vanished. An utter silence fell. Then from this void, there began emerging other noises, distant and faint, getting louder. The chittering of voices not quite human. Some were laughing and cheering. Others were crying, sobbing plaintively. There was a momentary burst of applause—loud clapping and hooting—over an

unsettling, grinding noise underneath, like an old machine
winding down. Like the gnashing of teeth.

Chan saw himself sitting in the dealer chair. He was
inspecting himself in very fine detail, down to the most
minuscule point on his iris. Each molecule was alive, moving,
and from their mixture would emerge snatches of moments.
Barbara playing poker at Thanksgiving, brandishing a card
with zest, cheerful and happy. Dumonde jumping up and
down on the grandstand next to him, making it tremble
underfoot. Mannheim smiling with fondness, taking his
hand and shaking it, telling him he was hired. There
were thousands—tens of thousands—of such accumulated
moments, and Chan relived them in all the intensity of their
experience, the entire span of his consciousness.

Years passed—or the briefest part of a second. He was
walking down a dark hallway, toward the clack of tiles behind
a study door. The door was ajar, and streaks of orange-and-
blue light seeped from the edges, bathing the walls. From
inside, the man with the painted eyes was shouting "Trey!"
in a high-pitched voice, over and over. Chan placed both his
hands on the door and pushed it open. The orange-and-blue
light dazzled him, and he shaded his eyes. At the gaming
table sat the Countess, and she was young, a child no more
than ten. She was laughing, playing a hand of Stud Poker
versus the painted man—her thin fingers moved freely and
easily over the cards, snappish and quick-paced. She hovered
her index finger on the back of her hidden card for a brief
moment. Then she seized the card and flung it on the table—

Mannheim placed a hand on Chan's shoulder. "It's time,
Chan. Let's see the hock."

Chan opened his eyes. The Countess seemed the only
person still attending to the formality of revealing the final
card. She looked at Chan curiously, the same way she had
first regarded him so many months ago:

Can you?

Chan lowered his hand slowly and extended his index finger, hovering, over the final card. Then, with the faintest, deftest movement, he issued the card through the slot. It spun out, revolving lengthwise in the air, describing an ancient, flawless arc as it fell toward the table.

What the people crowded around that table witnessed (although many more would attest to having seen it after) was the card, while descending on its journey to the felt, clearly loaded with paint—for it was the Queen of Spades still. But as it neared the table, the image blurred, becoming arcane and incomprehensible. The color was draining from it, leaving trails Chan swore he could see. By the time it settled gently on the green felt, light as a feather, there was hardly any color on the card at all.

The card was now the Trey of Spades!

There was an audible gasp as the card appeared: it was the Countess sucking in her breath between her teeth. Chan stared in amazement at the card.

"It can't be," Mannheim was saying behind him. "I saw the setup—we all saw it!"

"What just happened?" a voice asked from the crowd.

"It's a misdeal!"

"What?"

"A misdeal! A misdeal!"

"We all get our bets back, don't we?" Barbara said amid the cacophony. "Please tell me we do."

"I don't understand this," Chan heard Mannheim say. "It doesn't make any sense!"

Chan turned his head. "Sir," he said. "What should we do?"

"Hush!"

"Quiet, everyone!"

"Ladies and gentlemen, please!"

The room was silent, awaiting Mannheim's words. He composed himself, straightened his tie, and told Chan, "Go ahead—spread the deck and count it down." Then he moved to the phone and called upstairs to surveillance.

Chan carefully collected the deck, squared it, and gently fanned it face up on the table, with no expectation as to what would emerge. The first thing he noticed was that the Queen of Spades, which he was certain had not appeared during the deal, was situated early in the deck, where the Trey of Spades had originally been. The murmuring in the crowd grew as they saw, like Chan, that somehow the positions of the two cards—the Trey and the Queen—had switched mid-deal.

Otherwise, the deck was entirely complete, with all fifty-two cards.

"They can't even begin to say how," Mannheim said after he got off the phone. "But surveillance confirms the deck was legitimate both before and after the deal. They also said there was no mistake made on the case-keep."

"We could have told you that," said Barbara.

Mannheim cleared his throat. "Ladies and gentlemen, your attention!" Chan thought his boss sounded different now. "I officially declare this hand a misdeal. All players are allowed to rescind their bets."

Above the peal of applause, Chan heard a very distinctive noise, like the cawing of a crow. The Countess's mouth was wide open—she was laughing so hard she had to hold her chest with both arms. Thomas Eccleston, standing behind her, had raised his dark glasses to his forehead, and was still staring at the board in astonishment.

Chan could breathe again. He felt light-headed, as light as the last card falling toward the table, transforming as it fell.

CHAN WAS IMMEDIATELY TAPPED OUT after the hand. He turned to Mannheim and told him that his standing so close had been what enabled the card to change. "For a moment, there was a pathway—I believe it was yours, sir." Then he hugged Mannheim, which he had never done before. "Good-bye, sir. And good luck."

Afterward, Chan drove home and collapsed into bed. For the first time in Snoqualmie, he was able to sleep in his apartment, soundlessly and dreamlessly, and when he awoke the next afternoon, he felt refreshed, relieved, and very, very hungry.

A New Setup

AFTER THE COMMOTION DIED DOWN—AND it did not for almost a quarter hour—play resumed at the other tables. The Faro table, however, remained closed. Mannheim ordered its shutdown, overriding the pleas of the crowd that had gathered, many of whom wanted to place their own bets. Not until the surveillance tapes could be reviewed, he told them.

Then, after asking Dayna to relieve him, Mannheim exited the High-Limit Salon. His steps took him through the passage in the casino known only to its longest-serving employees, a winding corridor that led out the back entrance to where the staff lot stretched all the way to the first line of trees. Mannheim felt the night breeze keenly, the swaying pines and heavens above the Royal Casino seeming more vast in his dazed state, and he half expected to find his car, which he had not driven in several days, gone. But of course, there it was. He opened its door and left his key and wallet on the driver's seat, in full view of any passersby. Then he closed the door halfway, leaving it ajar.

Afterward, Mannheim re-entered the casino through the front entrance, a mirrored revolving door that required only a gentle nudge from his shoulder. His gaze passed over the walls and floor of the bright lobby, which were paneled in a warm, vivid cedar. As he used to in the old days, Mannheim took a moment to inspect each of the five suits of armor lining the wall, feeling their weight and contours with his fingers, admiring the progression in material from leather to links of chain to heavy, forged plate. Beside the armor, the maw of the massive, raised portcullis gaped before Mannheim, inviting him to step through. Boldly, he did, and emerged into the pit.

Immediately, Mannheim could sense the liveliness in the air. The casino floor was buzzing in the aftermath of the hand, and as he walked across it, many of his old regulars— the small-timers—wanted to find out "what really happened" in the high-limit room. One young woman unknown to Mannheim shook his hand vigorously, asking him to touch her pocketbook in order to "pass the luck." Others kept their distance, but whispered and pointed as he passed: "There he goes—he oversaw it!"

The employee lounge, where he'd spent innumerable hours, was Mannheim's sanctuary on the casino floor, and he headed there now. It had recently been renovated, much to his taste, the walls freshly painted a robin's-egg blue and lit in each corner by a tall floor lamp with a red shade. There was a sink, a tray of drying mugs and dishes beside it, and a new, more powerful microwave oven installed over the stove. Leanne and Bao sat at their usual table drinking coffee and chatting, and very soon, they spotted him by the door. Standing up, they pulled out a chair for him, entreating him to sit and provide his own account of the hand. So Mannheim told them what he knew, as sensibly as he could:

"Somehow, Chan switched the Queen and the Trey."

He could have said more, that he felt his standing so closely behind Chan had affected the course of action. Chan

had essentially confirmed this fact afterward. But to offer
this seemed needless.

Mannheim spoke with Leanne and Bao until their break
was over, and then the next group came in, this one including
Derek and Rumi, and Mannheim related the incident anew.
He added more details: Barbara slamming a fist on the table,
the Countess cawing with laughter. They had never heard her
laugh before. Four more times, for four more sets of dealers,
Mannheim spoke of the hand until, at six a.m., the first of the
day shift began to appear through the lounge's doors. By that
time, Mannheim felt utterly worn out, and he greatly desired
rest. Excusing himself, he left the morning crew, who were
mostly strangers hired by Lederhaus, to be apprised of the
events of the evening through secondhand information.

Mannheim was certain a headache was coming—every
time he blinked now, he saw bright flashes of light, as if he
were wading through a field of sparklers. Unsteadily, he
made his way down the stairs, clutching at the banister with
both hands. Around him, a stillness lay heavy in the air,
underneath the surface noise and exclamations, the clatter
of chips exchanging hands. The casino itself was still and
silent, like some great beast keeping its own counsel, waiting,
it seemed, for Mannheim in the changing room.

There, in the darkness, he lay down and closed his eyes.

THE NEXT TIME THEY OPENED—HOW much time seemed to
have passed!—his old, shrunken body lay on the pallet, his
breath hardly moving. Most curiously, the flashes of light that
had previously dazzled his vision were *escaping* now, radiating
from his eyes and mouth, illuminating the entire bedchamber
in an eerie, colorless glow. Was this what Dr. Eccleston and
Theo had called his aura? Mannheim could sense, like the ad-
vance of a momentous tide, the light filling the room, then
slowly washing through the hallway, up the stairs, into the

offices, into the pit, immersing the gaming tables and ornate carpets, the ceiling painted to look like the night sky, the suits of armor standing neatly in a row. The light sank into every crevice, chip, and inhabitant inside the Royal Casino, and a great and joyful sadness welled up inside his old body, still on its back on the pallet, and Mannheim could taste with his lips the salt of his tears.

NEARBY, A PHONE RANG.

The body on the floor stirred, rising in the darkness with great effort. The bell rang, and instinctively, the body must respond. On leaden feet, it shuffled forward down the long tunnel, toward the far end of the hall, toward the small, half-sized door. The top of the door was arched, lit on each side by a smoky lamp, their hot oil mixing with the thick dust of desiccated bones and paper, filling the old lungs with a fine, gray ash.

The body coughed and coughed, but walked on. The bell seemed to ring continuously now, one long deafening trill. From the other side, the doorknob of the half-sized door began shaking violently.

The parched mouth ventured to open, to articulate the question "Who's over there?" but the jaws were full of ash and sand, grains spilling out and onto the floor, packed inside all the way down the throat to the pit. The body wobbled, staggered, and fell against the wall. Then, no longer able to bear its own weight, it collapsed, knees shattering into pieces on the cold stone floor.

The doorknob rattled—then *click!* And for a brief moment of clarity, Mannheim saw his twisted legs on the floor in front of him, felt himself surrounded by beings, murmuring among themselves over the gray shell before them.

Was he dreaming? No—distantly, he heard his own voice, rising above the whispers. Coming toward him, from behind

the door. It was a child's voice—*his* voice—ascending over
the bell of the phone, overmastering it. The voice was singing.

> *They fly so high,*
> *Nearly reach the sky,*
> *Then in my dreams,*
> *They fade and die.*

When he finished the song, the crowd before him, his
teachers, schoolmates, and friends at Saint Agatha's Home
for Children, burst into applause, and Mannheim smiled
and received it all, standing before them. The year was 1935,
and it was springtime. The future, so brilliant and so brittle,
moved through him, quickening his breath, something
impossible to grasp, to seize firmly, a last, powerful wave of
sensation the gray shell could no longer contain.

Mannheim shuddered once, twice. Then hands were laid
upon him, and Mannheim was no more.

SEVERAL WEEKS LATER, DR. ECCLESTON and Theo were
sitting in the shop, still talking about their great fortune.

"It's astonishing," Dr. Eccleston said. "You are rich,
child—rich!"

"I wonder if Mr. Mannheim knew all along." Theo looked
older now, dressed in new clothes. "He changed everything
for us."

The night of his passing, Dr. Eccleston had called
Mannheim to tell him the good news. There had been three
lottery tickets in his junk drawer, over a year old, and she'd
taken them to their place of purchase, a twenty-four-hour
gas station, to ascertain their value. The first two were
losers, but upon the third, the clerk's eyes had widened and
he gasped, "I can't believe it!" He'd come around the counter
to shake her hand, yelling to someone in the back. "She's

here! She's finally here! We've been waiting," he told her with a smile, "for a very long time!"

The jackpot was an almost ludicrous $1.7 million.

Then, two days after Christmas, after the services were over, a lawyer had come into the shop and informed them that upon his death, Mr. Stephen Mannheim, with no next of kin, had left a will that distributed his personal effects between Dr. Eccleston and Theo Sommerville. Mannheim's house belonged to the bank, the lawyer said, but the rest of his possessions would be sold in an auction, with proceeds after service fees to go directly toward Theo's college education. The will further stipulated that any additional monies would be placed in trust under Dr. Eccleston's guidance until the child turned eighteen.

With the ticket safely redeemed and the processing of its jackpot underway, Dr. Eccleston felt she was finally entitled to relax, although the phone kept ringing from local and even national news media. One of the most curious, a woman named Faye, had even come to the shop under the pretense of being an interested new client, although Theo had immediately seen through her. "You don't have to pretend with us, ma'am," he had told her. "We'll tell you everything you need to know about Mr. Mannheim."

This particular afternoon in the first week of the New Year, Dr. Eccleston and Theo received another unexpected visitor. He was a young, dark-haired man Theo had never seen before, dressed in a gray chauffeur's uniform—his name was Thomas, and Dr. Eccleston was his mother. This was a fact that delighted young Theo, who'd only rarely heard mention of his cousin's existence before, and always in the past tense. But here he was, standing before them in the flesh: Thomas told them he had come to say good-bye, as he and his employer were leaving Snoqualmie for good.

"Where will you go, mister?" Theo asked.

"Cousin, Theo," Dr. Eccleston gently reminded. "Thomas is your cousin."

"Göttingen," Thomas said, smiling. "It's an old city in Germany. My employer is a scientist, and there's a new line of inquiry open to us there."

Dr. Eccleston, for her part, said she was so glad Thomas had come to see her before he left—so glad and so happy.

From what Theo could gather as he silently listened, observing their body language and sensing the tenor of their unarticulated thoughts, mother and son had been estranged for over a decade, the result of an argument over Thomas's future. She, of course, had wanted her talented son to pursue the divinatory arts, as he (like Theo himself) had shown much promise at a young age. Despite his gifts, however, Thomas's mind leaned more toward the logical and mathematical—he craved explanations, proofs that could be documented, disseminated, archived. At college, he had fallen under the spell of one of his professors, a woman much older than he was, and when she left the university to continue her own personal investigations into the relationship between long-term probability and deep gravity, he had followed her as an assistant.

At the time, Dr. Eccleston could not help but suspect something untoward in the old professor's seduction of her only son: his dropping out of school had been the final straw in their turbulent relationship. After a series of raging rows over his plans, in which the mother decried her son's path as false, and he in return discredited his mother's intuitions as so much bunk, they had mutually decided to withdraw relations until this deeply personal, deeply ideological resentment erected between them—this impenetrable blank wall—had, through the passage of years, finally crumbled.

The mood was festive in Dr. Eccleston's small shop, where Thomas stayed for over two hours, talking excitedly with both of them about the future. Dr. Eccleston could not stop beaming and rubbing her son's hands and shoulders with affection as they sat around the table. Both their auras, Theo noticed, were the same shade of deep blue, and beautiful. He closed his eyes and listened to their chatter, hearing more than their words, paying attention to their intonations, their inflections, their long separation in the spaces and pauses in between. By the time Thomas left, it was dark outside, and as Dr. Eccleston and Theo watched the headlights of Thomas's long, fancy car recede from the shop window, he was surprised to see it had snowed, a fine blanket of flakes covering the ground.

NEITHER THE COUNTESS NOR HER driver ever appeared in Snoqualmie again, a fact that surprised many at the Royal, but not Chan. As the months passed, the incident of the changed card faded into legend around him, becoming a dusty relic like the Countess's old chair, which joined the suits of armor in the entrance vestibule, and the Faro table, which was eventually folded and stored in a closet in the changing room.

Chan knew there had been only one previously documented case of exchanged cards—in late-eighteenth-century France, also, perhaps not so coincidentally, in a hand of Faro, immortalized by Pushkin in his famous short story. This hand would, in time, join this predecessor in the annals of gambling as a true historical oddity.

But in Chan's memories, the hand never lost its luster—on damp Snoqualmie nights, the experience of its magic warmed him, and reminded him of the unknowability of the world, and its sweetness.

TODAY, YOU MAY STILL FIND him dealing in the High-Limit Salon at the Royal, his tables full and lively, and many of the players leaving substantial winners.

About the Author

BORN AND RAISED IN HOUSTON, Texas, Michael Shou-Yung Shum eventually found himself dealing poker in a dead-end casino in Lake Stevens, Washington. Two doctorates bookend this strange turn of events: the first in Psychology from Northwestern, and the second in English from the University of Tennessee. Along the way, Michael spent a dozen years in Chicago, touring the country as a rave DJ, and three years in Corvallis, Oregon, where he received his MFA in Fiction Writing. He currently resides in Astoria, New York, with Jaclyn Watterson and three cats. *Queen of Spades* is his first novel.

Acknowledgments

ETERNAL GRATITUDE TO LAURA STANFILL for believing in *Queen of Spades*, and for being the best advocate a writer can have. To the talented team at Forest Avenue, including Gigi Little who designed the gorgeous cover, thank you for bringing the manuscript to its beautiful, flawless fruition.

To my talented cousins, Ciaran and Byron Parr, much love and thanks for the two exquisite interior illustrations and the author photo, respectively.

To all the writers and booksellers kind enough to read the early galleys and provide blurbs, thank you.

For everyone who helped shape *Queen of Spades* from draft to manuscript, especially my first readers and committee members at the University of Tennessee, I will forever remain indebted.

To my friends at Oregon State University, thank you for supporting me and my writing when I was finding my way.

Finally, unending love to my spirit companion, Jaclyn Watterson, and our guides, Woodsy, Basil, and Zoe—it wouldn't be a world without you.

An early draft of the first chapters appeared in *Spolia* in 2014.

QUEEN
OF
SPADES

READERS'
GUIDE

A Note on Faro

FARO, THE GAME AROUND WHICH *Queen of Spades* is centered, was once the most popular gambling game in the world. Most famously, Doc Holliday banked a (reputedly crooked) Faro game in Tombstone, South Dakota, in the 1870s—but as the twentieth century loomed, Faro had already begun to disappear from casinos and gaming parlors, eclipsed in popularity by Blackjack and Craps. Please note that for the sake of readability, I've simplified the rules of Faro slightly, although the climactic final hand conforms to the original rules, as well as the rules of the Faro-like game used by Pushkin in "The Queen of Spades."

Casino Terminology

Bust—a hand in Blackjack that exceeds 21.

Checks—casino chips. Common casino denominations are White ($1), Red ($5), Green ($25), Black ($100), and Purple ($500).

Cut—the final act of an official shuffle, involving separating the deck into two parts at an arbitrary point (either selected by the dealer, as in Poker, or the player, as in Blackjack) and placing the bottom portion on top.

Cut Card—each dealer's unique plastic card (typically of a uniform color such as yellow or blue) cut the same size as a deck, upon which the one-handed cut at the end of an official shuffle is performed.

Daily Double—a single bet involving the winners of two different horse races.

Dime—$1,000. Also "Grand" and "Large."

Down—a dealer shift at a table, usually half an hour.

E.O.—an Early Out or Early Off, leaving a shift early.

Exacta—a bet on the first- and second-place finishers in a horse race.

Felt—to bust another player in Poker.

Floor—the on-duty manager and settler of all disputes.

Muck—to fold in Poker. Also, the discards in a hand.

Paint—Jacks, Queens, and Kings.

Pitch—to professionally deal a card to a player.

Push—to tie in a casino, in games such as Blackjack or Poker.

Redbird—a red $5 chip.

Reload—to buy more chips.

Riffle—the traditional shuffle where the deck is separated into halves and interwoven with the thumb.

Set-Up—a new deck of cards, usually upon request by a player, or due to the current deck being compromised in some way.

Scramble—the first shuffle of a new deck, giving it a "good scramble" face down, using circular motions of both hands in order to thoroughly mix the cards.

Shuffle—an official casino shuffle is two riffle shuffles followed by a strip cut, another riffle shuffle, finishing with a one-handed cut onto a cut card.

Strip Cut—the most challenging shuffle, where the deck is held in one hand and cards are successively "stripped" by the other hand from the top of the deck to the bottom.

Tap out—tapping a dealer on their right shoulder to indicate replacement after the current hand is finished. Not to be confused with "tapped out," a gambling term meaning broke.

Book Club Questions

1. How did reading *Queen of Spades* change your ideas about casinos and the world of gambling?

2. What choices did the author make approaching the issue of gambling as an addictive behavior?

3. Close your eyes, and for several minutes, imagine the Queen of Spades in as much detail as you can. Why is this one card so significant?

4. Barbara is a strong woman whose relationships do not define her, yet two men—Dimsberg and Chimsky—are over-eager for her attention. How does she manage to keep each at bay?

5. Do you believe in luck or chance? What role does risk play in your life?

6. At what point in the novel does Chan decide to stay at the Royal Casino instead of moving on, and why?

7. Consider the paths taken by the four main characters who are present for the final deal. How has each changed by story's end?

8. How does the time and setting influence the feel and mood of the story? Would the story have to change if it were set today?

9. Read Pushkin's short story "The Queen of Spades," upon which this novel is based. Discuss the many similarities and differences.

Read These
Forest Avenue Titles

The Hour of Daydreams
Renee Macalino Rutledge

"*The Hour of Daydreams* is a gorgeous read that should be relished as one would a piece of dark chocolate cake. Rich with tantalizing characters and delicious prose, this is a novel that readers, both young and old alike, won't be able to help but savor."

—Leslye Walton, author of *The Strange and Beautiful Sorrows of Ava Lavender*

City of Weird:
30 Otherworldly Portland Tales
edited by Gigi Little

"*City of Weird* is a dark, imaginative and entertaining exploration of the bizarre, set against the backdrop of Bridgetown. From the career troubles of the undead to what's lurking in the basement at Powell's, this book is perfect for readers who want to know what truly keeps Portland weird."

—Ian Doescher, author of the *William Shakespeare's Star Wars* series

Froelich's Ladder
Jamie Duclos-Yourdon

"At once a fantastical, madcap adventure and a poignant meditation on independence and solitude, it's the kind of book that captivates you quickly and whisks you high into the atmosphere. I was in thrall to the surreal Oregon landscape, populated by tycoons and grifters, cross-dressers and hungry clouds. This debut is clever, irreverent, and ultimately unforgettable."

—Leslie Parry, author of *Church of Marvels*

The Remnants
Robert Hill

"Reading *The Remnants* reminded me of Pound's conviction 'that music begins to atrophy when it departs too far from the dance; that poetry begins to atrophy when it gets too far from music.' Robert Hill bridges this gulf even more directly, writing sentences that not only sing but dance, full of whisks and sways and sprightly little sidesteps of language. How would they look, I began to wonder, if you diagrammed them? Like pinwheels, I imagine. Like fireworks. Try to fasten them down and they'd still keep moving."

—Kevin Brockmeier, author of *The Illumination*

Landfall
Ellen Urbani

"With her new novel *Landfall*, Ellen Urbani enters the world of American fiction with a bang and a flourish. She brings back the terrible Hurricane Katrina that tore some of the heart out of the matchless city of New Orleans, but did not lay a finger on its soul. It is the story of people caught in that storm and the lives both ruined and glorified in its passage. Her descriptions of the flooding of the Ninth Ward are Faulknerian in their powers. It's a hell of a book and worthy of the storm and times it describes."

—Pat Conroy, author of *The Prince of Tides*

Carry the Sky
Kate Gray

"In the rich rarified world of a prep school, Kate Gray has woven two powerful personal stories into a charged and compelling human novel which shows us that swimming under that quirky, antic, off-beat community are also life and death. Gray has a sharp eye and tells her story with verve and a deft touch."

—Ron Carlson, author of *The Signal*

The Night, and the Rain, and the River:
22 Oregon Stories
edited by Liz Prato

"I love this book like I love the ocean. *The Night, and the Rain, and the River* gets under your skin and travels your body from the first page. Each story brings you to the edge of your own heart, or life, or death, or gut grabbing laughter, and as the stories accumulate, you slowly realize you've been allowed into a world. These writers will mark you for life; remember their names. We are nothing without each other."
—Lidia Yuknavitch, author of *The Book of Joan*

The Gods of Second Chances
Dan Berne

"Every so often a novel comes along that feels like nothing you've read before. Dan Berne's *The Gods of Second Chances* is one of those, soulful and shattering in equal measure. Berne shines a light on rarely visited corners of both the world and the human heart in a page-turning story that stays with you long after you've reached the end. Be prepared to be amazed."
—Karen Karbo, author of *Julia Child Rules*

A Simplified Map of the Real World
Stevan Allred

"Funny, sensual, piercing, honest, witty, and a braided woven webbed stitch of stories and people unlike anything I ever read. It catches something deep and true about the brave and nutty shaggy defiant grace of this place. Fun to read and funner to recommend."
—Brian Doyle, author of *Mink River*